BONHIST

Cheyenne Medicine Woman

Jack Frazier

QUILL HAWK PUBLISHING

ISBN: 978-1-965142-88-2 (Paperback)

ISBN: 978-1-965142-89-9 (Hardback)

Book Cover by Ava Wood, Fins and Feathers Design

Edmond, OK

CONTENTS

Prologue   VI

1. Chapter 1   1

2. Chapter 2   8

3. Chapter 3   14

4. Chapter 4   20

5. Chapter 5   26

6. Chapter 6   34

7. Chapter 7   41

8. Chapter 8   49

9. Chapter 9   55

10. Chapter 10   60

11. Chapter 11   66

12. Chapter 12   72

13. Chapter 13   79

14. Chapter 14   85

15. Chapter 15   93

16. Chapter 16   98

17. Chapter 17   105

18. Chapter 18   110

19. Chapter 19   116

20. Chapter 20   121

21. Chapter 21   127

22. Chapter 22   133

23. Chapter 23   140

24. Chapter 24   146

25. Chapter 25   152

26. Chapter 26   159

27. Chapter 27   164

28. Chapter 28   170

29. Chapter 29   178

30. Chapter 30   184

31. Chapter 31   189

32. Chapter 32   196

33. Chapter 33   201

34. Chapter 34   206

35. Chapter 35   212

36. Chapter 36   218

37. Chapter 37   224

38. Chapter 38   230

39. Chapter 39   236

40. Chapter 40   242

41. Chapter 41   250

42. Chapter 42   256

43. Chapter 43   264

44. Epilogue   269

45. Acknowledgements   272

46. About the Author   273

PROLOGUE

COLORADO, 1868

The immense mountain was one of many; still, its distinct peak, white and jagged, set it apart from the rest. Clear water filled the cool air with a mist as it tumbled from the mountain top to the green valley below. One could recognize its solid rock face rising like a giant through feathery white clouds to a summit thousands of feet above sea level, cutting through the clear blue sky.

This mountain was special to a small band of Lakota Sioux and Cheyenne who were camped at its base just above the tree line. They called it Spirit Mountain. One of the Lakota, called Star, talked about Crow, a Cheyenne who had crossed over at Sand Creek, who had climbed this mountain. She had been Crow's wife and knew how Crow had led her through a secret passageway to the top, where a mysterious tiered valley was hidden. Bonhist, the daughter of Crow and Star, was only six winters; she had been born on Spirit Mountain and still held its memories.

Star had told the story repeatedly while she displayed a small golden headband that sparkled as brightly as her beautiful dark eyes. She claimed that Spirit Mountain was full of the white man's medicine—gold. Yet, to her amazement, after four winters of intense effort, they had failed to rediscover the entrance. Many of them had given up hope of finding the secret passage and had begun to doubt the story; yet they had lived in peace for four winters without seeing even a single enemy. The hunting had been good, so they said nothing.

Now, the entire group watched as the pony soldiers slowly climbed the mountain, moving in their direction. Bonhist stood beside her mother, who had already notched an arrow. Star looked to her left; there were her aging parents, Red Eyes, Coyote Ears. Beside them were their lifetime Lakota friends, Goes Ahead, and his wife, Woman From the North. Beaver Tail and his wife, Prairie Fire, were stationed close to Goes Ahead. The men notched arrows and waited. The Cheyenne were positioned to Star's right. The Squirrel, husband of Bob Tailed Wolf, stretched up proud and tall with his bow half drawn and ready before his wife crossed over at Sand Creek. To his side was Pretty Dove, now his wife and the sister of Bob Tailed Wolf. Pretty Dove had been the wife of One Eye, who had crossed over at Sand Creek with Crow and Bob Tailed Wolf. Behind the Squirrel, the children watched with big eyes as Pretty Dove was wringing her hands and praying to the Great One. The party, seven adults and five children, bravely waited for the twenty-seven pony soldiers that approached from the green valley below. Led by a large man sitting erect in his saddle as if he were a mighty chief. On either side of the captain rode two Pawnee scouts dressed in the uniform of the pony soldier.

As the pony soldiers confronted the small band of Indians, they spread out as their captain approached with the Pawnee scouts at his sides. In an instant, Star raised her bow and shot an arrow into the ground in front of the approaching captain. "Come no closer," she signaled in sign talk. She then notched another arrow and stood her ground.

The captain gave the order, and the soldiers all dismounted at once and raised their rifles. One Pawnee scout stepped forward, using sign talk, and addressed the small party of Indians.

"We are under orders to retrieve stolen horses and lead you back to the Indian agency."

In the silence that followed these commands, only the roaring rush of falling water could be heard. This moment, tense and grave, chilled their hearts. Everyone knew that their lives hung delicately in the balance of Star.

The captain of the pony soldiers held his hand above his head, ready to give the order to shoot. His men leveled their firearms and waited. With twenty-six rifles against five bows, Star stood steadfast and unmoved by the overpowering odds.

The captain looked a bit nervous as the Indians glared straight toward him. It was apparent who their number one target would be. Their accuracy and quickness were well known among the pony soldiers. The captain, looking at Star, guessed that she might be their leader, since she had shot the warning arrow. Surprisingly, she had a delicate beauty, yet no hint of fear showed in her face. She would fight, no doubt about it.

Star now faced the same pony soldiers who she believed had killed her husband, Crow, at Sand Creek. An intense hatred for these men filled her. Knowing they had come to take their horses and force the party back to the white man's world. All hope seemed gone. Tension grew when suddenly Goes Ahead and Beaver Tail began singing their death songs.

But Star was determined not to yield to these white eyes. The muscles in her forearms tensed as she focused on the captain's heart. At that precise moment when everyone expected Star to shoot, a child's voice rang out.

Bonhist spoke out clearly to her mother, "Mother, Father has closed the entrance to Spirit Mountain. Today is not a good day to die. He will lead us through the clouds to Spirit Mountain when we cross over. Throw down your bow."

The child's words shocked the Indians. Star lost her concentration and looked down at her daughter's soft, beautiful face with tears in her eyes. "Bonhist, there comes a time when we must hold our ground and fight."

"Yes, Mother, but I believe there is more to fighting than holding your ground and shooting an arrow," answered Bonhist.

"What else is there?" Star asked, in wonder at her small child.

"Winning," Bonhist whispered.

In an instant, Star threw down her bow.

CHAPTER 1

The pony soldiers escorted the small group of Lakota and Cheyenne, led by Star, back to Bent's Fort.

Shortly after, Red Eyes spoke with his daughter. "Star, why stay here in this white man's world? Let us escape and travel north, where the Sioux and Northern Cheyenne are living free. Remember who you are—the niece to the great Chief Sitting Bull."

So it came to pass that Bonhist traveled with her mother and grandparents north. They joined a large encampment of Sioux and Cheyenne led by Chief Sitting Bull.

It gave Bonhist much pleasure to watch her proud grandfather as he rode beside Star to the lodge of the great chief. In the days that followed, they were happy, enjoying the hunting and the beauty of the great northern country. Red Eyes' only disappointment was that Star still showed no interest in any of the chiefs who pursued her. Then the day came when Red Eyes crossed over, and was soon joined the following winter by Coyote Ears, his wife. Now, Bonhist had only her mother to rely on. The few Lakota relatives that she knew were not close to her heart, so she kept her distance.

To her delight, she found herself growing close to Chief Sitting Bull. Star had always been a favorite of the great chief. Chief Sitting Bull was Bonhist's great-uncle, but according to Indian custom, Bonhist called Chief Sitting Bull grandfather.

Bonhist, in her fourteenth winter, was a rare beauty with a curious, delightful personality and, like her mother, very independent. Since Star was a woman warrior with exceptional bow skills and Bonhist possessed similar characteristics, the great chief delighted in giving Bonhist tips on shooting her bow, riding her pony, or just talking. No matter how discouraged the chief felt, Bonhist could always make him laugh and feel lighthearted. One evening when he seemed concerned, she approached him with a smile. "Grandfather, why do you look so sad this evening? Have you not had a good day?"

Chief Sitting Bull looked up at the beautiful Bonhist and, with some effort, returned the smile.

"You are right, my granddaughter, today has brought sad news. I worry about our people. I do not know how we can continue to live in peace with the white man."

"Tell me, Grandfather, what kind of news would bring such a sad face?" Bonhist said as she leaned over and tenderly touched the old chief's face.

Instantly, Chief Sitting Bull brightened with a smile that rewarded Bonhist's efforts. "The wolves bring news of the pony soldiers. They are led by Yellow Hair, the same one who killed Chief Black Kettle at the Washita in the Indian territory. They now come to make war on us."

"But, Grandfather, we have lived in peace for these last few years. Why do they come now?" Bonhist asked with a curious look.

"Two winters back, the white man discovered the golden stones in our sacred Black Hills. We have tried to rid our land of these white eyes, but more come each day. Now the pony soldiers will try to drive us from our land."

"Aiee, Grandfather, now I understand your sad face; mine is sad also," Bonhist said, making a face that made Chief Sitting Bull smile widely. "Do not worry, Grandfather, Mother, and I will stand at your side. We will never allow anything to happen to you. We will shoot Yellow Hair with arrows," Bonhist vowed.

"Yellow Hair is a great warrior and will not be so easy to kill," sighed Chief Sitting Bull without looking at Bonhist.

"Will you lead our warriors against Yellow Hair?" asked Bonhist with wide eyes.

"No, the Sioux and Cheyenne do not fight with a leader. Each man fights his own battle. There is much honor in counting a coup or taking an enemy's scalp, but the other chiefs and I have offered a plan. We hope Yellow Hair only wants to talk, but I feel that we will be forced to fight."

"The pony soldiers will have a leader. Their warriors will not even get off their horses without his orders. They do not shoot their firesticks without the wave of his hand. White men do not fight for honor; they fight to win," answered Bonhist.

"Where does my beautiful granddaughter get such wisdom?" the mighty chief asked, smiling at his granddaughter.

"I have seen the white man. Many act as one. What is your plan, Grandfather?"

"There are those among us who want to go out first to face the enemy alone. This is a great honor in riding out in front. We have about fifty of these warriors. Still, they have agreed in council to run out in front of Yellow Hair like a bird with a broken wing and lead him back north to our main body of warriors. Then, we have those among us who have pledged to die in this battle. These are the young, mainly Cheyenne, who no longer want to live. They have agreed to wait until Yellow Hair is in position, then they will ride into his arms. This will force the pony soldiers to fight us in a hand-to-hand battle instead of shooting and reloading their firesticks from a distance. When this happens, we will rush in from every direction like a multitude of ants."

The great chief paused and stared grimly into the fire as if he were rehearsing the battle in his mind. His thoughts were interrupted by his bright-eyed, curious granddaughter.

"Grandfather, that is a good plan. May mother and I ride at your side?"

"Yes, my granddaughter, I want you and your mother to be at my side." As Bonhist smiled proudly at her grandfather's words, he added quickly, "Still, it is my prayer that Yellow Hair will only want to talk."

Suddenly, a quick rap caught their attention. Bonhist quickly opened the lodge flap, and a young warrior stepped in, looking very strong and fierce. She looked toward her grandfather, who continued staring at the fire.

"My chief," said the young warrior. "Yellow Hair, he comes!"

The following morning, June 25, 1876—a date that would be recorded for all time in American history as the day that General Custer and the Seventh Cavalry attacked the Sioux and Cheyenne encampment at the Little Bighorn.

On the hillside, looking down at the valley, the chiefs sat on their ponies waiting. Bonhist and Star were near Chief Sitting Bull. Bonhist looked across the meadow; on the far hillside were hundreds of Sioux and Cheyenne warriors. She then looked all around at the warriors covering the hills. As they waited, Bonhist felt a tension that generated enormous energy. Finally, the warriors who were playing the part of the bird with the broken wing appeared. They were running their horses at full speed, dust flying high as they fled.

Bonhist looked toward her mother, who tensed her muscles as she drew her bow from its case. She felt her heartbeat faster as the pony soldiers came into view. They were in full pursuit, and Yellow Hair rode out in front of his men with his saber raised high over his head. Turning, she looked toward the chiefs. None of them showed any excitement; it was like an eagle waiting for the rabbit. Finally, the warriors who had led the pony soldiers into the trap wheeled around and formed a line facing the enemy. Yellow Hair did not slow down, nor did he see the charging suicide warriors who were carrying only their lances or war axes.

Bonhist looked at her mother and saw she was eager to join the battle. The Sioux and Cheyenne warriors dashed from the surrounding hills in such significant numbers that it looked as if the hills were sliding into the valley.

This was the same enemy that had murdered their people at Sand Creek and the Washita. Warriors from everywhere were attacking with hate in their hearts. This was the multitude of ants that her grandfather had envisioned.

"Mother," Bonhist shouted, "go ahead! You are a warrior; join the others, and I will be at your side. We will fight together!"

As Bonhist had anticipated, this statement stopped her mother, who wanted desperately to join the battle. Star's frustration brought a slight smile to Chief Sitting Bull, for he knew that Star's first obligation was the safety of her daughter.

Star turned with a stern face and said, "Do not play the fox with me. You are much like your father. We will stay here; perhaps your grandfather will need our bows."

Now, Bonhist watched the battle. Her heart fell in sadness as she recalled her grandfather's grave face when he realized they must fight. This battle was a terrible thing. Yellow Hair had made a wide path as he turned his horse, returning to his men. They formed a circle and were fighting gallantly. Her grandfather planned to work as the pony soldiers were now using their fire sticks as clubs, engaging in a hand-to-hand battle with the Sioux and Cheyenne. Bonhist tried to locate Yellow Hair, but the rush made it impossible to pick out any individual.

Chief Sitting Bull rode next to his granddaughter and said in a gravelly voice, "The pony soldiers are not waiting for their leader to tell them to get off their horses. They are now fighting like the Indians; each man fights his own battle." Bonhist felt suddenly small next to the great chief. She would guard her thoughts more carefully in the future.

The chiefs began moving down to the valley battleground. The fight was over, and the war cries filled the air.

The scalp dances continued through the night and into the next day. Following the excitement of the great victory, Chief Sitting Bull announced that he and the Sioux would soon move north to Canada.

"The white men are as many as the leaves of the trees," he said. "They will keep coming. We will be safe for a time in the far north country."

During the twilight of the evening, Star looked at Bonhist while she watched an almost perfect V-formation of geese flying south. The last glimpse of the sun painted a beautiful red sky in the far west. "The Cheyenne are staying in this area. They plan to go hunting. The Sioux go north to Canada. Which way shall we go, my daughter?"

Bonhist did not take her eyes from the geese. She felt a sudden tug in her heart that she did not understand. In an instant, she replied almost in a whisper, "We go south to the lands they call the Indian Territory."

Chapter 2

Bonhist looked into the sad eyes of Chief Sitting Bull. She thought her heart would break to see his dismal face. "Grandfather, my mother and I will start in the morning on our journey. Many sleeps will separate us, but our hearts will always be close."

"I am proud of you, Granddaughter, for you are wise beyond your years. I believe that you will be safe in the territory that is called Oklahoma. They have not found golden stones in that area. Perhaps nothing of value can be found in that land, and you will be left in peace."

Tears rolled from the black eyes of Bonhist as she hugged the old man. "We will be together again; may the Great One above watch over you."

"I have given your mother four of my best horses for your journey, and you have plenty of dried meat. This small gift is for you. This eagle feather has been strong medicine for me since I first proved my manhood and became a warrior. I now want you to have it. It will make me proud if you choose to wear it on your wedding day."

Bonhist's face broke into a river of tears as she hugged Chief Sitting Bull. He carefully secured the eagle feather with a strip of red cloth to her long, black hair.

"Grandfather," she sobbed. "Plan your battles well when the pony soldiers come near."

The following morning, Star and Bonhist started their journey back to Colorado. From there they planned to go on to the Indian Nations, the land where Crow's people, the Southern Cheyenne lived. There they would make their home and start a new life.

As they passed through the Cheyenne village, Pretty Dove waved as Squirrel called, "Star, where are you and Bonhist going?"

"We are going to the Indian Territory they call Oklahoma," Star answered. "They tell me that it is not good hunting, but at least the People can live in peace."

"We have decided to stay on this beautiful land. If we must fight the white pony soldiers, we will," Squirrel said with a grim look on his face.

"Good hunting and may the Great Spirit guide your arrows against the whites," Star answered.

"You are mounted well. May strong medicine keep your journey safe. You should be with our friends the Southern Cheyenne by the moon when the leaves fall."

It is true, thought Bonhist. *We have six beautiful ponies. Four were gifts from Chief Sitting Bull.* Her dark eyes quickly assessed the lot. Two pintos they used as pack horses; one black pony pulled a travois; they rode their two favorite Appaloosas and led one spirited red mare.

As Star and Bonhist rode from Cheyenne village, they heard a war cry. Turning to the noise, they recognized a young warrior riding toward them on a slow-footed gray pony. It was Roaring Waters, the son of Spirit Walking and her husband, the Elk. The pony soldiers had killed both Spirit Walking and the Elk along with Crow, Bonhist's father, during the Sand Creek Massacre. Roaring Waters was now sixteen winters and had been raised by an uncle.

"Bonhist! Star! Where are you going?" yelled Roaring Waters.

"We are going to the Indian territory to join the Southern Cheyenne," Bonhist answered.

"May I go with you? Another bow would make you stronger."

"Nevertheless, why would you want to leave this land to go to the Indian Nations?" Bonhist asked.

"They killed my uncle in the battle with the pony soldiers and Yellow Hair. It was I, Roaring Waters, who vowed to die. I was a member of the suicide warriors and among the first to attack. I rode straight to the pony soldiers without even a weapon. As I rode, I held my arms and hands high and offered my chest to their firesticks. It amazed me that they missed such an easy target. As I rode among the enemy, one of them knocked down my beautiful gray Thunder Bolt using his firestick as a club." This statement brought an instant smile to both Star and Bonhist since the gray pony looked to be a very slow and a very poor mount. "I jumped up to attack him; he easily threw me to the ground and straddled my body as he raised his big knife. I looked to the blue sky above and smiled since I knew that I would soon cross over to see my mother and father. The pony soldier hesitated for only a heartbeat, and the next thing I knew, he fell forward over my body with three arrows through his chest. Rolling him off my chest, I took his knife. It worried me that I might not find my way to the spirit world so easily, so I charged the closest enemy. Just as I believed that he was going to shoot me with his little firestick, a lance struck him square in the chest. The spirits must have been laughing at me, for the battle was over and I stood in the middle of the fight still in this world. Afterward my brothers gave me an eagle feather for bravery. Now, I am low in spirit and have decided to return to my mother and father's people."

"You are welcome to join us," Star answered. "Your mother and father died at my husband Crow's side at Sand Creek. You are like a son to me."

"And like a brother to me," responded Bonhist, smiling.

"We will see many pony soldiers in the area and must travel mainly at night while we keep our camp well-hidden during the day," Star remarked.

"The soldiers look for my grandfather. Once we are several sleeps south, we will travel quickly without worrying about the pony soldiers," Bonhist added.

The three had no sooner cleared Cheyenne village when they heard the shrieks of three riders. Turning, they looked to see who approached.

"Perhaps, you do not remember me. I am Red Leaf. I grew up with your husband, Crow. We were childhood enemies. I always resented him, and I thought he was a burden to our tribe. Since he was without parents, everyone had to feed him. But it was the bravery of your husband, Crow, that saved my life and that of my son, Charging Bull, at Sand Creek. This is my son, and this is my daughter, Soft Winds. We want to travel with you to the Indian Nations."

Bonhist looked at the three. Red Leaf looked much older than her mother, while Charging Bull had the look of a fierce warrior although he was only perhaps fifteen winters. Soft Winds was just the opposite of her brother. She looked very shy and was perhaps twelve winters. Bonhist looked toward her mother and for a moment saw a hard look. Her face then softened, and she responded to Red Leaf. "Yes, I do remember you. You are like a sister to me. You and your children are welcome." Star then turned in her saddle and rode south.

That evening as the sun set in its home in the far west, Star turned to the small party and announced, "Tonight, we will not make camp but will continue riding. Before dawn, we will make our camp in those distant mountains. We must be careful of the pony soldiers and watch for any enemy. Roaring Waters, you and Charging Bull will be our wolves. Ride ahead and watch for any signs of the enemy."

By the gray of morning, the party of travelers had selected a well-hidden camp. It was on the hillside and offered a good sweeping view of the wide valley. Star was a little incensed with Charging Bull since he proudly rode in with a fat deer that he had shot. She had not wanted to take the time for cleaning and butchering a kill, and lighting a fire was dangerous.

"In the future," she said, "do not hunt as we travel, it slows us."

Without help, Charging Bull dressed out the deer and started working the hide. He started a small fire and roasted the meat. When Star awoke, she could see the young warrior near her robe. Charging Bull brought her part of his fresh kill. Star accepted the roasted steak and looked carefully into the face of Charging Bull. She said nothing, hoping to see what type of man he was.

"I am sorry for my mistake. I am not as experienced as you. I will learn much from the wife of Crow.

With that Star smiled at the young warrior. Watching, Bonhist was glad to see the tension lift between the two. She decided that she was going to like Charging Bull.

At dust, Star again started the party on their journey. Again, with Charging Bull and Roaring Waters acting as wolves, they traveled cautiously through the night. Once they saw a large encampment with many campfires. Knowing that these were pony soldiers, they made a wide path around the camp while continuing to move south.

As the eastern mountains started to light from the morning sun, Star picked out a good camping area. It was, again, well hidden in a thick grove of blue spruce on a hillside.

No sooner had they settled into their sleeping robes than Charging Bull came rushing into camp, shouting, "Riders have found our trail; they are coming!"

CHAPTER 3

"Quick," whispered Star, for all to hear. "We must abandon our camp. Clean the area so not even a trace is left."

"No mother," Bonhist whispered. "We do not have time, let us make the camp appear as if we are sleeping. We will quickly hide and wait with our bows ready. If it is an enemy, we will shoot from the shadows. If it is a friend, we will come out and invite them into our camp."

"Yes, that is a good plan. Your grandfather has taught you well," Star agreed.

Quickly, everyone placed a pack in their sleeping robes and crept back into the cover of darkness. The morning sun had not yet cleared the horizon, and the hidden camp provided an excellent area for an ambush. With arrows notched, they waited in silence. Bonhist could neither see nor hear any members of her party, still, she felt the tension. At last, they could plainly hear the hooves of several ponies as riders approached.

Seeing clearly was difficult, but a soft voice spoke out, "Star, it is I, the Squirrel and Pretty Dove. We and our daughters, Crow Wings and White Dove, have decided to join you on your journey. We have been following your trail for two sleeps."

Star walked from the shadows of the trees with an arrow still notched in her bow. "Welcome my brother and sisters to our camp. We will journey to the Indian Nations together."

Ten people now made up the traveling party. Since Star and Bonhist had thought they would have to make the journey alone, they welcomed their friends but knew that both good and evil could result from traveling in a larger party. Bonhist looked at her old friends. Crow Wings with her wide eyes brought a smile to Bonhist's face. Crow Wings and White Dove were half-sisters and fifteen winters old. White Dove's father was the Squirrel, while Crow Wings' father was One Eye. White Dove looked like her mother, Pretty Dove. She liked nothing better than talking. When she saw Bonhist, she shrieked greetings. "Aiee, Bonhist, it is good to see my little sister."

"Yes, White Dove, I enjoy seeing my older sister, but where are your brother, Gray Hawk, and your sister, Night Woman?"

"They are both married with lodges of their own. They have decided to remain with the Northern Cheyenne. The rest of us feel the Indian Territory is better. We fear that the white man will kill us in our sleep if we stay in this beautiful land of our fathers."

"Yes, White Dove, still, if you keep talking, we will never get to this Indian Territory they call Oklahoma. The pony soldiers surround us. We must be very quiet and travel mainly during the darkness of night. Now we rest, and this evening, we will continue our journey."

Though Bonhist was the youngest of the girls, except for Soft Winds, who was twelve winters, she was half a head taller. Bonhist was even taller than her mother, Star. No one really noticed Bonhist's height since she was very slender, but her womanhood showed with well-developed breasts and long, shapely legs.

As evening approached, the party moved with Charging Bull, Roaring Waters, and the Squirrel acting as wolves. The men spread out, keeping a constant watch for any signs of the pony soldiers. The women, led by Star, kept close to the trees as they traveled south. Just before the sun came up, Bonhist took the spare red mare to Roaring Waters. "Would you like to ride this fine red mare?" she asked. "She is a gift from Chief Sitting Bull and a very fast mount. Her name is White Feet."

"Thank you, Bonhist. You are the best sister that I have ever had, yet it will hurt Thunder Bolt's feelings if I choose another mount. Thunder Bolt is more than a mount. She is my friend," Roaring Water answered with a sincere expression.

"I understand. If you change your mind anytime or if you want to rest Thunder Bolt, the offer still stands."

As the gray of morning approached, the party came upon the Yellowstone River. It was a magnificent sight as they could see from their vantage point well above the water. As they came closer, they recognized that they were on a high cliff at least one hundred feet above the river. The walls of the cliff shot straight down into the rushing blue mountain water. Next to the cliff, the water was slower and darker, revealing a deeper section. The trees across the river seemed dwarfed by the height. It was a breathtaking view as the river seemed to flow into a vast canyon.

Everyone crept cautiously to the edge for a peek into the deep canyon.

"It makes me dizzy looking down. How far does this canyon go, and will we have to cross that river?" blurted out White Dove in a loud voice.

The Squirrel chastised her at once. "You must be quiet, my daughter. There are many pony soldiers in this area."

"We will not have to cross this river, at least not at this point," said Star.

"Who would dare jump from here?" asked White Dove with a laugh.

"Please, be quiet, my sister," whispered Bonhist.

"Come," said Star. "We must quickly find a hiding place for our daytime camp."

The party turned their ponies from the great canyon walls and rode across a meadow toward the nearest hillside thick with pines and aspens. Reaching the middle of the open field, a small mound rose before them. It was no higher than two horses. Charging Bull rode upon the rise and quickly signaled. The party froze in their tracks; coming straight at them was a large force of pony soldiers. They had been caught out in the open and were now totally unprotected. The pony soldiers numbered more than two hundred and fifty. And yet, they were unaware of the Indians.

Star notched an arrow and said, "I will fight them." Everyone quietly removed their bows and started humming their death songs.

"No, mother," Bonhist said. "We must surrender. We cannot win against so many."

Then Roaring Waters let out the Cheyenne war cry at the top of his lungs and charged. It alarmed Cheyenne, and with wide eyes, everyone peeked over the mound. Roaring Waters was at least three bow shots away from the pony soldiers. Still, he shot three arrows in rapid succession before turning to ride away. Immediately, the entire force charged after the young Cheyenne warrior.

"What is he doing?" snapped Star.

"He is still trying to commit suicide and cross over to the spirit world. This time, I think he will succeed," Bonhist said.

"Look," said Charging Bull. "His old gray runs slowly as if someone has tied his hind legs together. They will catch him soon."

"He rides to the cliffs of the canyon and leads the pony soldiers away. We must hurry and hide in those trees before they see us," instructed Bonhist.

They had one last glimpse of Roaring Waters as he and Lightning Bolt jumped from the canyon wall. The pony soldiers rushed behind him and immediately began firing their firesticks.

The party of travelers was now on the hillside among a thick clump of pines. Soft Winds was crying, and Crow Wings was hugging her. "Do you think Roaring Waters live?" asked Charging Bull.

"No, the fall alone will kill him," answered the Squirrel in a whisper.

No one slept that day, and the women all mourned and cried for Roaring Waters. The Squirrel and Charging Bull went off by themselves on the hillside. They were all tired when darkness fell, yet they continued riding south.

Three sleeps later, they rode out upon a barren prairie. This was a different kind of landscape from the one they were used to seeing.

"In many sleeps, we will reach the mountains. We will then be back in our old home—Colorado," announced Star.

"Mother, we have not seen an enemy for three sleeps. Can we now travel during the day?" Bonhist asked.

"We will fill our water skins, let the horses graze, and rest so that tomorrow morning we can start again," agreed Star.

This announcement brought a grin to all faces as they looked upon the vast, dry prairie.

"You will not believe what I see beyond the ridge," Charging Bull said eagerly.

"What could it possibly be?" Star asked in response.

"It is a small herd of buffalo."

"Have you forgotten already that we are traveling and do not have time to hunt?" Star asked.

"I know. Still, it makes my heart full to see such a sight."

"My heart is also happy to see the buffalo, Charging Bull. I, too, wish we had time for a good hunt." She smiled at Charging Bull, then mounted her pony with the rest. Suddenly, a loud war cry filled the air, and a war arrow struck the ground.

Chapter 4

The arrow struck the ground with a loud thud. Was this a warning from a potential enemy?

"It is a stripe-feathered arrow from a Cheyenne bow," Star shrieked with an amazed expression.

Everyone turned on their ponies, trying to see who had shot the arrow. A lone warrior suddenly appeared, walking slowly toward them.

"It cannot be, but it looks like Roaring Waters!" shouted Charging Bull.

"It is Roaring Waters, but is he of this world, or is he a spirit?" Bonhist asked.

He slumped to his knees as the riders approached.

"Are you still of this world?" Bonhist asked.

"Yes, the spirits have cheated me again. They do not allow me to cross over, but my fast horse, Lightning Bolt, died in the fall. I spent a day covering her with stones so the coyotes and buzzards would not disturb her on her journey to the spirit world."

"How did you escape so many pony soldiers?" Star asked.

"They shot their firesticks at me. Believing that I would die, I relaxed and let the river carry me downstream. They must have thought the same thing. When I realized that I was apparently still alive, I angrily jumped up after being washed onto a sandbar. Later, I found Lightning Bolt. I expected the pony soldiers to find me, but, to my disappointment, I never saw them again. I have been trying to catch up and have not eaten for three days. Go on with your journey. Just leave me some dried meat and a water skin; I will catch up later."

"No," Star said. "We will stay with you until your strength returns. Charging Bull, you and the Squirrel will go with me to hunt the buffalo. Some raw liver will put Roaring Waters back on his feet."

"You will take White Feet as your pony. White Feet may not be as fast as Lightning Bolt, but she will do," Bonhist said. This brought a smile to everyone's faces as Charging Bull let out a war cry.

Star, the Squirrel, and Charging Bull looked down on the small herd of buffalo. From the side of the hill, Star picked out a young, fat yearling. The three rode into the herd, and Charging Bull made a quick kill. Everyone helped with the butchering, and it was not long until Roaring Waters feasted on raw liver and buffalo tongue. Roasted hump ribs came later, with everyone enjoying the fresh kill. Bonhist and the young women worked the hide more from habit and custom than necessity. It was another restful day for the travelers as all had plenty to eat and drink. It also gave the horses another day to graze and regain their strength. The Squirrel and Charging Bull kept a sharp eye over the countryside, watching for any signs of danger.

The following morning, they began traveling south through a barren prairie. Roaring Waters led, riding the red mare with four stocking feet, while the Squirrel and Charging Bull rode in flanking positions. They served as the wolves, watching for any sign of danger as the party continued south toward Colorado.

After several sleeps, they saw the outline of the far purple mountains. This sight brought excitement and laughter to the small party. They were back in a familiar country. This had been the home of the Sioux and Cheyenne for many years. Bonhist could see tears running down her mother's cheeks. She knew only too well that Star was reminiscing about the days when Crow had climbed and lived in those mountains. Somewhere, far to the west, was the mountain that Star called Spirit Mountain. It had been the home of Crow and Star; it was the birthplace of Bonhist.

Bonhist could remember how her grandfather, Red Eyes, doubted the story of Spirit Mountain. She felt the large twin medicine bags that Crow had left her. Still carrying his medicine, she had grown accustomed to its weight and often examined its contents. Each contained one feather of the magpie; the rest was gold! Her mother, Star, who was skilled at storytelling and a gifted healer, often wore the golden headband that resembled a glowing sun. She claimed to have made the golden piece herself with gold from Spirit Mountain.

"Mother," Bonhist said. "Tell me again about the first time the father took you up on Spirit Mountain."

Bonhist felt sadness as she watched her mother wipe away the tears and begin the old story again. Although it made Bonhist feel sad that she had never known her own father, her primary concern was for her mother, who, after twelve seasons, could not forget the love she felt for Crow and refused any other men.

Suddenly, Charging Bull shouted, pointing toward a rock cliff that dropped several hundred feet. Standing on its edge was Roaring Waters. Everyone looked, expecting Roaring Waters to jump at any moment. Instead, a small figure crawled out beside him; it was Soft Winds. Everyone sighed in relief when the two stepped back and sat down together, silhouetted against the distant mountains.

Four sleeps later, the small party was deep in Ute country, moving to the southeast toward Bent's Fort and the Indian Agency. The rocky hillsides offered hidden camping spots as the party moved slowly and cautiously, enjoying each day in this beautiful country, like a condemned man eating his last meal.

One evening, as everyone was settling down on another peaceful night, Charging Bull rode into camp leading two strange horses. He dismounted and proudly showed off two mouse-colored ponies, well-built and mountain-bred. These were apparently Indian ponies.

"A Piute camp is one sleep west," Charging Bull said with a big smile. "I watched two Piute warriors taking honey from a dead tree. While they were busy with the bees, I took their ponies. Look, these bags are full of honey!"

The Piutes were the natural enemy of the Cheyenne and Sioux. For years, they had fought with each other, stealing horses and women, taking scalps, and counting coup. Under normal circumstances, Charging Bull would be a hero, greatly rewarded for his bravery. Yet, Star now glared at him while his mother, Red Leaf, threw her hands up in despair.

"I have raised a son who is no smarter than a rabbit. No, even a rabbit does not run into a wolf den to steal a crumb of food."

"Still, mother, you do not understand. These are Piute, our enemy. If I had a chance, I would have also counted a coup."

"Did you say we are only one sleep from the Piute camp?" Star asked.

"Yes, that is a great distance to travel. Besides, I was careful to cover my trail."

"Quick, everyone, we will break camp. Leave those horses with honey bags. Perhaps we can still make it to safety," Star instructed.

Charging Bull looked at his elders in disbelief, unable to hide his annoyance as he threw down the reins to the Piute ponies.

"If we were a war party, this would have been a great act. But we are poorly armed, and your bravery could bring much trouble," Squirrel whispered.

The party moved quickly with Star leading toward the high country. Leaving the ponies behind, they traveled all night and continued all the next day. Finally, Star gave the order to make camp. The Squirrel, Roaring Waters, and Charging Bull all took their turns at watch. The following morning, all seemed normal, so everyone relaxed a little. They continued moving the next day, very cautiously, and found a well-hidden camp that evening. Again, the men kept watch throughout the night. The next morning, Bonhist felt that something was wrong, but she said nothing to her mother. As the camp stirred around, White Dove screamed out, "The horses are gone!"

To the amazement of the wolves, all the horses were missing! Only a short distance from their sleeping robes was a Piute war lance. They had stuck it in the ground with a small bag of honey hanging from its handle.

25

Chapter 5

"It is my fault, my responsibility. I will get the horses back," Charging Bull said.

"I will go with you," Roaring Waters responded.

"I will go also," Squirrel said.

"No," said Bonhist. "You will not leave seven women unprotected. We need your strength. What if none of you returned? Besides, Charging Bull is no more at fault than a duck would be for swimming in water or a bear for climbing a tree looking for honey. It is a natural reaction for a Cheyenne warrior to attack the Piute. We all make mistakes; this time the Piutes won, but another day will come. Now, we must walk and carry what we can. We can replace the horses."

"Yes, but our fine lodges and cooking equipment, our furs and clothes, we cannot carry them all," Pretty Dove complained.

"Now, we will lose everything and must walk a great distance through dangerous country," White Dove added, with Crow Wings nodding in agreement.

"Quiet! My daughter is right. The Piute left us our lives. We will carry what we can; we need our weapons, water, food, a sleeping robe, and perhaps a skin for a lean-to on rainy nights," Star said as she looked closely into the eyes of the entire group. Then she added, "We will walk to Bent's Fort and, if we have to, we will walk to the Indian Territory they call the nations."

"This is your fault," said Roaring Waters, pointing at Charging Bull. "You may be a good hunter, but you think like a rabbit."

"And you may be strong in the war games, yet you rush toward death like a sage hen. They took the horses during your watch," Charging Bull snarled in response.

Meanwhile, the women led by Star lifted their packs and began walking.

"You two can stand here and argue, or you can join the rest of us," said the Squirrel with a stern face.

"Why do they call you the Squirrel?" asked Roaring Waters. "You do not look like a squirrel."

"When I was young, I had the habit of storing food in a hiding place like a squirrel—the name stuck."

Roaring Waters and Charging Bull stood toe to toe and did not move as the others walked down the mountainside. Finally, Soft Winds ran back and gently took Roaring Waters by the hand and led him away from the staring confrontation. Bonhist watched with great interest. This was not a happy group, especially her mother, who had left behind a beautiful lodge she had carried on a travois from Chief Sitting Bull's camp. The young women were also annoyed and threw angry glances at Charging Bull.

That evening, Star selected a camping spot, and everyone ate in silence. Bonhist watched her mother climb to the side of the mountain, where she sat on a rock overlooking the camp. Soft Winds sat near Roaring Waters, and they talked quietly. Crow Wings, who had a quick change of heart about Charging Bull, was sitting near him as they smiled at each other. White Dove was talking loudly to Grandmother Moon, who was full and bright. Seated near the campfire and looking tired, Pretty Dove, the Squirrel, and Red Leaf hung their heads in silence. The Squirrel was handling a small ceremonial drum as he slowly turned his eyes toward the moon.

They are pulling apart, and their spirits are dead, Bonhist thought. "Squirrel," she said, "can you play a social dance on your drum? I want to dance."

The Squirrel only nodded in response and began beating his drum. As Red Leaf and Pretty Dove sang in high pitched voices to the rhythm of the drum, everyone, including Star, watched as Bonhist began the familiar steps of the dance. She moved in a circle with her buffalo robe wrapped around her slender body.

After walking all day, no one was in the mood to join her except White Dove, who smiled and asked, "May I dance with my little sister?"

"Yes, please do."

"Do you feel the strong spirit of these mountains?" White Dove asked.

A natural impulse to entertain stirred inside Bonhist. She realized that everyone's attention was focused on her, and she took full advantage. "Hello, Grandmother Moon," she said, raising her hands toward the sky. "Mother Earth and Father Sky have been good to us, and Grandfather Sun has gone to his home in the west. I feel the spirit of my father, Crow, in these mountains." The drum grew louder as Bonhist played to her audience.

Star now stood and started making her way to her daughter. Suddenly, Bonhist screamed, "They called me, I must go!" She whirled her buffalo robe above her head and, as it fell to earth over her body, it appeared to lie flat on the surface of the ground. In the dark shadows of dusk, it looked at the party as if this strange, beautiful girl had disappeared. Bonhist had managed the illusion so well that everyone stood and moved closer. Finally, White Dove picked up Bonhist's robe and screamed, "She is gone!"

Bonhist had noticed a depression in the ground that led to a small crack just large enough for her slender body to slide through. Under the small ledge, she quickly worked her way up to a large rock that overlooked the camp. It delighted her heart to have pulled off the trick. But now to continue the game—she could see that her trick had stunned them. She fought hard to keep from laughing and instead leaped upon the rock in full view and said, "My father, Crow, has spoken. He said that true Striped Feathers would join in brotherhood for our journey is long and our enemies are many. We should be happy with what we have and dance. Play the drum!" She leaped from the rock, picking up her robe. As she and White Dove continued dancing, everyone joined in. Despite tired feet, they danced until the moon was bright white and well overhead.

"Now," Bonhist said, "tell us the stories of Crow."

Everyone listened as Star stood to tell still another story in the life of her husband.

"Please," interrupted Red Leaf, "I have never told the story of Sand Creek and how Crow saved my life and that of Charging Bull, who was then only four winters." Everyone listened with immense interest while Red Leaf, with tears in her eyes, told of how she had always hated Crow. Yet it was Crow who gave his life for her and others at Sand Creek. Her description of his marksmanship was almost unbelievable for those who had known Crow.

Finally, Star, with tears rolling down her cheeks, said, "Good night, my brothers and sisters. Let us get some sleep, for Grandfather Sun will be laughing at us before long."

Charging Bull and Roaring Waters looked at each other. Their hands gripped as they shouted the Cheyenne war cry.

"I will be the wolf tonight. You two get some sleep," Squirrel said.

Everyone slept well in their robes until the morning sun. Bonhist woke as she did every day, with a smile on her lips and a sparkle in her eyes, speaking to the Great Spirit, the trees, and the rocks.

Three sleeps later, they reached a river and turned east. No one had to announce that it was the Arkansas River, for they all felt its spirit. Eight sleeps after reaching the river, Bent's Fort was in sight. They hoped that the Indian Agency and the man called Boone would still be found there. Since William Bent had resigned, Boone had been popular with the Indians. They felt that he would help them.

"This is my plan," said Star to the travelers. "We will seek out the Indian Agency and talk with Boone. Perhaps he will supply our food stock and help us to replace our horses. We are only passing through on our way to the Oklahoma Indian Territory. I am led to believe that the quicker we pass through Bent's Fort, the safer we will be." Star smiled at the group, and everyone nodded in agreement.

Lieutenant Henry Bartholomew Fry sat in the shade of the porch outside the officer's quarters in Bent's Fort. This easy duty suited him fine. His commanding officer happily assigned the high-tempered lieutenant an out-of-the-way post. He was young, good-looking, and used to having his way. His father, an eastern banker, had used his influence and money to secure his son's commission. Henry Bartholomew Fry had been in serious trouble. He had become involved with another man's wife. A fight occurred, and Henry had left the woman's husband dead. He was sent west and placed in a non-threatening situation. He had ten men under his command, who all disliked him intensely. Lieutenant Fry was of average size, 5'10" in height, and one hundred and eighty pounds. Now, his green eyes squinted as he ran his hand through his thick brown hair and took note of a small band of Indians entering the fort. "As usual," he reasoned, "they will go to the Indian Agency looking for a handout." He appraised the group quickly and noticed several young women. Perhaps this evening would be more fun than usual. He had not been with a woman in a long time. This looked like a good opportunity. He had no idea which tribe they belonged to and did not care one bit. They were ragged and poor. He could see that.

The Squirrel and Star walked into the agency while the rest threw their packs on the ground near a horse corral and sat resting.

Upon entering the Indian Agency, Star and the Squirrel faced an elderly Indian woman sitting at a desk. She looked up with surprise and, without smiling, spoke in the tongue of the Cheyenne. "Who are you, and what are you doing here?"

Both Star and the Squirrel relaxed, expecting a white man who could not speak their tongue.

"We are a small party of Cheyenne from up north. We are now traveling south to Indian Territory and were expecting to see Boone," Star said.

"My name is White Moon, and I am Cheyenne, as you are. I have worked here for many winters. Boone is now in Washington. He counsels with the great white chief. He has been gone for two moons. Still, I am surprised to see you since the Cheyenne have all gone to Oklahoma."

"We will soon be there as well. However, the Piute stole our horses several sleeps ago. We were hoping to get new horses and food before we continued," Star explained.

"This is not a good time. We have no horses for you, and our food supply is low. They have assigned a crazy pony soldier to this post, and I suggest that you leave here quickly."

"Is there nothing you can do for us?" Squirrel asked.

"I will open the stock room so that you may take what pleases you. An old Cheyenne man who is blind lives a short distance downriver. I feed him and try to help him the best I can. His name is Whirlwind, and he has many dogs. Perhaps, he would give you a few dogs to pull your drag poles."

"Was Whirlwind of Chief Thin Face's tribe?" Squirrel asked. "I think I know him."

"Yes, he was once a fierce warrior blinded by white men who believed he knew the location of their gold. He has adjusted well."

"Why did he not go to Indian Territory with the rest of the Cheyenne?" Star asked.

"Since he is blind, no one would take the responsibility for leading him."

"Why is Boone counseling with the big white chief?" Star asked again.

"The white man has thought of a new plan for the Indians. They call it reservations. They will require all Indians to live on these reservations and never leave. They will give the Indians food, blankets, and seeds to become growers."

"If we live in the Indian Territory, will we be free?" Star asked.

"Yes, that is why old Whirlwind yearns to travel to Indian Territory, where he can die free and with his own people."

"Get on your damn feet! I must question and search you," Lieutenant Fry shouted.

"No, it is too late," White Moon said.

Chapter 6

White Moon rushed from the agency office and stormed up to the lieutenant, speaking in the white man's tongue. "What are you doing? These are Southern Cheyenne, traveling to the Indian Territory. They have come for help since they have neither horses nor food. Leave them alone, or I will report your actions!"

Bonhist thought for a moment that the pony soldier would backhand the old Cheyenne woman, but instead he shouted back to her in his own tongue, a language Bonhist did not understand.

"These are renegades, enemies of the U. S. Government. Possibly, they were part of the force that attacked and killed General Custer and the Seventh Cavalry. I will search and question them before they continue to the Indian Territory."

"You are crazy! Can you not see that these Cheyenne are mainly young women with two half-grown boys and an older man? They are no threat to anyone. They came in peace, looking for help; let them go in peace."

"Get out of my way!" shouted Lieutenant Fry, shoving White Moon aside, causing her to lose her balance and fall to the ground. Bonhist immediately rushed to White Moon to help her to her feet. At that exact moment, Bonhist saw her mother reach for her bow.

When White Moon was on her feet, Bonhist turned to the pony soldier and, using sign language, asked, "What do you want?"

Henry Bartholomew Fry did not understand a word, yet he smiled instantly. He had seen many beautiful young women in the east, but the sight of this young Indian maiden gave him the shock of his life. For a moment, it stopped the thought process of his cunning mind from formulating a plan. Lieutenant Fry was determined to have a woman, even a young Indian maiden would satisfy his needs, but this was too good. In front of him, within touching distance, stood the most beautiful young woman he had ever seen. He suddenly turned to White Moon and demanded, "What is she saying?

"She is asking what you want."

"Tell her that it is my duty to search and question their party," responded Lieutenant Fry, who now had a sly smile on his face.

As Bonhist watched the pony soldier, she felt danger. *This is an evil man; we cannot trust him,* she thought.

White Moon turned to the small group and said, "He is demanding that they search your packs and question you. He will look for scalps."

"Here," Bonhist said. "Search my pack. We have nothing to hide from this evil man." Bonhist quickly threw her pack on the ground in front of the lieutenant. Immediately, the rest followed her lead and laid out their packs for search.

Bonhist glanced toward her mother, who was still holding her bow, debating whether to notch an arrow or roll out her pack with the rest.

Lieutenant Fry ordered two of his men to search the packs. With much reservation, the men followed their orders and haphazardly went through the packs.

"Nothing here, Lieutenant," a trooper said.

"That's fine. Now, if that young lady will follow me to my quarters for questioning, the rest may carry on with their business," the lieutenant said.

Bonhist's every instinct was screaming danger! Do not trust this man! She had worked her way to the back of the group near the corral. When Lieutenant Fry pointed at her, she desperately whirled her robe above her head as she had done before. The robe floated to the ground and lay flat. As all turned, they could not believe their eyes; Bonhist had disappeared again.

White Dove slowly picked up the robe and screamed, "She has done it again. Bonhist has disappeared into the air."

Star then spoke to White Moon. "Tell this dog that my daughter can vanish into the air. I will answer his questions."

"No!" said the Squirrel. "Tell him I will answer his questions."

Now, the lieutenant had the attention of all ten of his men. They went through the corral and around back. Once out of sight, they mocked the lieutenant, laughing. After a few minutes, they returned to report that the young woman had vanished, nowhere to be found.

The lieutenant flew into a rage. "Throw this entire group into the stockade. No one will leave here until I talk with that girl!"

"Sir, don't you think this is getting out of hand? The government has filed no charges against these people. And that girl is just a little bit young for you to take to bed," the sergeant said.

The truth stopped the lieutenant in his tracks, and he took a grim look at the sergeant. "You forget who is in charge around here. I want these dirty redskins held for further questioning." He then turned and walked back to his quarters. The sergeant spoke to White Moon loud enough for the retreating lieutenant to hear, "Tell them that they are to wait for questioning." The sergeant signaled to White Moon, "Tell them to leave now."

When the lieutenant slammed his door, White Moon whispered to Star. "I will lead you to the camp of Whirlwind. You will be safe there for this evening. He can supply you with dogs if you want them. Just follow the Arkansas River well past Flint Hills. You will come to a point where a branch of the river flows south. Follow that stream into Indian Territory. You will have water and good hunting all the way!

Star smiled at White Moon and said, "Thank you, Mother, you have been kind. Now, take us quickly to Whirlwind's camp." At that, White Moon began to lead the small party east to the camp.

Bonhist quickly slipped out of the robe that was around Red Leaf's shoulders. Red Leaf had welcomed her under the robe as she had thrown her own robe into the air. Bonhist had again pulled off her disappearing act, with only Red Leaf knowing the truth. She now concealed herself by wrapping herself in her robe and joining the group.

"Where is Bonhist?" Star asked.

"I am here, Mother."

Everyone turned and stared.

"How do you do that?" Roaring Waters asked.

"My father has given me strong medicine," answered Bonhist with a satisfied grin as she lifted the twin medicine bags that hung around her slender neck. Red Leaf smiled to herself while the rest stared in awe.

After several minutes, the group entered Whirlwind's camp. The aroma of a roasting turkey filled their nostrils even before they saw the lodge. Everything there was neat and orderly. A filled water skin hung from a tree limb. But the old man was not in sight. White Moon smiled and walked to his campfire, slowly turning the turkey secured to a sharp stick, the stick piercing the bird. She then said, "It's okay, Whirlwind; I bring friends. These are your people, the Southern Cheyenne." Suddenly, from the shadows, a figure moved. He had been in plain sight all the time, yet no one had seen him, not even White Moon. Whirlwind did not speak as he moved among the Cheyenne and finally sat on his robe in front of the roasting bird. He had carried a heavy walking stick, which he now laid by his side. His hair was still black with streaks of white that shot from his forehead all the way back past his shoulders. His hair was not braided, yet he was well-groomed in other ways. He dressed in the traditional Cheyenne buckskins, a loincloth, and leggings. The beadwork was the clear sign of a Cheyenne warrior.

"What are the names of these friends you have brought?" he finally asked.

Sitting in a circle around Whirlwind, who proudly lifted his head so all could see his scars and sightless eyes, White Moon started around the circle by introducing Star and the Squirrel. She then let Star introduce the rest. Whirlwind knew the Squirrel and Red Leaf.

When Star said that she was the wife of Crow, a smile came to the face of the old blind man. "Yes, I remember Crow well. They say that he had a daughter. Is this true?"

"Yes, this is Crow's daughter. Her name is Bonhist," Star answered with a smile.

"Come, child," the old man said.

Bonhist, without hesitation, walked to Whirlwind and sat beside him. "I am here, Grandfather. I am pleased to know you."

"May I touch you?" Whirlwind asked.

Bonhist reached over, lifted the old man's hands, and placed them on her face. This gave Whirlwind great pleasure; his face lit up in delight.

"Yes, this is the daughter of Crow. You are much like your father. Your father gave me many laughs. I was very sad to hear of Sand Creek."

"Grandfather, why do you live here by yourself?" Bonhist asked.

"The People have all gone to the Indian Territory. As you can see, I have no eyes. I fear that I will die alone since I cannot travel to my people."

"You will come with us, Grandfather. I will be your eyes and walk with you every step until we are together again, back in Indian Territory.

Around the circle, obvious displeasure was felt at Bonhist's invitation to the old blind man. Yet, no one said a word or spoke out against the folly of such an act.

"Thank you, Bonhist, that is what your father, Crow, would have said. You will do his memory honor. Still, I would put your party in danger, and it is a long way to go. I will stay here and die in this land."

"No, you will not, Grandfather. You will come with us. We are always in danger, so you will add nothing new to our trip to Oklahoma."

"I hear the sound of many horses," Whirlwind said.

Instantly, both Roaring Waters and Charging Bull jumped to their feet and ran to a high point above the camp. "The pony soldier! The crazy one comes."

Chapter 7

As Lieutenant Henry Bartholomew Fry rode over the ridge and into the camp of Whirlwind, he saw only Whirlwind, White Moon, the Squirrel, and Star. The rest were hidden with their bows notched and ready. Leading a string of nine government horses, two of them carrying packs, he was alone with only a determined expression on his face.

Whirlwind raised his hand to the lieutenant and spoke in the Cheyenne tongue. "You are not welcome in my camp. Leave now, or the buzzards will eat your flesh by morning."

Lieutenant Fry turned to White Moon, "What did that old coot say?"

White Moon then spoke to the Lieutenant in his own tongue. "He said you honored him by your visit, and he would like for you to state your business quickly."

"That is none of his business. I came to speak to the mother of the girl that I saw this afternoon. I do not know her name, but she is the one they said could vanish into thin air."

White Moon turned to Whirlwind and Star, giving her own translation. "He said he came in peace and that he is very honored to be in the camp of Whirlwind. He wishes to speak with Star about Bonhist."

Star stepped forward quickly and spoke sharply, "I should have killed you this afternoon. However, I will shoot you off that horse if you even talk to my daughter."

Again, White Moon translated to the lieutenant. "This is the mother of the child you saw this afternoon. They call her Rabbit Teeth with Breath of Skunk. She asks what you want."

"I will never understand the stupidity of Indians. How could they name a pretty, young woman such a name? Tell the mother that I will marry her daughter. I have brought these horses and two packs full of tobacco, coffee, cooking utensils, and food in trade for the young woman."

White Moon turned to Star with a smile and said, "He wants to marry Bonhist. He will trade the horses and packs that are full of food, tobacco, and coffee for her."

"Tell him he is dead. I will kill him and leave him for the ants. Bonhist will never marry a white man. But we will take the horses anyway," Star said.

"His safety is very important to you all. If we kill him or he does not return to the fort, they will send many pony soldiers who will tie ropes around all your necks and hang you from the trees. You will all die, and the ropes will trap your spirits so that you cannot cross over into the spirit world to be with your husband and loved ones."

"Tell him the answer is no! We do not want anything from him. Tell him to go and leave us in peace," Star ordered.

White Moon turned again to the lieutenant and translated, "Star, the mother to Rabbit Teeth with Breath of Skunk, has said that you are very handsome and strong. You will make her a fine son. She is concerned since her daughter is only ten winters, has a very flat chest, and is skinny. Still, we will prepare for the torture ceremony. After you have completed this act, then Rabbit Teeth with Breath of Skunk will be prepared for your wedding. We are all so happy for her."

"What the hell is a torture ceremony? Is that some stupid Indian thing? I will not do anything that hurts me. Hell, I just want the girl. Maybe I was wrong; I have decided that the child is too young for what I want. I will go now."

"However, lieutenant, we have a much older woman over there," she said, pointing toward Red Leaf. "She thinks you would be good in the blanket. She will come with you tonight for the horses; however, her last husband died of some disease."

"No! I will leave now," Henry said as he turned in his saddle, leading his string of government horses back to the fort.

White Moon turned with a smile and said, "He honors your wishes. He will bother you no more."

Bonhist watched the entire proceedings with great interest. She greatly admired White Moon for knowing the white man's tongue. *Someday*, she thought, *I too will learn to speak the tongue of the white man.*

The following morning, Whirlwind called his dogs. They cut and trimmed poles and loaded the packs. Bonhist had now convinced the blind Whirlwind that he could wait for death alone or come with them to the Indian Territory, where he would be with the

People again. White Moon was also encouraged to come; however, she refused, explaining that with this new plan to put the Indians on reservations, she would be needed here at the agency. Final words were spoken, and the traveling party pulled out, five dogs hauling five small travois. Bonhist smiled widely as she held the hand of Whirlwind. She talked endlessly, describing the sky, birds, clouds, and other features of the terrain. Glancing at her mother, she could see that she was relieved to be away from the fort again, walking to the land of the People.

"Roaring Waters, you and Charging Bull will spread out and walk on the north side of the river. Star and I will hunt the south side. We will be the wolves for the main group, keeping a sharp eye for game. We now must hunt for our food," said the Squirrel. Star smiled, happy that the Squirrel was assuming some leadership and had moved out walking along the river well in front of the women and Whirlwind.

Several sleeps later, they came upon the Flint Hills of Kansas. This had been the hunting ground of the Striped Feathers, who now called themselves the Cheyenne. They had often gathered flint stones for their arrows and lances from this area. A strong spirit existed here. Everyone felt a little sad to leave the Colorado mountains behind and travel through the Flint Hills, perhaps for the last time. Still, they hunted with success and kept moving along the river.

The sun was high overhead when the Squirrel came running, "Hide everyone, the pony soldiers are coming."

Within minutes, the landscape showed no sign of the traveling party; even the dogs, packs, and pull poles were well concealed.

Riding in columns, a small group of pony soldiers soon passed. No one was surprised to see Lieutenant Fry lead them. They stopped in the bend of the river where the lieutenant dismounted and studied the ground as if he were trying to read the trail. His men wore broad grins on their faces as they watched in silence. He then remounted, and the pony soldiers rode on.

The sun moved high in the sky before Star readied the traveling party. "They look for us and will bring much trouble if they catch us. Roaring Waters, you and Charging Bull will lead by a half day's travel in front and be our wolves. The Squirrel will follow you by a short morning's walk, and I will be right behind him. If you spot the pony soldiers returning, you will send a signal and hide. We must see our enemy and camouflage ourselves before they see us."

Bonhist walked beside Whirlwind. She held his hand and continued talking with him as if nothing had happened. They fell behind, and Bonhist could see the dust rising from the trail of the travois. They could see the trail too easily left by the drag poles. *How could the white man miss such obvious signs?* she thought.

Finally, Whirlwind spoke. "You are a very beautiful young woman, that is obvious. More than that, you have a rare quality among the People. Your father, Crow, had that quality. It is a compassion for your people and all men."

"Grandfather, how do you know what I look like. Remember, I am your eyes. How do you know my heart? I am not my father or my mother. I am only Bonhist, the sage woman. Still, the chief of the pony soldiers frightens me. I sense an evil in this man."

"Bonhist, do not be deceived in the thought that I cannot see you; I see through my hands, my ears, and my nose. I know you are beautiful; the fact that the pony soldier has gone to so much effort to find you tells me he thinks you are beautiful, too. Your instincts are true about this man; he must never find you. I know from the way you treat me that your heart is good—like your father, Crow."

"Do not worry, Grandfather, this man cannot read our trail; he is no smarter than a rabbit."

A wide grin spread across the face of the old blind man as he listened to Bonhist. He swung his heavy walking stick with one hand as the other squeezed a little tighter to the soft, slender hand of the sage woman.

As evening approached, Star gathered the party well away from the river in a hidden gorge. It was perfect for their camp. As the women were preparing the evening meal, Charging Bull entered camp with a big smile. From his buckskin shirt, he dumped a generous supply of fresh corn. "An abandoned corn field is not far from here. It has as many tender ears of corn as stars in the sky."

"With the dogs, we could carry enough corn to last all the way to Indian Territory," Pretty Dove said.

"The light from Grandfather Sun is almost in his home. Let us look at this abandoned corn field in the morning," Star suggested.

As the sun came up the following morning, the party of travelers stood looking upon a lush green corn field that ran parallel to the river. No one was around, and it appeared abandoned entirely as Charging Bull had said.

"This is hard to believe that such a fine field of corn is just left for the birds and animals," Bonhist said.

"Still, who is there to keep us from gathering a big supply for our trip?" White Dove said, with Crow Wings agreeing.

So, the party entered the field, picked big ears of corn, and put them in extra packs. Suddenly, a shot sounded. As its thunder vibrated through the morning air like a great bolt of lightning, the Squirrel grabbed his chest and fell face down in the corn field.

Everyone looked to the source of the thunder, where a white man stood beside two mules pulling a wooden wagon. White smoke rose from his fire stick, and he reloaded, looking for another target.

The travelers stood in disbelief, except Roaring Waters, who screamed the Cheyenne war cry and charged the man. He ran through the field, raising his hand with the big knife shining in the morning sun. Exposing his chest, he invited a bullet. Instead, the man threw his rifle into the wagon, jumped to the seat, and turned the mules with a shout.

In an instant, the mules were running, pulling the wagon and the man out of sight, leaving only dust flying high in the air. Pretty Dove ran to her husband, rolled him over, and wailed with a terrible cry. "Squirrel is dead."

Leaving the corn behind, they lifted the Squirrel and carried his body back to their morning camp. Pretty Dove was holding her husband and crying while White Dove and Crow Wings joined their mother in her wailing.

Minutes later, Roaring Waters came running into camp. "The white man returns with the pony soldiers. The crazy one is leading. I will go and fight them."

CHAPTER 8

"No! Roaring Waters, you and Charging Bull can lead us down the gorge to get off the river and head south. Since the pony soldiers are looking for us along the river, we will take a new route," insisted Bonhist with a sense of urgency.

"You do not understand," retorted Roaring Waters. "The white man with the mules is leading the pony soldiers to us while we talk. We must fight now!"

"Yes, but we must have a proper burial for the Squirrel," Pretty Dove sobbed.

"Lay him here," said Bonhist. "Grandfather, give me your walking stick." In an instant, Bonhist had caved in an edge of the gully. The embankment fell in one big torrent, covering the body of the Squirrel whom they had wrapped in his buffalo robe and laid with his weapons. "There, we have buried him. We have no more time for a ceremony. Now, listen! We will leave a false trail by leading the dogs with the drag poles to the river. Near that thick grove of ash trees is a good place. They will see my tracks entering the river, and they will believe that we are hiding among the groves. Meanwhile, you will travel to that far ridge and wait for me," Bonhist said, pointing south.

"No!" Star said. "That is too dangerous. The pony soldiers search for a prize, and you are the prize. I will lead the dogs to the river."

"No, Mother, they would shoot you, but the crazy one wants me alive. Have you forgotten how I can disappear? Do not worry, and do not look for me. I will return to you by nightfall."

Without another word, Bonhist led the dogs quickly to the river. The party followed her instructions, walking with their packs down the gorge, which was no more than a gully stretched in the direction of the distant ridge that Bonhist had noticed.

The dogs reclined almost immediately upon reaching the river's edge. Bonhist did not take the time to tie them, quickly leaving her tracks and leaping into the water. Pulling herself from the river, she looked up to see the loping horses carrying the pony soldiers coming around the bend. Without time to select a good hiding spot, she dived forward rolling in the sand until her back was up against an embankment. Her only concealment was some scrubby buffalo grass that grew along its upper surface and hung down across her face. She looked quickly at her buckskin clothing, covered with wet sand, so that she blended into the embankment. She was lying in plain sight. By making herself quiet and still like a rock, she hoped to seem to disappear into thin air.

The white man, who had grown the corn, leaned forward on the mule's back, pointing toward the dogs. A few heartbeats later, the entire group of pony soldiers was within thirty feet of Bonhist. She had never been so scared but allowed herself to peek at her pursuers as they dismounted to look over the dogs and drag poles. "They're close! I can feel it! You men surround these trees. Sergeant, take a man and ride downstream. They may be trying to drift with the current. We have them, and, by God, I do not want that girl hurt. Kill the rest if they resist," ordered Lieutenant Fry.

"Sir, may I remind you that Bent's Fort is mainly just a trading post. We have no business trying to capture these poor people. All they are trying to do is go home to the Indian Territory so they can be with their own tribe."

"Poor, hell! Sergeant, these thieving Redskins are guilty of a felony. It is our duty to apprehend them. Now follow your orders."

"Stealing two bits' worth of corn does not make them the enemy. All you want is that girl."

Bonhist heard plainly the strange words that the white men spoke, but she understood nothing. As her fear subsided, she found that these men were entertaining to watch. One man was clumsily climbing a tree as two others rode their horses downstream. The search was intense as they examined every rock and tree. After the sun was well overhead, one man started a campfire within twenty feet of Bonhist. He had a pot of water heating. Another pony soldier brought a load of corn that they shucked and threw into the large pan of water. "They are going to eat," thought Bonhist. "If they do not see me, I will thank the Great Spirit every day of my life. Surely when darkness comes, I can slip away."

"What the hell is going on here!" shouted the lieutenant.

"Sir, it is only a small amount of corn; we will enjoy having something different," the cook answered.

"Hell, I don't mean that. I mean, why are we stopping the search? They have to be here; we can eat at another time."

"Sir, the men have to eat. Them Injuns can hide like rattlesnakes. When you step on one, he'll reach out and stick a knife in you. They aren't going nowhere; let's eat."

The men ate, smoked, and finally, the lieutenant ordered them back to their task. Bonhist smiled again as men were now wading along the riverbanks looking for possible hiding places. All this amused her, and she wished more than ever to understand their words.

"I will tell you one damn thing; we are not leaving until we find them Injuns!" the lieutenant screamed as late evening approached. Everyone just shook their heads and looked at the dogs.

"Why don't we turn them dogs loose? Maybe they'll lead us to the Injuns?" one trooper asked.

"Turn them damn dogs loose!" shouted the lieutenant. He was disappointed to see that the dogs hardly moved except to approach the cook, looking for some scraps of food. One wagged his tail, moved toward Bonhist, and, within a foot, rolled over wagging his tail.

"Them are Injun dogs; they are not gonna lead us to them Indians. Hell, don't you know, Injuns eat dogs," a sandy-haired trooper commented.

As the sun set, the cook again stirred up a fire and put on the coffee and beans. Soon, everyone gathered around for his evening meal. "We'll camp here tonight and continue our search for the fugitives by the first sunlight," the lieutenant said.

Everyone moaned and gathered their sleeping rolls. One man threw his gear down beside Bonhist, waking the sleeping dog, who walked away.

The men ate, smoked, and leaned back on their sleeping gear using their saddles as pillows. It was late summer, and in the west, a beautiful orange and purple sky gave way to evening darkness. The cook threw an old log across the fire to assure a hot bed of embers for the morning breakfast. "Lieutenant," the sergeant said for all to hear. "Has it occurred to you that them Redskins might just be miles from here laughing at us?"

"I am in a bad mood, Sergeant. I hope you have a good point for bringing up such a dumb remark. Why would they leave their dogs and enter the river? What are you suggesting?"

"Well, sir, Indians can be quite crafty. Hell, see what they did to General Custer? Maybe they just wanted us to think they entered the river by leaving their dogs there. What I am saying is they could be anywhere—maybe miles away."

"No, sir!" announced the sandy-haired trooper. "One of 'um is right here." He reached over, grabbed Bonhist by the arm, and yanked her to her feet.

The lieutenant jumped to his feet and shouted, "That's her! Bring her over to the light. I want to get a good look at her this time."

The men formed a semicircle around Bonhist and the lieutenant. Everyone wanted to see the young woman who had prompted the lieutenant to take this unusual and unnecessary excursion. Bonhist shook the sand from her body and went without resisting. It was evident this was no ordinary woman. She was every man's dream. "Open your mouth," the lieutenant ordered. He then took his hands and forced open Bonhist's mouth. He saw beautiful, even, white teeth surrounded by healthy, pink gums.

"I will kill White Moon when I see her again," the lieutenant declared. He could already see her legs. They were long, slender, and beautiful. "Now," he said with lust in his eyes, "let's see what a ten-year-old child looks like." His trembling hands reached for her well-developed breasts.

Chapter 9

Facing Lieutenant Fry and within his grasp was the woman of his dreams. With long, silky black hair, flowing over her shoulders like water, she lifted her chin. A Cheyenne, wild and free, she had the face of an angel. The lieutenant looked upon this rare beauty as if she were a beautiful wild horse. She would be his and his alone to break and train as any wild mustang. Catching the young woman had been difficult, and his men had resisted him at every turn of the river. Still, it was well worth the trouble, and he would certainly do it again. Smiling as he reached out for his prize, he planned to rip her buckskins from her body and take a good look. White Moon had tried to deceive him, but his eyes could not have been mistaken—she was a beautiful woman. He glanced at his men, seeing that they stood in awe as he did. Just before he touched her, she raised a short skinning knife to her throat and gave a hand signal.

"Lieutenant, she's Cheyenne. She will kill herself before allowing you to touch her. Try to talk to her; her hand sign means stop," the sergeant said.

"Move back, she is frightened and will kill herself," the sandy-haired trooper repeated.

The two men stopped the lieutenant for only a moment. Turning his head toward his men, he said, "I do not need advice from any of you. Hell, no one cuts his own throat." He took another step toward Bonhist, which prompted the Cheyenne maiden to touch the knife to her throat, causing a drop of blood to trickle down her neck.

As he hesitated for a second, a heavy club from out of the darkness landed squarely on his back. Henry Bartholomew fell like a tree, unconscious and face down. Moving into the pony soldiers with his club swinging like a whirlwind was the old, blind Cheyenne. His black hair was streaked with white, and he had painted his face for war. Instantly, Bonhist yelled into the darkness, "Do not shoot! These are not bad men. Give them their lives."

She signaled the sergeant quickly, advising the men to lay down their weapons. "Do not follow us! We will continue our journey along the river to Indian Territory," she said in the tongue of the Cheyenne and in sign talk. She turned sharply and reached for the hand of Whirlwind, who had stopped swinging his walking stick, saying, "Come, Grandfather, you have done well. You are a brave and true warrior of the Striped Feathers."

Whirlwind took the young woman's hand with a smile as they walked into the darkness, where Star and the rest waited with notched arrows. The men crouched low, expecting arrows to fill the air, but to their surprise, the Indians were gone.

At sunrise, the Indians lay along the ridge watching the pony soldiers. The lieutenant moved like an old man barely able to mount. Turning slowly in his saddle, he shouted a command. They rode in a column of twos down the stream in the direction of the rising sun.

"Look, the crazy one still searches for our trail, looking for Bonhist. He will not give up," Red Leaf said, pointing at the soldiers.

"We will go south and take a new route to the Indian Territory. He will look for us along the river," announced Star.

"Another river is many sleeps to the south, the land is dry, and hunting is poor," Whirlwind said.

"Let us not be foolish," said Bonhist. "We will take the time to return to the river, fill our water skins, pack a load of corn, and then head south to this river of which Whirlwind speaks."

With a good supply of food and water, the party headed south through barren land that looked like nothing could live on it. The going was dry, hot, and dusty, but they still felt safe. Not even Charging Bull could find food, either plants or animals.

They did not know the distance they had traveled, but after their sixth sleep, they ran out of both food and water. Two days later, as they roasted one of the dogs in the shade of a washed-out gully, they were tired, thirsty, and hungry, but most of all discouraged.

"We will die in this land," White Dove said while eating her small portion of the dog. She was the only one who had the energy or desire to talk. "Birds do not even fly across this barren, worthless land. I am surprised that they have not made this into a reservation for the People."

"Get the water skins ready," said Whirlwind. "I can see rain. We will have water soon."

Each night, they roasted another dog till they were all gone. Then two days passed without food. "I cannot go any farther. I cannot even remember when we last ate. I will die on this spot," White Dove cried.

"You are not alone, White Dove. We all feel the same. I should have gone with the crazy one so that the party could have remained on the Arkansas River," Bonhist said.

"I should have killed him at the fort. He has caused us much grief. I would never allow my daughter to go with such a man," a tired Star uttered.

"Do you think someone will one day cross this lifeless land and find our bones?" Crow Wings asked.

"We will not die. Roaring Waters and Charging Bull will find game," whispered Soft Winds. Bonhist smiled at that. Only twelve winters old, she had great courage and faith and was perhaps in love with Roaring Waters.

Soft Winds' words brought good luck, for the following morning, Charging Bull killed an antelope. The unfortunate animal was even smaller than the dogs. Yet, by drinking the blood of the fresh kill and eating its flesh practically raw, the party of ten felt a little stronger. Out of water again, they walked south for two more days. Approaching the shade of a thicket of scrub cedar trees, they collapsed one by one to the hot sandy soil. By mid-afternoon, not even White Dove had spoken as each realized that this was the end, and no one would ever get up again. When the sun went down, Bonhist turned and looked into the sky where the stars and moon shone brightly. "I had a vision. Both food and water are nearby. We must turn west."

Nothing was stronger to the Indians than a vision even though most of them did not have this gift. Often a medicine man or a chief would base an important decision on such a sign. With great effort, Bonhist rose to her feet. Seconds later, Star rose and joined her daughter.

"If we find food and water, we will return hopefully before the buzzards come," Bonhist said.

Walking only ten feet, she noticed that everyone was now up and following her.

CHAPTER 10

As the sun rose in the east, the rugged, dry land appeared to have a haze of blue. Perhaps it was only a reflection of the giant clear blue morning sky. The party had been stumbling along following Bonhist since the middle of the night. Suddenly, Red Leaf fell to her knees and moaned loudly. Then Pretty Dove and her daughter White Dove slumped to the ground. Bonhist stopped and raised her hands to the sky. "Oh, Great Spirit of the sky, we thank you for the vision you have shown my eyes. I know the canyons are near because you have shown me both food and water. I see now that you will guide us to the Indian Territory, and gratefully it is so."

Within fifty feet of where Bonhist stood was the unseen rim of a canyon. Stumbling upon the sight of the canyon, they were amazed. Bonhist seemed to make it appear—like magic. "Stop Grandfather! Before you step from the edge of the canyon wall, there is a sharp drop."

"Look," Charging Bull said. "Water!"

Finding a likely spot to descend, they rushed down the side of the canyon's sloping wall and fell face first into a stream that had no more than two inches of water in its bed. Only Bonhist and Star helped the blind Whirlwind down the embankment to the water.

"Look, red berries grow along the walls of the canyon," Charging Bull observed.

"Yes, and look—trees. Cottonwood, elms, and over there are cedars," Roaring Waters added, pointing to their surroundings.

"I hear falling water," Whirlwind said.

Charging Bull rose to his feet. "I hear nothing," he said. Walking to the next turn of the canyon, he yelled, "Come, the water falls to a lower valley where there is a deep pool."

White Dove, Crow Wings, Red Leaf, Pretty Dove, and Soft Winds stumbled to the red berries. They each ate as fast as they could pick them. Bonhist, leading Whirlwind, walked beside Star and Roaring Waters to the spot where Charging Bull had seen the falling water.

"This is amazing," Star said. "It is beautiful to my eyes."

Grass and trees covered the valley. A good stream continued through the wide canyon. Charging Bull had already found a way to the lower valley and dived into the pool of water with a splash. Roaring Waters was right behind, and the two young Cheyenne warriors swam across the life-giving, clear water with a war cry. Soon, Bonhist had helped Whirlwind down to a spot below the falls where he sat beside the cool pool of water.

"Look, the berries are even thicker here," Roaring Waters said.

Bonhist picked berries as fast as she could and gave them to Whirlwind. As they all ate the berries, the rest of the party followed to the lower valley. Bonhist smiled at Charging Bull as he wandered down the stream with his bow in hand.

He soon returned with a bullfrog. "I have seen turtles and frogs."

The women were cooking the turtles and frogs that the boys had killed when Star walked in with a fat rabbit. "This is not much for ten people; however, I feel that good hunting exists in this canyon. The cold man of the north will come before we reach the Indian Territory. This would be a good place for our winter camp," Star announced.

Red Leaf grunted and said, "We need buffalo to survive the winter."

"It is true; we cannot live on frogs, turtles, and rabbits. Nevertheless, the Great Spirit has brought us here. Surely, we will not starve," Bonhist answered.

"Yes, Bonhist, you have strong medicine. Your vision was accurate. This is good. We have plenty of water; and we will find food," Whirlwind said.

Among the Cheyenne and the other Plains Indians, girls were taught the use of weapons and skills of hunting with the boys. The women now used these skills as their stomachs still growled with hunger. With throwing sticks and their bows, they combed the area. Still, even with their combined efforts they could not produce a steady supply of meat. Even digging for roots had provided only poor results; hunger would not go away.

Two sleeps later, Charging Bull came rushing into camp with great excitement. He had hunted by himself, and no one had seen him all day. "Come! I have seen the white man's buffalo. They call them steers. They have been abandoned and now run free like buffalo. We must kill one before we all starve."

"They are abandoned like the corn field. Which of us will die for one of the white man's steers?" Star asked.

"Who cares? I will offer myself, or I will fight the white man for one," Roaring Waters said. "Come, brother, we will hunt."

"No, we will all go. Perhaps Charging Bull has seen some wild steers; if so, we will all be needed to hunt and to butcher," Star said.

So, the party gathered their packs and marched down the canyon. "It is almost dark, and still, it is a long walk to the cattle. We will camp here and hunt in the morning," Charging Bull explained.

When morning came, everyone woke up with great hunger. They had eaten many berries and rabbits, yet their stomachs ached. After a half day's journey, the canyon opened into a wide valley with a river. The river was almost dry, and on either side were hundreds of trees, mainly cottonwoods. Charging Bull signaled, and everyone stopped to look. Movement in the trees caught their attention. It was cattle, and many. Star gathered the party and said, "Do not be fooled; I am led to believe that the white man who owns these steers will be close. We must scout the area before we shoot one. Let us meet back here before Grandfather Sun has gone to his home in the west."

Everyone nodded their understanding and quickly spread out, reading signs. They were trying to detect anything that would suggest the presence of the white man. By late evening, they met for a council. They agreed that they would kill one steer, as no one had seen anything that would show danger.

They made the kill silently and quickly with the great shooting eye of Star. Roaring Waters rushed in and cut the steer's throat, smearing blood across his face; he screamed the Cheyenne war cry. Soon, they began the butchering and lit a fire, all of them starving.

The aroma of roasting steaks soon filled the air. This was their first experience eating the white man's beef. It was not as good as buffalo, but all agreed that it was better than dog. Nevertheless, everyone ate until they could eat no more. It was good to have full stomachs, and all felt content as the sun went to its home in the west. Everyone slept soundly.

Jesus Travoris, known as Chewy, was assigned to keep track of Milburn's cattle. He was living in the line cabin. His cousin, Ramone Estrada, would replace him sometime after Christmas. Chewy was happy about his assignment. The line cabin was set back in a grove of cottonwoods along the North Canadian River. It was well built and comfortable. Near the cabin was a corral. Chewy smiled as he looked at a pile of magazines near his bunk bed. He could not read the English, but he loved to thumb through the articles and illustrations. Mainly, he loved the idea that the other hands would not bother him. Never had there been any trouble, at least, not for six years back. Sr. Milburn had caught three young men red-handed. They were rustling eight steers, and not one rustler was more than sixteen years old. Sr. Milburn hung them from the closest tree. Still, he liked working for the old man.

Sr. Milburn was very old and had led an interesting life. As a young man, he had been a mountain man and had married a pretty Blackfoot Indian. They had a son named David William Milburn. Milburn's wife died young, leaving Milburn to raise his son. He had worked for years at the Four Rivers Ranch in Colorado and never remarried. Still, Milburn wanted to leave a legacy to his son. He had sent him back to an eastern school; however, things did not work out as David showed no interest in the academic world. Instead, he liked horses, guns, and the West. This ranch, named the Milburn Canadian River Ranch, was Milburn's last effort to secure his son's future. Milburn was a good man, but he hated nesters. They knew that he would hang or shoot anyone caught rustling his cattle.

Three horses were kept in the corral. Sr. Milburn had told Chewy that his job was to hit the leather daily and ride, observing the eastern edge of Milburn's spread. It was a pain; yet, without exception, Chewy did his duty. On this day, Chewy could not believe his eyes. Through Milburn's old field glasses, he saw the Indians. It made him shake and tremble, for they had just killed one of the bosses' steers. It was a good fourteen-mile ride to the main ranch house; nevertheless, turning the buckskin, he rode at full speed without looking back.

Chapter 11

"Señor Milburn! We have trouble! Indians!" called Chewy as he slid from his horse, still wet from its long run.

Milburn's ranch was not a shoestring outfit. He had built it knowing that one day it would belong to his son, David. The ranch hands, under the supervision of the best carpenters that he could hire, had constructed the house. It sat high on a hillside overlooking the Canadian River, with a veranda along the front that offered a sweeping view. This was Milburn's favorite place to sit. He had flowering plants hanging from the roof and a heavy wooden table for eating outdoors. They had divided the home into two. The smaller section housed the kitchen, where the cook, a Mexican Woman named Marie Carrillo, and her husband, Rojo, lived. The larger area contained three bedrooms and a living area with a massive rock fireplace. Adjacent to the living area was an office with a heavy oak desk. Bookcases filled with the classics lined the walls. A formal dining room, rarely used, was the last addition. A wide hall separating these two sections of the house was open at both ends. They called it a "gallery" or, as some preferred, a "dogtrot" because the dogs often lay there.

Behind the house were three working corrals, a large barn with a blacksmith shed, and a bunk house. In addition, Milburn was proud of his vegetable garden and fruit trees, which an elderly Asian man named Moo Nguyen tended.

Chewy had arrived just before first sunlight, but all the ranch hands were up, sitting around the old wooden table on the veranda, eating biscuits, bacon, and drinking coffee.

Milburn jumped back from the table upon hearing the news, knocking over his chair. When he violently threw his coffee cup to the ground, David cautioned, with his usual smile, "Take it easy, Dad!" David, taller than his dad, with a thick crop of long black hair and gray eyes, was slender through the waist, had well-developed arms and shoulders from hard work, and carried a rifle as if he were born with it. "This is nothing we can't handle. They are no threat to us. The boys and I will take care of it."

"I may be old, but I can still ride. I will decide whether they are a threat or not."

"Señor Milburn, I could not tell the number of renegades nor the number of steers they have killed," Chewy offered as he grabbed a hot biscuit and jammed three slices of greasy bacon inside.

"We haven't seen Indians around here in a while. Did you recognize their tribe?" Milburn asked as he reached for his gun belt.

"No, Señor, I do not know—maybe Apache."

"Well, hell, get saddled; we have a fight. Everyone's going except Marie and Moo; we will pull out in five minutes."

"Me, too?" asked Chewy as he gulped down some coffee and reached for another biscuit.

"Hell, yes, you too, Chewy. You are the one who spotted 'em. Get a fresh mount. You almost killed that buckskin." Everyone laughed as Chewy put a couple more biscuits coated with bacon grease under his shirt.

Thirteen men rode for Milburn, all armed to the utmost and as proficient with a pistol, knife, or rifle as they were with a ranch hand. They had fourteen miles to cover and no time to waste. When they reached the ridge overlooking the river where Chewy had first spotted the Indians, Milburn called for a halt. It was just past noon with the sun straight overhead. "Tell us what you saw," Milburn ordered, cutting himself a chew of tobacco.

Chewy, tired from riding all night, maintained his excitement. "I saw them, Sr. Milburn, through the glasses." His eyes were dancing as he pointed to a spot on the river. "Many Indians moved through those woods; they shot a steer. I saw it bellowing and pawing up the ground right over there. That's all I remember before I turned and rode for the ranch."

"You look tired, Chewy. Here you deserve a good chew," said Milburn, offering his plug of tobacco.

"No, Señor, remember I do not chew."

"Have a chew!"

"Sí, Señor," Chewy said, taking a small piece from his angry boss. Everyone grinned, remembering how sick Chewy got from his last experience with Milburn's tobacco. Milburn turned, standing before his men angrily, and said, "I have been around Indians; they are quick and deadly. If you make a mistake this afternoon, you will never see another day. They could be anywhere, and in a second, you could be dead. I mean to kill every one of them; still, I will do the talking before we hang them. Hit the leather; let's ride."

Milburn turned and mounted his horse while Chewy heaved up the contents of his stomach. Milburn did not seem to notice; however, the men got a big chuckle. "Lead the way, Chewy; show me where they shot the steer."

As Chewy rode upon the area where the steer had been shot, he swept his sweat-stained black hat from his head and dismounted. "I swear, it was here," he said in amazement. He looked around; there were no signs that anyone had ever been in the area. David rode up beside Chewy and dismounted. Kneeling to the ground, he whispered, "They were here."

David reached into his saddle bags and removed a small bundle containing soft moccasins, a loincloth, leggings, and a buckskin shirt. In minutes, he transformed himself from a ranch hand to a Blackfoot warrior. He completed the transformation by painting four black marks across his face.

Chewy looked up from his biscuit and said, "Yi-ee, I hate it when he does that."

A round of chuckles filled the air as David turned to the men. "Stay here until I return. I will give the call of the crow three times before I enter camp. I do not want any of you shooting at me."

David armed himself with his Bowie knife and his rifle. A heartbeat later, he was gone. "Fix some coffee, Rojo, and you might as well fry up some bacon. We'll be here for a spell, I reckon. Chewy, get some sleep," ordered Milburn.

The crow call sounded dust. Milburn reminded everyone that David was returning. Shortly, David appeared and walked to the coffee. Pouring himself a cup, he turned to his dad and said, "They're up a canyon 'bout four to five miles."

Rojo quickly brought David a plate with hot beans, fried bacon, and sourdough biscuits. "Well, how many are they? Can we take them?" asked Milburn.

"I suppose that if we can get the jump on them, it might be a fair fight."

David maintained a straight face as he soaked his sourdough biscuit in the beans. "Well, what kind are they? Is this a hunting party or a war party?"

David looked at all the rough hombres who had stepped forward, clinching their fists.

"Neither," David said as he poured himself another cup of coffee. "As far as I could see, they were seven women, two young warriors, and an old man. They're Cheyenne, and they must be starving. They've half eaten that steer already. They do not have a rifle or pistols among them. I figure they're on their way either to the Indian Territory or going back north. Just passing through, I expect."

"Cheyenne! Hell, they're meaner than a bunch of rattlesnakes, and that old man could be plenty of trouble," said Milburn.

"Oh yeah, I forgot to tell you—the old man is blind."

Now everyone relaxed and smiled. "Sr. Milburn," said Jose as he shifted from one boot to the other. "Will we hang the women also?"

"Well now," said Milburn in answer to Jose's question. "I do not condone to killing women. Matter of fact, I've never killed one in my life. Nevertheless, we will hang those men and escort the women off our land. We will point them in whatever direction they want to go. And we will confiscate the rest of the uneaten steer."

David threw the rest of his coffee into the fire, then tossed the cup and plate to the ground. He looked hard at his father. Turning abruptly, he walked away.

"Where are you going?" Milburn asked.

"To the house. I don't want to witness this."

"Well, what would you do? Suppose I had passed on to my reward. How'd you handle this?"

David slowed down at that question. He turned to face his father, "I expect I would cut out a couple more steers for them; maybe give them a horse; and send them on their way."

"Hell, they do not even have horses. Now that's what I call a ragtag outfit. Ok, if you'll come to show us where they be, I'll let the old blind man live, but I'm kicking their asses all the way out of Texas."

"I'll show you where they are, but I don't want any shooting, and you will let them keep that half of a steer."

"Chewy, when I pass on, I am leaving you in charge. There ought to be someone with brains running this outfit."

"Sr. Milburn, if they do not have rifles or pistols, how did they killed that steer?" Chewy asked.

"They have bows and arrows, and they're damned good shots," David answered.

"Ok, boys, let's get some shut-eye. We need to get up before sunrise. I want to get this done by the break of dawn."

Chapter 12

The eastern sky turned gray as the sun approached, and a chill in the air suggested an early winter. A pot of coffee, black and hot, sat steaming on a rock near the campfire. Rojo stacked tin cups next to the pot. Bacon sizzled in one big skillet while sourdough biscuits fried in another. Rojo, husband to Marie, was the trail cook. He worked feverishly to get the morning off to a good start.

Milburn stood drinking his coffee, watching the men, one by one, roll from their blankets. It would be an easy day. His victims were practically defenseless, caught red-handed stealing his cattle. He had to be careful, though, how he handled this situation. His son, David, was susceptible to any rough stuff. Yet, if it came to a fight, you always wanted David on your side. He was a fighter, and the men respected him. Since the Indians were stealing his property, he would be justified in any action he chose—he would be the law and the executioner. One steer was not worth more than ten dollars unless it was in Dodge City at a premium price. Besides, he had more cattle than he could count along this stretch of the Canadian River. But stealing even one cow was not to be tolerated!

"Let's get a move on," Milburn said. "We've wasted enough time on these cattle rustlers. I want to be back at the ranch by this evening."

The men tended to their bedrolls and saddled up before coming to coffee. As everyone sat finishing the last of their breakfasts, David took a small stick and outlined the canyon in the dirt. "They are here," he said, pointing to his crude drawing. Looking up at the men he knew well, he planned the confrontation. "We will ride down the canyon to this point. Dad, Buck, and I will ride on down to their camp, while the rest of you will leave your horses and walk on each side of the canyon rim. We will have them in a crossfire in case there is trouble." David knew that Buck would not walk that last mile. He was a top cowhand out of West Texas and did not do anything that he couldn't do from a horse's back.

"Rodriguez, you will take half the men along the west canyon wall. Carlos, you will take the other half along the east wall," he continued as the riders reached a point about a mile from the Indian camp. Slowly, they approached as the sun threw its light on the western wall. The smell of smoke and roasting meat filled the air.

Bonhist sat with her mother and Pretty Dove near the racks. They were drying the meat and storing it for future use. Red Leaf and the rest of the women were tanning the steer's hide. They had it stretched and staked while everyone else worked. Smiles filled their faces as they had full stomachs. The men were not in the camp area or in sight. Suddenly, the women saw the riders. Silently, they reached for their bows and notched arrows.

Star stepped forward in defiance. "Do not come closer," she said in the Cheyenne tongue. "What is your business in our camp?"

The three men apparently did not understand the Indian words and kept coming. Star gave the hand signal to stop, but they ignored her and kept going. Finally, she shot a warning arrow that stuck in a small root near the riders. Again, she told them to stop in both words and sign language. This time, the riders stopped, and Milburn dismounted. He stooped down, pulled the arrow from the root, broke it, and in perfect sign talk said, "You have killed one of my little buffalo. I own this land and the steer. You have broken the white man's law, and now we must punish you."

"We were starving and needed this meat to travel to the Indian Territory. Your loss will be greater if you come closer; the next arrow will go through your heart. Leave now and live," Star said.

Milburn smiled and signaled to his men on the canyon rim to show themselves. "A show of strength will frighten these women," Milburn whispered to David.

Suddenly, Whirlwind appeared. He held Chewy in a stranglehold using his walking stick across Chewy's Adam's apple. Charging Bull stood on the west canyon wall with his arrow full-drawn and pointed at Rodriquez's chest. Roaring Water held his position on the eastern wall, Carlos his target.

"You may kill us all, but some of you will die too, including you," Star said to Milburn.

Bonhist could see that the white man was furious and would fight. Many were going to die over this steer. Milburn then gripped his rifle, shouting, "Well, Cheyenne, I have never backed down from a fight, and I won't now."

Silence fell; there seemed to be no solution to the predicament. Just as Milburn started to make his move, Bonhist stepped forward and spoke to the Cheyenne. "Listen to me, my brothers and sisters. I have seen this man in my vision. Now trust me, for my vision is true—these are not bad men. Throw down your weapons, let me talk with this man."

Bonhist could see that no one was moving or following her instructions, so she tried again. "Whirlwind! Let that poor man go! Charging Bull, throw down your bow; you are frightening that man! Roaring Waters! Throw down your bow. Today is a bad day to die."

Milburn looked up in amazement. The Indians were throwing down their weapons, and this young Cheyenne maiden was walking toward him with the most beautiful smile he had ever seen. He blinked, for suddenly, she reminded him of his late Blackfoot wife. "What powers does this child have?" he whispered to himself.

Bonhist walked right up to old Milburn. Using sign talk, she said, "You have lived among the Indians. Your wife was a member of what tribe?"

"Blackfoot," muttered the dumbfounded Milburn.

"Is this handsome one that rides by your side your son?"

Again, she caught Milburn off guard. All he could do was nod.

"Yes, I felt his spirit last night when he spied on our camp. He is very quiet, but these clumsy men along the canyon walls are too loud to sneak up on anyone."

David, understanding sign language as well as his father, now became interested in this conversation. "You knew I was here last night?" he asked.

Bonhist smiled and at once won his heart. "Oh yes, even the blind Whirlwind saw you with his ears. We expected you to show up sooner."

"Why did you not hide from us?" asked David.

"We do not hide. We have too much work to do to prepare for the cold season. It will come soon. Now, let us talk about the livestock. We have taken one of your steers, and we will need two more to get through the cold season and to the Indian Territory. I will talk trade," she said.

Milburn looked around to his men. They stood like statues waiting for his orders. "Put down your weapons. I will talk with these people. Chewy, are you alright?"

"Si, Sr. Milburn. I feel like a chicken who had its head under a broomstick."

Milburn smiled to himself and turned back to the young woman. He suddenly realized that he was enjoying this business transaction. "What do you have to trade? That steer was valuable."

"It is no more valuable than the many buffalo killed by the white man on our hunting grounds. Still, I have this very precious golden stone that my father left me before he died at Sand Creek."

Milburn, who had come to hang these cattle rustlers, now found himself apologizing to this young woman. Amazed, David thought he knew how to work his dad, but this young woman could teach him a thing or two. He tilted his big black Stetson hat back on his head, relaxed, and enjoyed the entire affair.

"I have heard of the Sand Creek massacre, a terrible thing. I never cottoned to it. It was low down and cowardly. I've never killed a buffalo that I did not eat, including the tail."

"I know you are a good man. I can see that in you," Bonhist answered.

"Let me see that stone," ordered Milburn, reaching out to Bonhist.

Like magic, a large gold nugget appeared in Bonhist's palm.

"Is this the only one you have?"

Bonhist smiled and looked deeply into Milburn's eyes. "This one will buy three steers and a pony. A pony could pull a large travois, and Whirlwind, who is blind, could ride."

Milburn stuck the gold nugget into his mouth and bit down. He appraised the stone and continued, "You have a deal. But I would like to know your name."

David laughed and yelled to Chewy. "Come on down, Chewy. We need someone with brains to lead this outfit. I will not have any inheritance left by the time my dad goes to the great beyond to receive his reward." David was getting a big kick out of the whole affair; every one of the cowhands could see the humor and laughed as well.

Milburn, a little red in the face, turned to his men. "Go round up two more steers. Chewy, bring your horse. You can walk back to the line cabin."

"Si, Sr. Milburn. Do you want me to bring them the iron cooking pot as well?"

Everyone roared at Chewy's words, and David almost fell from his horse laughing.

Bonhist got Milburn's attention one more time and said, "Do not let my mother know that I gave away the gold stone. She would be very upset since it was the last thing my father gave to me."

"Which one is your mother?" Milburn asked.

"She shot the warning arrow and first spoke to you."

"Yes, now I see where you get your beauty. I will keep your secret. However, I would like to know where your father found this stone." Milburn looked to see if David or any of his hands were watching. They were laughing at Chewy, so he quickly slipped the nugget back into Bonhist's hand. "You keep it," he whispered.

Bonhist's smile penetrated all the way to Milburn's heart. She then said, "My name is Bonhist which means sage woman."

Chapter 13

"Tell me, Bonhist, where did your father find the golden nugget?" Milburn asked.

"They tell me that my father found it on Spirit Mountain."

"Where is this Spirit Mountain?"

"In Colorado, where we used to live."

"You don't say! I used to live in Colorado myself. Can you remember the area around Spirit Mountain?"

Bonhist smiled at Milburn. "I will try," she said. "It sits like a giant among many tall mountains. It is always white on top, and water falls from its summit. They said that my father once climbed it all the way to the top. A nearby river flows east to a valley where it joins three other rivers. A white man has built his lodge there and has many steers like you."

Milburn let out a whoop and slapped his knee. "That would be the Four Rivers Ranch. I used to ride for that brand. A man from across the big waters, an Englishman, owns the ranch."

Bonhist smiled and asked Milburn his name. "My name is James Milburn, and this is my son, David. These men work for me. I want to invite you and your people to winter here if it pleases you."

Bonhist motioned to Star, asking her to join them. Star walked proudly toward the group.

"Chief Milburn, this is my mother, Star. She is leading us to the territory. Mother, this good man is named Chief Milburn. This handsome one on the black horse is his son, David. The rest of these men are his warriors. He is giving us two more of his steers and a horse and has invited us to camp here for the winter. It happens that he used to live near Spirit Mountain, where the four rivers meet."

Star looked at Milburn without smiling. She then used sign language as Bonhist had been doing. "I have seen you. You led some men with a Cheyenne wolf called Snake. You chased my husband, Crow, and me to Spirit Mountain. If it had not been for the good heart of my husband, I would have ridden back and killed you that day. Today, Crow's daughter, Bonhist, has saved you again. She is too much like her father."

"That was you! You and your husband just vanished. It still troubles my mind, a mystery never solved. How did you do it?"

Star allowed herself a small smile, but tears sprang into her eyes. "Crow knew of a hidden passage. We had just married, and he was taking me to our mountain home."

Milburn could at once see Star's beauty and her love for Crow. "What has happened to Crow?"

"They killed him at Sand Creek along with your wolf, Snake."

"That was a sad day! Perhaps I can help," said Milburn. "I've told Bonhist that you may winter here, but I now have a better idea. I'll send a wagon and bring all of you to the ranch. You would be safe and comfortable through the cold season."

"No, it is kind of you to allow us to camp here. This much we will accept. Do not forget that we are the People; we would not enjoy living in the white man's lodge."

Milburn looked around. Everyone had settled down and was waiting for the conference to end. "Well, hell! Let's get back to the ranch. Run a couple of yearling steers down here for these people, and, Chewy, bring your horse. Bonhist will need him." Turning, he swung into the saddle and waved goodbye.

The cold man of the north came hard and swift. Even in Montana, they had not experienced a harsher freeze. Snow filled the canyon, leaving it a frozen wonderland. Star and the rest quickly realized that without their warm lodges and ample furs, life in the panhandle of Texas would be hard. Even in the canyon, strong winds frequently provided blizzard-like conditions. They dug into the canyon walls, forming caves. Their food and water were sufficient, so keeping warm became their top priority. Working hard every day, they kept up a good supply of wood.

Bonhist could see Whirlwind growing weaker day by day, and the faces of the others were drawn and unhappy. One morning, everyone gathered in the cave of Roaring Waters and Charging Bull, where a good fire was burning with the smoke pouring out of a hole dug for that purpose. Since they had left everything behind after they roasted the dogs, there were no cooking pots or warm buffalo robes. Stew was prepared the old way by heating rocks and placing them in rawhide containers.

"I have had a vision," Bonhist announced, and everyone looked up with interest. "I have seen the white men. They come to take us to their ranch. All will be good; we will learn from them and have a warm place to sleep."

"Still, we must walk a long distance through the ice and snow," Pretty Dove said.

"We will need a pole drag to pull our food supply behind the red horse," Roaring Waters said.

"We will freeze walking that long distance, and we do not know the exact location of the ranch," Red Leaf added.

"I would like to see the white man's lodge," Soft Winds whispered.

"My vision has shown me that we are neither cold nor do we have to walk. We must gather our belongings and prepare to travel. We will learn much from these white men."

No one questioned the validity of Bonhist's vision. They had grown used to her powers. Still, when all was ready, they stood outside their caves looking at each other. "Will the white man have tobacco?" Whirlwind asked.

"Perhaps you were just having a dream instead of a vision," White Dove said after they had stood for a lengthy period. The snow was beginning to fall again, and there still was no sign of the white men.

"I do not believe the white man knows of Bonhist's vision. They do not come," Crow Wings said.

"Let us eat so we will be prepared for travel," Whirlwind said.

As they began to chew on some dried meat, Charging Bull rode the red pony into camp. "We have visitors," he said as he slid from the pony's back.

It was no surprise to Star when David and two of the ranch hands arrived. They brought a wagon pulled by two mules. The wagon was full of prairie hay and blankets. "It is too cold out here even for the People," David announced, using sign language. "My father has sent me to bring you back to the ranch."

Bonhist, smiling, walked toward David, wrapped in a flimsy hide over a buckskin dress. "We have been waiting. What has taken you so long?"

"Traveling conditions," he answered.

"Do you want us in there?" Bonhist asked, pointing to the wagon.

"Yes," replied David. "Blankets are stacked in the wagon. You should be warm. We will travel to the line cabin tonight, and tomorrow we will go on to the ranch."

They amazed David with how quickly they prepared for the trip. Climbing into the wagon, they wrapped themselves in the blankets in only minutes while Charging Bull mounted the red pony that would pull the travois.

Once at the line cabin, Chewy prepared a big pot of red beans spiced with peppers and a large skillet of fried potatoes. His meal was completed with sourdough biscuits and coffee, black as sin. Star refused to enter the cabin, staying in the wagon wrapped in a blanket. "Mother, take this food," Bonhist said, handing her mother a tin plate of Chewy's cooking. "We will no longer live as we did in the north country. We will learn to live in the white man's world and learn new ways," Bonhist said, looking at the sad expression on her mother's face.

"You have already forgotten," Star muttered.

"No, mother, I have forgotten nothing. Still, my spirit and my heart must lead me. The People will all die if we cannot bend like the willow. Look into my heart. Am I not your daughter?"

Star glanced at her and said, "Yes, Bonhist, you are my daughter whom I love more than life."

"Then trust my vision and my heart."

Star looked deeply into Bonhist's face. She reached over and took the plate of food. "I could never win an argument with your father either. You are just like him. Still, remember this, men like these killed your father. I will always hate the white man for this thing as well as their lies."

"Yes, I know how you feel. We can only live in this moment, not the past."

On the following afternoon, as the wagon rolled over the crest of a hill, the ranch came into view. Bonhist smiled for there before her was a new world—the white man's world. She would enjoy exploring it. It was just as amazing to her as Spirit Mountain.

<h1 style="text-align:center">CHAPTER 14</h1>

Bonhist made several important discoveries on her first day on the ranch. Her sense of smell led to the greatest impression. "Whirlwind, they call this a barn. Can you smell it? It has a peculiar odor. They feed their horses here even during the cold season with the prairie hay they cut and store in the loft. They throw it down through a hole to the horses along with a measure of oats."

"The barn does have a strong spirit and smell," Whirlwind agreed without a smile. "It is a bad custom to keep their horses strong so they can war even during the cold season."

"I like the smell of the hay loft," Bonhist said as she pulled Whirlwind toward another area of the barn. "This is their tack room where they keep saddles and bridles. The saddles are made from the hides of steers treated with water or oil. Feel it, does it not smell good?"

"Only a bear would live here. I prefer the smells of the open prairie and the buffalo and the high mountains," Whirlwind said in his gravel voice.

"Yes, of course. Still, we are not learning about you and me; we are learning about these white men and their strange customs."

Bonhist turned toward the sound of footsteps—it was David. "Bonhist, it pleases me that you are interested in the ranch. I want you and Whirlwind to learn all you can. Here's a message from my father for you," said David. "He'd like you and all your people to join him for his evening meal in the main ranch house."

"Some of us will be delighted to see Milburn again and eat a meal with him. Still others, like my mother, will not go into his lodge," answered Bonhist.

David shrugged his shoulders and smiled at the pretty young maiden. "All right, the ones who want to come are welcome."

"David," Bonhist said in the spoken word, then continuing in sign language. "Do you have time to show us around the ranch?"

"Yes, but there is very little to see. This is just an ordinary ranch. We'll have a roundup this spring and drive our cattle north to Dodge City."

"Why would you do that? You could eat one each day for the rest of your life and still not eat them all. What good will they do you in Dodge City?"

David laughed at this and answered in amusement. "We'll sell our cattle in Dodge City. They then ship the cattle east on the iron horse. People in big cities in the east will eat our cattle, not us."

"Why? I do not see the purpose of this. White men do many crazy things."

"Bonhist, you must understand one important fact about the white world. Gold controls it, like the gold nugget you gave my father for the three steers and the pony. When we sell our cattle in Dodge City, they will give us gold."

"Yes, gold is your medicine. I have heard this before. My father knew this, and my mother told stories of gold. Still, I do not understand. Why is it such strong medicine?" Bonhist asked.

"The value of something is determined by how much gold it would take to buy it. If you had enough gold, you could buy this ranch, a home in Denver, or whatever pleases you," he answered.

"David," said Bonhist. "Your medicine is strong. I admire you and would like to ask you a favor."

David smiled and said, "You want me to give you some gold?"

"No, David, I want you to teach me the white man's tongue. That is more important to me than gold."

"Okay, but it takes many moons to learn to speak in the white tongue."

As they strolled on from the barn to the blacksmith building, Bonhist continued with her questioning.

"What is this? There's a different smell that I do not like."

"This is a blacksmith building. We make things from metal here like a wagon tongue, wheels or the metal shoes we put on our horses."

"David, could I watch you do this? Can you make metal knives? Is this where you make your fire sticks?"

Again, David laughed, "Hold on, not so many questions at once. Yes, you may watch when we shoe a horse. Yes, we can make metal knives. And no, this is not where they make our weapons."

"Do you spend much time in this blacksmith building?"

Throughout the conversation, Bonhist repeated her questions in Cheyenne so Whirlwind could understand. Finally, he spoke, "Are metal arrowheads made in this building, too?" Bonhist used sign language to repeat the question to David.

"Yes, making arrowheads from metal is easy. In fact, our blacksmith, Randy Pendleton, has made me many. I keep a full quiver of arrows and a bow made by my mother's people."

"Do you prefer the bow to your fire stick?" Bonhist asked.

"No, not normally. Still, often a silent kill is better. We have had trouble with the Comancheros. They have burned down our barn twice. They like this part of Texas since many canyons offer them a place to hide. When we drive our cattle north, my father and a few men will stay to protect the ranch."

"Aiee, these men, the Comancheros, you shoot with arrows?"

"I will dress as my mother's people and paint my face. I can hurt them under the cover of darkness with a knife and arrows. They have learned to fear us and do not come close."

"So, you will lead the men north with the cattle while your father will stay here at the ranch to protect all of your gold from the Comancheros. Gold is a lot of trouble. White men are very strange."

"It is the way of the white world," agreed David.

"Why do you not have a wife? A Cheyenne man of your age would have a wife, maybe two."

David laughed at this question, "Women are very scarce in this country. I have never seen one that I wanted."

"Can I ask another question?" Bonhist said with a smile.

David looked up to the roof, expecting another personal, probing question, and nodded. "Could your blacksmith warrior teach Roaring Waters and Charging Bull to make metal arrowheads? This would help them pass the time, and our supply of arrows is almost gone."

David agreed as the tour continued. Later, when the Cheyenne gathered in the loft of the barn, Bonhist spoke, "Chief Milburn has invited us to his lodge for an evening meal and storytelling. It would be an insult to refuse."

"I will not enter his lodge. I do not like the smell of the white men or their lodges," Star said.

"Nor I," Red Leaf said. "I remember Sand Creek and will never sit in the same camp with a white man."

"I will go with Bonhist. She is now my eyes," Whirlwind said.

"I will also go," Pretty Dove said.

The rest simply nodded and signaled with their hands that they would go with Bonhist. So as the overcast day slowly turned to darkness, the group of Cheyenne led by Bonhist prepared to leave the loft. Suddenly, before the entire group stood David dressed as a Blackfoot warrior. Recognizing that this was the same man that she had talked with only that afternoon was hard for Bonhist. "Is that you, David?" she asked.

He made quite an impression since Blackfoot had been a traditional enemy of the People. Now he stood before them and looked as much of a warrior as any of them.

"When I was born, my mother gave me the name Black Wolf. My white man's name is David William Milburn. She died with my sister at the hands of white men when I was only five winters."

"You live with one foot in the world of the Blackfoot nation and the other foot in the white man's world. How do you do it?" Bonhist asked.

"It is very hard. My father once sent me out east to a school where I learned many things. Still, my heart was with my father here on this ranch, so I returned. I did not like the way people looked at me. Here, with my father, I have learned to live in both worlds. Come, I will lead you to my home; you are all welcome."

"I have changed my mind. I will also come," Star said.

"I will also come," Red Leaf said.

So, the entire group followed David to his home, where Milburn greeted them. The white-haired old man surprised them all when he chose to wear his buckskins. The beadwork was undeniably Blackfoot. They were led to the dining room and introduced to chairs. Roaring Waters was the first to sit. "Have I crossed over?" he asked.

"No, the spirits have cheated you again. Yet you have shown much bravery to trust the lean backs perched on wooden sticks," Bonhist said with a smile.

The evening was full of surprises. First, they met Marie Carrillo, the cook. They had never seen a Mexican woman before, and her red-cloth dress caught their attention. Bonhist insisted on seeing her kitchen, where she had prepared the food. So they all followed her across the dog trot to her domain. "I like this room most of all. Smell!" the smiling Bonhist said.

They spent several minutes looking at the two wood-burning iron stoves and ovens. Metal pots, pans, and iron skillets lined the walls.

Scarlet peppers hung from the ceiling, and a basket of jalapenos caught their eye. "What are these?" Bonhist asked, pointing to the peppers.

David interpreted Bonhist's words, "It gives the spicy hot flavor to Marie's cooking. We like our food prepared this way. This is salt. We also like it in our food. Tonight, Marie made tortillas with beans and beef. You will like them, I think." Marie's smile warmed the hearts of the Cheyenne.

"David," Bonhist said, "when you are not teaching me the white tongue, I would like to work with Marie and learn the medicine of tortillas and spicy hot cooking. Is this possible?"

Immediately, all the young women wanted to work with Marie and learn the white man's words. "Yes, all of you can work anywhere, and I will try to teach. We can start in the morning."

The evening was exciting and enlightening for the Cheyenne. Bonhist insisted that David show them everything about their ranch house. The beds were especially a marvel. Finally, the meal was served. *Delicious*, Bonhist thought. The corn tortillas were favorites, but Bonhist noticed that Star ate little of the spicy-hot beans.

At last, the storytelling began as Milburn gave Whirlwind a cigar. He had never seen one before and liked it very much. Milburn told the first story of how he had started the ranch. Star told a story of the first time Crow had taken her on a frightening mountain climb. Finally, Bonhist removed a beautiful eagle feather and announced, "I will tell the story of this eagle feather." She looked around the room and continued, "My grandfather—Chief Sitting Bull—gave it to me. I promised him that I would wear it on the day I marry. This spring

I will be fifteen winters and will soon reach the marrying age. It is my dream to teach my people of this ranch and of its many strong medicines. I hope that they will allow the People in the territory to have such ranches. We would be good at raising horses." She then told her story of the battle with Yellow Hair at the Little Bighorn. "Each person there has his own version of the battle. Still, I was near my grandfather, Chief Sitting Bull. Through his eyes, I could see that the white man gave us no choice but to fight. It is my dream that in the future, we can have other choices and build a new life in the Oklahoma Indian Territory."

<h1 style="text-align:center">CHAPTER 15</h1>

As the days and weeks passed, Bonhist and the other young women helped Marie with her cooking and housekeeping, happily practicing their new language. "Hello, goodbye. My name is Bonhist. What is your name? These words are strong. Still, I do not understand when David talks to his father or his warriors. I want to understand more words," Bonhist said with a disappointed expression on her face.

Roaring Waters and Charging Bull spent most of their time in the blacksmith building. They had made fifteen good metal arrowheads and a dozen more that were rejected. David had led them to an ash grove, where they found several limbs suitable for arrow shafts. Charley Wallace, the blacksmith, liked the boys and could see where they could become skilled workers.

With Carlos's help, Whirlwind enjoyed feeding the horses. It was not long before Whirlwind knew where and how much hay to drop. He also fed oats to each horse and knew them by name. At some point in the day, Milburn would find Whirlwind for a chew. This pleased them both.

Star, Red Leaf, and Pretty Dove began working on new lodges. They had gathered lodge poles from along the Canadian River, and Milburn generously supplied them with skins.

One afternoon, White Dove spoke in private to Bonhist. "Sister, do you have ears for my words?"

"Yes, my sister, what troubles you?" Bonhist asked.

"I will soon be sixteen winters. I am old enough to marry. I wish to speak from my heart. Can I trust you?"

"Yes, White Dove. You can trust me with your heart."

"I have fallen in love. Still, I do not know what I should do. Can you help me?"

"I will try to help you, White Dove."

"Bonhist, I love David. Still, he only looks at you. He does not even know I am standing by your side. Do you love David, too?"

Bonhist was silent for a long heartbeat. She looked deep into White Dove's eyes and felt the bonding and love of a sister. White Dove was vulnerable like a tired rabbit in the jaws of a coyote. "I love David also, like a brother. I have not yet reached the marrying age, and I do not plan to marry until I have made a life for my mother in the Indian Territory."

White Dove's smile warmed Bonhist's heart. "Then will you help me win David's love?"

"Yes. However, it will not be easy. He has said that he has never seen a woman that he wanted. How can we make him want you?"

"First, you must spend less time with David. I know how you want to learn the white man's tongue. Still, do not come for more lessons. We could trade Marie some of her red cloth for a new dress. Is this not a good plan?"

Bonhist again hesitated for a lengthy period before answering, "Yes, your plan is good. I can learn the white tongue from another. I think Marie will help with the dress."

For the next week, Bonhist did not attend her lessons. White Dove was pleased to have David to herself, with only her sister, Crow Wings, and Soft Winds as her competition. As Bonhist had guessed, Marie helped make the red dress. She dressed White Dove as she would her own daughter with a white shell necklace and earrings. Bonhist had to admit the dress made White Dove look very pretty. Then one day, David cornered Bonhist, "Why have you been avoiding me? I have not seen you for a week. Did I do something that has made you angry with me?"

Bonhist gave David a surprised look. She felt terrible, and her heart fell to the ground. Still, she smiled and said, "No, David, I am no longer interested in learning the white man's tongue. I am a bad student."

"Yet, we have become friends. I enjoy your company more than anyone. Why do you run from me?"

"I have not been doing that. I have been busy with Marie. I love you like a brother and have missed you also."

"You love me like a brother! This hurts my ears, Bonhist. You are the only woman I have ever wanted. I want you to be my wife!"

Tears immediately filled Bonhist's eyes, and she stood without speaking for a long time. Finally, she said, "I am sorry, David. I have not reached the marrying age. I want to help my mother find a new life in the territory. I have seen a vision. I can see you very happy with someone who wears a red dress. I hope you will not hate me. My path lies in a different direction."

David turned with a jerk and left. Bonhist immediately fell to the ground sobbing.

The following week, Bonhist spent her time working with Marie and helping her mother with the lodge. She had seen David only once; he had turned his head without speaking. Still, White Dove seemed radiant as she wore her new red dress and was improving with her white man's tongue. At last, Milburn invited the entire group again for another evening meal. After the meal from Marie's kitchen, Milburn leaned back, pulled out a cigar, lit it, and passed it down to Whirlwind. "I have a proposal," he said. "Soon spring will be here. We will have our roundup and drive our cattle north. I have grown to know and love you. I believe that each of you can make a life for yourself here on this ranch. I would like you to stay. My son will soon own everything that I have. My greatest regret is that I have no grandchildren. I would love to see my son married and happy before I go to my reward. Among you is one who would make my heart happy to be my daughter."

Star stood and, using sign language, began speaking, "Milburn, you are a good man. I once heard a great chief say that not all white men are bad. I thought that was a false statement; however, you have proven him correct. Among us, some may accept your offer. I only speak for myself. My daughter and I started our journey from Montana after the great battle with Yellow Hair. Our destination was the Oklahoma Territory, the home of the Southern Cheyenne. The Striped Feathers are my late husband Crow's people." Star quickly made the sign for the dead and continued. "I will not stop until I have reached the People. Still, I must ask, which of these pretty young women would David choose as his wife?"

Quickly, Bonhist stood beside her mother. "I am not of marrying age yet, but I love David as I would a brother. I will go with my mother to the territory."

Without speaking, Soft Winds stood beside Bonhist. Whirlwind, Red Leaf, and Pretty Dove followed her. Next, Roaring Waters and Charging Bull stood. Finally, only White Dove and Crow Wings were still seated. "Which of these two would you take as your wife?" Star asked.

David rose and smiled. He then said, "I have always heard that the Cheyenne were beautiful people. This is so, and I have decided—I choose Crow Wings."

"I will take the other," Chewy said. "I love the red dress."

CHAPTER 16

Crow Wings and White Dove both screamed while collapsing in their chairs. This greatly concerned Milburn since he thought they were struck dead. Bonhist, however, quickly explained that too much excitement and happiness had sapped their wind. Crow Wings and White Dove were sisters born of different parents but were the same age. Crow Wings was sixteen winters and the younger daughter of Pretty Dove and One Eye, while White Dove was sixteen winters and the daughter of Bob Tailed Wolf and the Squirrel. After they killed One Eye and Bob Tailed Wolf at Sand Creek, the Elk took Bob Tailed Wolf's sister, Pretty Dove, as his wife. Bonhist did not know how hurt White Dove would be, since her loss came unexpectedly. However, Chewy's offer was valid, and Bonhist believed that Chewy and White Dove would make a good match since both were talkers. Bonhist looked at Crow Wings. She was beautiful in body, being both graceful and lith. Her skin was darker than White Dove's. However, she had beautiful, piercing black eyes and black hair that shone like a crow's wings in bright sunlight. Crow Wings had a wild, feline look and was the mysterious, quiet one. "She is lucky," Bonhist thought. "David wants her."

Pretty Dove finally decided to stay on the ranch as well, since both her daughters were staying, and to the surprise of everyone, she agreed to marry Carlos Estrada. So, in the spring, the marriages took place in two ceremonies. One was the white man's ceremony performed by a country preacher named Samuel Despain. The other was the Cheyenne ceremony done by Whirlwind.

"What bothers you, Bonhist?" Star asked one day, noticing a sad look on her daughter's face.

"Mother, I feel so empty. Do you realize that we will soon be moving again toward the Indian Nations, and may never see Pretty Dove or Crow Wings or White Dove ever again? I am lonely for them already."

"I, too, feel this emptiness. Yet, I am happy for Pretty Dove and her daughters. They will be safe and happy."

"Mother, I am also sad since David does not speak to me anymore. Soon we will go, and I will never see this ranch or David again. I wish David and I could part as friends."

"You must remember, my daughter, that David is now married to Crow Wings. He is happy, and she will give him many strong sons—like her father, One Eye."

Bonhist nodded, understanding, then quickly buried her face in her mother's bosom as tears ran silently down her cheeks.

"It is time for us to go," Star said the next morning.

"The chill in the air is very cold. How do you know this is the time?" Bonhist asked.

"I have heard a chick-a-dee sing, 'summer is near.'"

The seven travelers gathered their packs and placed them on the drag poles behind the red pony. They had acquired three new lodges during their winter's stay. Milburn approached Marie at his side. They placed a large sack of beans and one of corn on their travois. Marie also added some red peppers and a large bag of salt. She handed Bonhist a package with a smile. Bonhist immediately opened the gift. She exclaimed with joy as she pulled out a white cloth dress. It was trimmed along the skirt's fringe in black and red. She then saw the matching necklace, earrings, and bracelet. Marie made the necklace from corn, threading it with a small piece of wire. She dyed two black and one red. She made the bracelet from a heavier wire that coiled around the wrist. She chose to use black and red corn again. It was a wonderful present. Marie's tears ran from her eyes, and she said something to Bonhist in Spanish. Bonhist turned to Milburn, who immediately translated. "She said it is for you when you reach the marrying age." Bonhist gave Marie a long hug.

Milburn then gave Bonhist a piece of paper. "When you get to the territory, soldiers may question your ownership of the red horse. This is a bill of sale; it is strong medicine and proves that you own the horse. When you do business in the white world, always insist on a bill of sale."

Bonhist then spoke in English. "How you say?"

"Bill of Sale," Milburn answered.

"Yes, bill of sale—thank you, Chief Milburn," Bonhist said, as she gave Milburn a long hug.

Walking east along the North Canadian River, they turned for one last peek at the ranch. Whirlwind, sitting on top of the red pony, led the way while smoking a cigar. They had gone less than a mile when they heard a hoop. Turning, they saw David riding his black stallion. He pulled up beside Bonhist and slid from the saddle. Without a word, he lifted her off her feet with a hug.

"Were you trying to leave without a word?" he said with a big smile.

Tears ran down Bonhist's cheeks as she looked into David's eyes. "Take care of my sisters. Crow Wings is the daughter of a mighty chief. She is a princess and will give you many strong sons. Do not forget me, David, for I love you too."

"Why was I not lucky enough to win your love? Is it because you worry for your mother and your people? You are a strong leader, Bonhist. I will always remember you and will name my first daughter after you. Now, I have a present and a warning. First, the warning—this river is dangerous. Quicksand and whirlpools are common. However, the real danger is—Comancheros. Do not travel along the river, leaving signs for all to read. Ride away from the river and send one person to fill the water skins. Never camp within sight of the river. Find a safe canyon. Keep a sharp watch on these men; they are killers and fortune-hunters. They would rape you and your mother and sell you into slavery." David handed Bonhist a sack.

Bonhist's eyes sparkled, and her smile captured David's heart. "Is this for me?"

David gave her a nod, a quick hand signal, and a smile.

Inside the sack were a heavy wooden box, a smaller paper box, and a cloth bag. "What is this, David? I have never seen anything like it."

"Open it, you will see."

"How do you open this box? What is its secret?"

"It has a latch, here, let me show you." David opened the latch and lifted the lid. Bonhist was shocked; she had never seen anything like it before. It was a nickel-plated Colt revolver with ivory grips. She glided her hand over the revolver as if it were unreal and would soon evaporate.

"Is this for me? I do not know the medicine for such things."

David smiled as everyone gathered around. He removed the revolver and rolled it in his hand as if it were a part of him. "It is a Colt, single action, with a seven-and-one-half-inch barrel. This is the way you load it." Opening the cylinder, David carefully demonstrated. He flipped the cylinder back in place. Sliding the new revolver into his holster, he pointed toward a stump and drew quickly and smoothly. He shot twice so quickly it sounded like one shot. Everyone grabbed his ears and watched a knot in the stump fly out as if it had exploded. David again showed Bonhist how to open the cylinder. This time, he also showed the bright-eyed maiden how to release the barrel so they could look through it. "See. The gun is now dirty. You must keep it clean. Watch!" David then removed a small rod from the box. He attached a small piece of cloth and placed a drop of oil from a can onto it. Very quickly, he cleaned the revolver and rubbed some oil on the cylinder. "Now look," he said.

Smiling widely, Bonhist looked down at the clean barrel. David turned to his black horse and removed a leather gun belt and holster from his saddle bag. He filled the gun belt with bullets. The belt had been specially made for Bonhist. He then opened the paper box full of bullets. "You must learn to use this revolver. It is a weapon that can save your life," said David as he attached the gun belt around Bonhist's slim waist.

"David, what is in the bag?" Bonhist asked.

"It is for you and your people. One day it will help you buy your own ranch."

Bonhist picked up the heavy bag and removed the rawhide strap. With one peek, she could see the white man's gold dust.

Bonhist glanced at David. "Why?" she asked.

David's answer was brief: "Because I love you, Bonhist." Stepping into the stirrup, David swung into the saddle and, without another look, rode away.

"I will one day name one of my sons after you," Bonhist called. She watched David ride out of sight, wiped the tears from her eyes, and turned to her mother. Everyone stared at the ivory-handled Colt that hung at her waist. With annoyance, she turned and said, "What is everyone looking at? Oklahoma Indian territory is that way," she said, pointing east.

Coming to a bend in the river, Star decided to cross to the northern side. "We will do as David suggested and follow the river from a distance. Fill your water skins now."

Acting as wolves, Charging Bull and Roaring Waters walked near the rim of the river valley. They saw deer, cattle, and even a few horses. All belonged to Milburn, so not even Charging Bull dared to hunt. They made camp that evening in a canyon. The group was smaller now. Bonhist's heart dragged the ground thinking about Pretty Dove and her two daughters. She looked across the campfire toward Soft Winds and smiled. Soft Winds was now thirteen winters and was beginning to show her womanhood. *She is very pretty,* Bonhist thought. Red Leaf had taken charge of the cooking, and Bonhist smiled when she added a red pepper and a small amount of salt to a pot of beans. She also cooked stew from the corn and dried meat. Charging Bull had come in for his meal. He quickly ate and returned to his post. Roaring Waters finally came running into camp.

"I have seen many riders. They rode east," he said.

"Were they Milburn's men?" Star asked.

"No, I am led to believe that perhaps they are the Comancheros."

Chapter 17

As the Cheyenne party moved away from the river, Bonhist studied the group. She smiled as she realized that each member of the party had been greatly affected from wintering at Milburn's ranch. That is, all with the exception of her mother, Star. It was as if her mind was driven to return to Crow's people—the Southern Cheyenne. She hated the whites as much as ever, and her greatest concern was avoiding the bad men they called the Comancheros.

Whirlwind proudly sat on the red pony as he puffed his last cigar. He also held a good supply of tobacco. The old warrior will always remember Milburn's kindness.

Roaring Waters was greatly affected by the ranch. Before, he was looking for death. He was the son of Spirit Walking. Bonhist had heard stories of her gift and felt a strange kinship to this woman whom she had never known. But she had true visions and often scared the people with her insight into the future. Now her son, Roaring Waters, had nothing to live for, or at least before the ranch. He now had both an interest in working with metal as a blacksmith and eyes for Soft Winds. Outwardly, Roaring Waters seemed just as before; however, Bonhist could feel the change.

Like Roaring Waters, Charging Bull developed a new interest. He, too, liked working in the blacksmith shop, and like the rest, was greatly interested in horses. Still, Charging Bull was born for hunting and adventure. He loved the hunt even more than the kill. Yet, he lacked patience and would rush in too soon, missing his opportunity. Bonhist looked at Charging Bull and smiled, for she knew he had a good heart, and she loved him like a brother.

Soft Winds was the interesting one. She learned to sew and cook on the ranch. Her eyes would never leave Roaring Waters for long, and Bonhist knew that she was in love. Soft Wind had a strong but gentle spirit—she would do well in the Indian Territory.

Red Leaf came to the ranch, hating the white man as much as Star did. As time passed, Bonhist could see a change in her attitude. "These whites are builders," she would say while clicking her tongue as she worked. Yes, Red Leaf would have gladly stayed on the ranch, but she still dreamed that in the Oklahoma Indian Territory, there would be a life for her. Perhaps even a man would look at her with pleasure.

Star suddenly called for the party to stop. As everyone gathered around, she announced that they would camp in a well-hidden canyon while resting. "We will travel at night as we did in the far north country. These Comancheros must not find us. Charging Bull, you and Roaring Waters go back and wipe out our trail. You both are our wolves. Your eyes will keep us alert to the enemy."

They had a cold camp without a fire and chewed some dried meat. Soft Wind and Bonhist gathered berries while Roaring Waters and Charging Bull were nowhere to be seen. Everyone tried to sleep, but sleep would not come. Bonhist walked over to Whirlwind. "Grandfather, do you sleep?" she asked.

"No, my daughter, my ears are wide awake. Is it time to continue our journey?"

"Grandfather, have you ever heard war stories about these Comancheros? What kind of men are they?" she asked.

"I have never heard of the Comancheros, but I have fought the Utes, the Blackfeet, the Crow, and the Pawnee. These enemies are honorable men. They are brave and true warriors who will take your scalp or steal your women and horses—but they fight with honor. You can even find honor among the whites. It is hard to find honor, but if you search, you will find goodness even among the white eyes. I have experienced evil from all these groups, but I am led to believe that these Comancheros are pure evil with no honor to be found. I do not wish to encounter these men. Your mother is right to take such precautions."

"You are very wise, my grandfather," said Bonhist as she moved back to her sleeping robe.

As evening approached, everyone gathered their belongings and set off eastward. Suddenly, Roaring Waters and Charging Bull appeared. They had returned from the river with the water skins full.

"Do not worry, Star," Charging Bull said. "We have searched the area, and there are no tracks or any signs of the Comancheros."

"Charging Bull! Do not be so easily fooled. A rabbit also thinks he's safe when the eyes of a hawk have spotted him from the farthest tree. We cannot make mistakes. No corn fields, or steers, or any hunting.

We must move quietly and unnoticed until we reach the Indian territory," Star snapped.

"Can we at least light a fire at our next camp. We could all use a hot meal," smiled Charging Bull.

"Do not tease me, Charging Bull. Our situation is not funny. Now, lead us before Whirlwind rides the red pony over the rim of a canyon," responded Star with no humor in her voice.

At the break of day, Roaring Waters came in as he had been walking some distance ahead. "I have seen no canyon, but a thick stand of mesquite trees is about five bow shots ahead. Do we make camp there?" he asked.

Star nodded her head, and they spent the day in the sandy soil under the shade of the scrubby trees. On this day, everyone was tired and slept well. A cool breeze hit Bonhist's face in the late evening, and she felt inspired to look at her gift from David. The Colt revolver felt good in her hand. She practiced many times drawing the gun from its holster. If only she could handle the gun like David. She loaded the pistol and wanted badly to fire the weapon, but she knew that would not be wise. At last, she unloaded the revolver and cleaned the barrel just for practice. The silence was broken as Star spoke.

"Why do you waste your time with this white man's weapon? You are a good shot with the bow. It is foolish to touch such medicine. You will blow off your foot."

"Mother, it is a gift from David. He said it could save our lives. I must learn of it just as I must learn the white man's tongue," Bonhist replied.

"It is time to go. Each day we get closer to the territory where we will be safe," Star said.

"Mother, may I fire my revolver?" Bonhist asked.

Star laughed. "You and Charging Bull are as funny as a sage hen. When we are safe, then you can fire your weapon."

Before they traveled far, Roaring Waters and Charging Bull came running. "We have seen the Comancheros. They are camped in a canyon just ahead. They have an old man staked out. He is a ranchman like Milburn. He is dead, they have cut off his manhood and stuffed it in his mouth. His woman is like Maria; she is tied to their wagon, and the Comancheros have raped her many times," said Rushing Water, breathing heavily.

"Come, show me their camp," Bonhist said.

Soon, the Cheyenne were peering into their camp from the rim of the canyon. It took Bonhist's breath away to see the suffering of the Mexican woman and to see the ugliness of the sleeping men that lay around each with a bottle of the white man's firewater.

Chapter 18

"You will not go into that camp!" Star said. "If someone has to go, it will be I."

"No, I will go," offered Roaring Waters. "The spirits will not allow me to die. However, if that should happen, it would be unimportant and would please me."

"Roaring Waters! I never want to hear you talk like that again. Your life is precious to us all, and you are vital to our survival. Now I have seen a vision. You will wait here. If the wolves wake or if I have trouble, make a silent kill."

With those final words, Bonhist silently moved down the side of the canyon walls and into the camp of the Comancheros.

Star and Roaring Waters notched arrows and crept along the rim of the canyon as Bonhist calmly made her way to the bottom. In the dark, the only source of light was the glowing embers of the campfire and a pale moon. Slipping her knife from its sheath, Bonhist reached for the tied hands of the woman. It surprised Bonhist to find that the rope was so tight that it cut into her skin. As the knife cut the bonds, the woman's eyes opened, and she screamed. Quickly, Bonhist threw her hand over her mouth. "Be quiet," she said in the tongue of the Cheyenne. Then, remembering her limited English, she added, "Come."

Bonhist looked around, and in the darkness, she could see no movement from the Comancheros. The wolves slumped forward, sleeping soundly as if they were dead. The woman rose to her feet with a low groan. Wrapping the blanket around her, Bonhist held her tight, and they began moving away from the cart.

"What is this?" Panchito asked with a laughing voice. He lifted his machete to the chin of Bonhist. Her face met his with a smile. "Oh, it is the face of an angel. Who has sent such a señorita into the camp of El Diablo?" He lowered his machete and stepped forward for a better look. As he did, Bonhist pulled the colt from its holster, striking the old Comanchero across his temple. This act saved his life, for in the next instant, two Cheyenne war arrows passed where he had been standing and struck the cart. Panchito was out cold, sprawled on the sandy floor of the canyon. Returning the pistol to its holster, Bonhist moved the Mexican woman from the canyon where they joined her mother and Roaring Waters. Two hours later, they met the others who had stopped, waiting for their return. Star was so excited about the encounter with the Comancheros that she would not let them stop until the sun rose the following morning. They were now north of the river by several miles. Finding an ash grove, they made camp. It was a good place to hide, so for three days they hid, praying that the Comancheros would not find their trail.

Bonhist sat in front of the Mexican woman and, using sign language, asked, "What is your name?" The woman could not understand. She reached out, taking both of Bonhist's hands into her own. She lifted them to her lips and softly started kissing the hands that had saved her life. Warm tears ran from her brown eyes, dropping on Bonhist. Bonhist smiled, and this time she attempted English, "My name is Bonhist; what is your name?" It pleased Bonhist that she remembered these white man's words, yet she had no idea whether they were spoken clearly enough.

The Mexican woman met Bonhist's kind, beautiful eyes with her own and answered, "Carmen." Bonhist could see that this woman could not speak the white man's tongue very well either. However, it was the only way they could converse with each other. Nonetheless, every time Bonhist came in range, Carmen would grab her hand and kiss it.

Red Leaf found a buckskin dress for Carmen, and soon, Carmen was preparing their meals. She was a cook like Marie and knew what to do with the peppers.

Panchito awoke the following morning madder than hell. He wildly shot several rounds from his Colt .45, nearly missing both night guards. Slashing his machete through the air, he cursed, ranted, and raved. Panchito was stiff, sore, tired, and mad! His men kept their distance while he shouted, "A young woman penetrated our camp last night while we slept! She stole valuable property! Out of the darkness, someone clubbed me in the head, and what were you doing? You were sleeping on a full stomach and whiskey! I want that woman! She is of the highest quality. She is worth a thousand horses. We will not rest until I have her!"

"Si, Panchito. Still, these are the war arrows of the Cheyenne. It may not be so easy, and besides, we have many horses. Would it not be wiser to go to the Comanche camp and do business?" Juan Rivera asked.

"Idiots surround me! This one woman is priceless. Do you not understand? Is she an angel, and is she worth much gold? This one woman is worth more than all the wealth of the Comanche. We will not rest until we capture her."

"Juan has a point. Indians are damned hard to find, and this is a big country. They could be anywhere. Do you have a plan?" Max Ragsdale snarled. Max was a white renegade, and the only member of the group with the skills and strength to stand up to Panchito. Yet, he had not found the courage for a real confrontation. Panchito whipped out his machete and pointed it toward Max's right hand.

"Señor Max, even the Indians drink water—am I right. So they will stay on this river or one of these canyons. We will spread along the river until someone finds their trail. We will then take their women and kill the men."

The three-day rest was good for the red pony; however, the water skins were now empty. Star again started the party of eight moving east toward Indian Territory. They swung close to the river, while Roaring Waters and Charging Bull carried the water skins to the river. The sun was starting to drop fast in the western sky. Both saw the rider. He sat on a high point observing the river. Finally, as the sun set, he moved, and they retrieved the water and returned to their evening camp.

For the next three suns, the Cheyenne made good time toward the Indian Territory. They ran out of water, and again, Roaring Waters and Charging Bull were sent to fill the bags. They stumbled upon a beautiful canyon where clear, running water was abundant. Many turkeys and rabbits filled the area. It was an ideal camp. The young warriors quickly filled the water skins and returned with their story. It was too tempting, since everyone wanted to swim and cool off in the pools. Finally, Star agreed, and the party eagerly entered the canyon. They made camp, and the dusty, dry travelers soaked up the water.

While the women swam in a clear pool, Charging Bull prepared a turkey trap. "This is a beautiful spot," Star said. "I would like to live here rather than the Indian Territory."

"Mother, Roaring Waters has killed a rabbit. I wonder what Charging Bull is doing? We will have fresh meat tonight. Perhaps you will tell some stories. I would enjoy staying here for a few suns to rest," Bonhist said.

"Have you so quickly forgotten the Comancheros?"

"No, mother, nonetheless, we are all so tired. Walking on empty stomachs and dry mouths has made us weary; even the red pony can use a rest."

"This is a big empty country. We will be safe here for now to rest and hunt," Star agreed.

The next morning, Charging Bull brought in four large turkeys, and almost everyone except Whirlwind and Carmen had killed a rabbit or two. It was a good day, and joy filled Bonhist's heart as she watched her mother and the others rest by the clear pools of water. The sun had warmed up the day, and soon the moon of the red berries would come.

On the third day, Star said to Bonhist, "We should move on, yet I hate to leave this canyon."

"How much further can it be to that Indian land they call Oklahoma? Perhaps there, we will find a canyon like this one, where we can build our own ranch."

Star smiled at her daughter's remark and looked up quickly to see Charging Bull running into camp. "A Comanchero rider has seen our camp and is now carrying word to their leader. We must leave now."

Chapter 19

"At best, we are only one sun ahead of those gruesome men. They will uncover our trail without a doubt. Our only chance is to outrun them," reasoned Star as everyone but Bonhist ran to gather their belongings.

Bonhist sat beside Whirlwind, watching the frantic party of travelers preparing to leave. She lowered her head, and like magic, everyone glanced at the glowing countenance of her face. They stood quietly, anticipating her words, for they sensed she was about to speak. "I have had a vision."

"No! I am tired of your visions," said Star. "They always put you in danger, and I can no longer stand it."

"Mother, we cannot run faster than these evil men. We are on foot while they ride fast horses. We must use my vision, not our heads."

"Bonhist has words like a straight arrow. I trust her visions," Whirlwind said. "Let her speak."

"Why do they chase us? We have done them no harm, nor do we have anything of real value," Red Leaf snapped.

"They have looked into the face of Bonhist," Roaring Waters answered.

"Yes, perhaps Roaring Waters is correct; still, did not David warn us that they steal women for their own pleasure and to trade for gold?" Bonhist asked.

"I have seen what they do to men. They stake them to the ground and cut off their manhood," declared Roaring Waters.

"My vision will save us. Listen to me, my brothers and sisters. We will split up. The main party will conceal itself along the river, traveling only at night. I will take the pony with the drag poles and lead the Comancheros south. They will believe that we are trying to outrun them. When they catch up with me, I will allow the red pony to continue walking while I make myself disappear. I will later join you."

"No," Star cried, "I do not like this vision and will ride the red pony."

"It is a good vision, but I will take the pony," Roaring Waters said.

"No, my vision is clear. I will be their bait," Bonhist said.

"You will get caught in the open, and we will never see you again. I cannot stand to see my daughter captured by the Comancheros, and if it happens, I will kill every one of them," Star answered.

"Do not worry, Mother, things will go well for us, for today is not a good day to die," Bonhist said with her usual smile.

Bonhist led the red pony with the drag poles into the Canadian River. Following the shallow water for a short distance, she felt pleased. *They will think that I am trying to hide my trail.* Noticing a low bank, she led the pony up and away from the river. Going back, she took a branch and wiped away most of the tracks, leaving only a slight hint of her course. She looked over her shoulder, smiling. Star would not allow anyone to move. They hid waiting. The following day, just before high noon, the Comancheros arrived. They went up the canyon a short distance to study their old camp. Panchito, on his sleek gray stallion, led them. The eyes of the Indians watched as the Comancheros carefully followed Bonhist's trail down the river and up the bank. Picking up speed, they found her clear trail.

"The rest of you stay. I will follow from a distance. If they catch Bonhist—I will kill them all!" vowed Star. The group gazed upon the beautiful Star and saw in her a Lakota warrior. As she started in a jog following the trail of the Comancheros, Roaring Waters and Charging Bull followed.

Bonhist had made good time. Turning, she looked back at her trail; no sign of her pursuers could be seen. The bright morning sun had made her eyes blink. Since she had not stopped to rest during the night, both she and the red pony were tired and thirsty. She drank, then poured water from her water skin into a buckskin bag for the pony. Looking ahead, she saw hills. Something inside, an intuitive urge, told her to run for those hills. Without another thought, she mounted the red pony for the first time. Turning his head toward the hills, she rode.

Approaching the hills, the river surprised her, for it made a bend and now lay between her and the hills. Riding the pony across the river, she untied the drag poles. Climbing the hill on the red pony, she noticed a gully. Either side of the gully offered an excellent view of the Canadian River. The gully led to a high-rise, the highest point on the hill. Bonhist rode along the gully looking up. She dismounted and walked to a point where she looked back at her trail. Her heart dropped to the ground as she saw the Comancheros. They were still a good distance from the river. Nonetheless, escape seemed impossible. Suddenly, she smelled smoke. Someone close had a campfire! Leaving the red pony at the edge of the gully, she climbed up the rise to the top of the hill. There before her was an old man roasting meat from a fresh kill. He sat where he had a sweeping view of the valley. He turned and looked at Bonhist with a toothy smile. Stretching his long, gangly body on a tattered buffalo robe, he belched. "Who are you?" Bonhist asked in sign language.

He answered in the tongue of the Cheyenne. "Hello, Bonhist, I have been watching you. Here, have a roasted antelope steak. It is not as good as elk; however, these are the antelope hills, and the elk rarely migrate into this area."

Bonhist stood in awe. She did not know how to answer this old man. Finally, she asked, "How do you know my name? I do not remember seeing you. Are you Cheyenne or Sioux? Are you also traveling to the Indian Territory?"

The old man laughed and motioned for Bonhist to sit beside him as he again offered the simmering steak. "This is the Indian Territory of Oklahoma that you have just entered." He laughed again and said, "You are almost as entertaining as your father, Crow. Now eat. You do not have much time."

Bonhist accepted the steak and took a bite. She looked up into the wrinkled face of the old man. He had a twinkle in his eye and a mischievous smile. "Did you know my father? Tell me what he was like?"

"He was very much like you—full of tricks."

"I know who you are. You are my Grandfather Trickster. How much time do I have before those evil men capture me?"

The old man rolled over laughing. Finally, he rose to his feet and looked at the approaching Comancheros. His height amazed Bonhist. He was the tallest man she had ever seen.

"I have changed my mind. You are just as entertaining as Crow. Now, have you made a plan?" he asked.

CHAPTER 20

Soft Winds, picking up her pack, followed the trail of Roaring Waters and Charging Bull. "Where are you going?" asked her mother, Red Leaf.

"I can shoot a bow like the others; maybe Bonhist will need me too."

"And I can swing a club," said Whirlwind as the blind man followed the sound of the girl's footsteps.

"Come, Carmen, let us follow and be killed with the others. What difference does it make?" Red Leaf snapped. Carmen hesitated for only a moment, then, realizing that she would be left alone, followed.

Roaring Waters and Charging Bull found it difficult to keep pace with the one-time Lakota warrior. Star had always been a fast runner, and now she was running with a purpose. Panchito, too, kept a swift gait like a hungry wolf on a bloody trail. Nonetheless, the three fell well behind the Comancheros. Star, looking into the rising sun with tears in her eyes, feared that they would be too late.

Bonhist stood beside the old man as he pointed a bony finger up the river. "Riders come," he said with a sly grin.

It was true. Making things worse, as the Comancheros crossed the river around the bend, a line of soldiers rode in two columns.

"Who are these pony soldiers? Are they the ones from Colorado? Grandfather Trickster, what must I do?"

"They are the buffalo soldiers, the black, white men. Good fighters."

"I have never heard of black, white men, and why are they called buffalo soldiers?"

"They have hair like a buffalo and black faces—this is a good situation."

"The enemy surrounds us, and you say—this is good! Ha!"

"What would happen, Bonhist, if you rode down this gully and showed yourself to the Comancheros? Would they not ride hard to catch their prize? Then you could ride over the other ridge and show yourself to the buffalo soldiers while shooting your little fire stick. Would they not come after you, too? You could then climb back up to this spot to watch. It would be fun."

Bonhist wasted no further time, sliding down the hill and onto the back of the red pony. Crossing the gully, she rode over the ridge showing herself to the Comancheros. Panchito's heart jumped as he once again caught sight of the most beautiful woman he had ever seen. "That's her!" he shouted. "Do not harm her, she is worth a thousand horses." Bonhist had never fired the Colt, but she had handled the gun often and could draw and shoot. The kick of the revolver surprised her, and she almost dropped it. She had no idea which direction the bullet went, so she fired again and again. The buffalo soldiers, recognizing at once that they were under attack, drew their weapons and charged the hill. Bonhist had hardly made the top of the mountain when the first shot was fired. She turned, looking for the old man—he was gone. Looking up, she saw a red-tailed hawk swooping overhead with a scream. Smiling and waving, she turned back to watch the fight and noticed three Comancheros lying dead. The rest were running for their lives with Panchito in the lead. Her heart jumped with joy to see the dust flying high from the heels of the horses as they fled toward Texas. As she returned to the campfire, she felt suddenly tired and hungry. Adding wood to the fire, she cut more slices of antelope. A sharp stick lying near held the slices of meat over the fire to roast. Looking out over her back trail, she wondered where the others had gone.

"Look, the river! The shots came from that direction, but I see no one," observed Charging Bull to Star and Roaring Waters.

"Maybe they have already captured Bonhist and now ride back to the canyon country."

"I will follow their trail until I have killed them all," Star vowed.

"We stay with you wherever you go."

Star smiled slightly at the two young warriors as they followed the trail leading them straight into the river. In only a short time, they stood on the opposite bank where the drag poles and lodges had been dropped.

"On the side of the hill are three dead Comancheros killed by the fire stick," Roaring Waters guessed.

"Bonhist fought from the top of that hill," Charging Bull agreed.

"With David's little fire stick, I pray she killed them all," thought Star as the three started climbing the hill. Soon, they found the red pony and continued to follow the tracks until they reached the hill's peak. There they came upon Bonhist as she slept near her campfire.

"She sleeps without a scratch and is safe," Charging Bull announced excitedly.

"And she has killed an antelope—she has great medicine," Roaring Waters added.

Lifting her hands to the sky, Star thanked the Great Spirit as she collapsed over her daughter, crying.

"Mother! What is wrong? Are you injured?"

"Your mother has been running for almost two days without sleep, greatly concerned for your safety," stated Charging Bull.

"Did I not tell you that I had a vision? You were to stay with the others and not worry. I wish you were more concerned for your own safety."

"How can I think of myself when I have a daughter who runs toward the hand of death with every turn of the river?"

"Still, Mother, we are now in the Indian Territory of Oklahoma, and we have survived."

Everyone looked at Bonhist with amazement. "How do you know that this is the territory?"

Before Bonhist could answer, Roaring Waters interrupted, "And how did you defeat the Comancheros? Tell us the story."

The three continued to lash out with their questions as Star motioned toward the antelope, "And how did you have time to make a kill?"

Laughing Bonhist protested, "I will tell you everything, but first, where is the rest of our party? We must go back for Whirlwind, Soft Winds, Red Leaf, and Carmen."

"They will come soon. We must rest before we go anywhere," Star answered.

Bonhist told the story over and over for the next two sleeps as they rested and allowed the red pony to gain strength. Roaring Waters and Charging Bull claimed three revolvers and one rifle from the dead Comancheros. They also found gun belts and three metal knives.

As Whirlwind and the others caught up, Bonhist again had to tell the story of the trickster and his plan for the Comancheros. Everyone laughed continuously at Bonhist's stories. Finally, Whirlwind said, "Bonhist, you have great medicine even summoning the trickster."

The following morning, they attached the drag poles to the red pony and continued walking along the river deeper into the territory.

Four sleeps later, Star's group came upon three Cheyenne warriors sitting on bony and weary horses. Star raised her hand as the three approached. "Who are you?" one of the warriors asked.

"We have traveled a great distance from the far north country searching for a home where we will be safe. They told us that the People live in this country," Star said.

"Do you lead this group?" the same warrior asked.

"No, this is our leader," answered Star as she pointed toward Whirlwind. Whirlwind sat proudly on the red pony and slowly turned his sightless eyes toward the speaker.

"What is the name of this great warrior who sits on the splendid red pony?"

"His name is Whirlwind, once a member of the mountain band led by Chief Thin Face. I am Star. My husband Crow was killed at Sand Creek. This is our daughter Bonhist."

Bonhist looked up to the three warriors who looked like they had not eaten in days. She felt sadness in her heart. "Mother, we could make camp early and ask Carmen to make a good meal for us all."

"We will camp here. You are welcome to our camp," Star said.

The three warriors sliding from their horses were all tall and very slender from lack of food. "My name is Big Dog Fletcher; these are my brothers Willie and Whitebird."

Star laughed as Bonhist had never heard her laugh before. There was joy in her spirit, and it filled Bonhist's heart. "Why do you have white man's names? What does Fletcher mean?" Star asked.

"After we have eaten, I will have the energy to talk. For now, let me say that I once saw your husband Crow win a great race for the People riding a mule. He was a great warrior." The three Fletchers then spread their robes and fell asleep.

CHAPTER 21

With the help of Soft Winds and Bonhist, Carmen prepared the evening meal. The Fletchers sat up, sniffing the smell of beef stew. They stretched and smiled as Star brought each of them a serving on the shoulder blade of a buffalo. With spoons carved from buffalo horns, the men ate the beef as if they found it good. "We are beginning to adjust to the taste of this white man's buffalo. Sometimes they give us beef at the agency," Big Dog said.

"Where is the agency?" Star asked.

"It is at Fort Cantonment on the North Canadian River," Big Dog answered. "The Cheyenne are on the west bank while the Arapaho are on the east."

"There are too many; why do you stay?" Star asked.

Big Dog smiled, rolled over on his robe, and looked into the evening sky. "We have many problems in this land. Because the buffalo have vanished, the People starve, and many are sick. At Cantonment, they give us food, medicine, and a little paper money. We stay close since we do not want to starve."

Bonhist smiled at her mother as she talked to Big Dog Fletcher. Her head was full of questions, yet she kept silent, enjoying her mother's contentment. Finally, she could stand it no longer and asked, "Why do you have a white man's name?"

Everyone listened; each was curious about the name 'Fletcher.' "My brothers and I helped a white man work his horses for one moon. When we left, he said that he would like to pay us for our work, but he had no gold or even paper money. So he gave us his name—Fletcher. It is strong medicine." Star laughed along with everyone else.

"The white man is like a fox. He guards his gold well," said Bonhist. "This country is not so bad. I have seen many medicinal plants. Why have you not killed an antelope?" asked Bonhist.

"Look at our arrows." Big Dog took an arrow from his quiver and held it for all to see. The arrow held no arrowhead, only a sharp point that had been hardened from the heat of a campfire. "We have not found the flint for making arrowheads. This makes hunting harder."

"You have no arrowheads?" asked Star.

"Most do not have a horse. None have fire sticks. When the pony soldiers see your weapons, they will take them and perhaps your horse as well. Your red pony is the finest," Big Dog added.

"Wild horses and cattle live along this river. They stay in the canyon country they call Texas. We could catch a few," Charging Bull suggested.

"They do not allow Indians to leave the territory. You have heard the story of the Northern Cheyenne. They left during the night and went back north—many died," Big Dog said.

"Who would stop us? I cannot tell the territory from the canyon country," said Roaring Waters.

"Pony soldiers would stop you. We are not free in this land. We are safe but not free, and the food they give us is not good. That is why we must hunt even with these arrows," Big Dog said.

"We will give you some of our arrows. You will like them," Star said. She then removed three of her arrows with metal arrowheads and gave them to Big Dog. She signaled to Roaring Waters and Charging Bull to do the same. Soon, the Fletchers were smiling.

"Where did you get these arrowheads?" Big Dog asked.

"Roaring Waters and Charging Bull know the medicine of making the metal arrowheads. They made them during our winter camp. Yet they must have the white man's blacksmith shop," answered Star.

"There is a blacksmith shop at Cantonment," said Big Dog as he settled back in his blanket and fell asleep.

The following morning, the party followed their new guides as the three brothers walked north away from the river.The Fletchers' ponies were so poor that no one wanted to ride them. After only a short distance, Charging Bull came running. "A large herd of antelopes is just beyond that small hill," he said.

Lying down on top of the hill, everyone watched the antelope swishing their tails rapidly as they grazed. "I can tell that you have never hunted antelope. We cannot get off a shot. They are out in the open and not even the red pony could get close," said Big Dog as his brothers nodded in agreement. "Our ancestors, the old ones who lived before the time of the horse, could get off a shot," Bonhist claimed.

"What do you mean?" Big Dog asked.

"You have heard the stories of how a medicine man would put on a buffalo robe and go among the buffalo. He would guide them to the hunters."

"Yes, but they were hunting buffalo, not antelope. The medicine of such hunting has long been dead among the People," Big Dog answered.

"Nonetheless, I would like to summon the medicine of such hunting and walk among the antelope with this robe," Bonhist said as she held up the antelope hide.

As Big Dog started to laugh, a walking stick suddenly landed near his nose. It was Whirlwind. "You waste time and energy by laughing. You'd be wise to get your bow ready before Bonhist has the antelope running over us," he said.

Bonhist smiled at Whirlwind and said, "Thank you, Grandfather. Stay here and be very quiet."

"This I have to see," Willie Fletcher said.

Everyone looked surprised since those were Willie's first words. They were beginning to think that Big Dog was the only one among them who could speak. Bonhist took her hide and ran in a wide path around the antelope, so they were between her and the hunters. She had noticed that the wind was strong and from the southwest. If she were downwind, perhaps she would have a chance, and if not, then it would at least break the boredom of the day.

When she was in position, she slipped into the antelope hide. As usual, she had left the legs and head skin intact. She now tied the legs with a rawhide strap to her arms and legs. She pulled the head over her head and smiled. *This is only a joke, but I hope the antelope let me get close*, she thought.

Bonhist watched the antelope's movement. Every few heartbeats, one of them would look up, then continue eating. *They are so careful*, she thought. *I will imitate them.*

Gradually, Bonhist edged closer to the herd. Bringing her head up, she would take a quick look, as the antelope had done, then let it drop to graze. The nervous antelope would not allow her to get closer than a hundred yards. She wanted them to go left toward the hunters. She experimented by moving to the right side of the herd. They made little sporadic moves to the left. Now they were headed in the direction she wanted. As the antelope pulled away from her, Bonhist moved directly behind them. This made the herd move closer to the hunters again. *This is fun*, Bonhist thought as she played her little game. *I cannot believe that they are going just where I want them to go.* The hunters waited in surprise. Star watched her daughter with a smile. Bonhist was acting and looking just like an antelope. With great patience, they waited until the antelopes were right on top of them. Bonhist knew the southwest wind would help the hunters. Everyone rose and shot at once. Each brother brought down an antelope. Star shot two with excellent accuracy. Charging Bull shot his fire stick and missed, while Roaring Waters shot his revolver and missed. Soft Winds surprised everyone when she also shot an antelope. Altogether, six antelopes lay dead. They spent the rest of the day skinning, butchering, and drying meat. As everyone laughed and ate, Star told their story to the Fletchers.

During the evening, when everyone lay on their robes looking at the stars, Big Dog announced, "We will have council in two sleeps on the North Canadian River near our camp. All of the chiefs and medicine men will be there. I want Whirlwind to tell your story. Star will also come since she is a warrior of the Sioux."

CHAPTER 22

As the North Canadian River came sweeping into view, Bonhist looked down the stream toward the south. A bluish haze of smoke showed the presence of the Cheyenne encampment. Approaching the village, Bonhist realized that their long trip was over. They had walked from Colorado to the territory. Here they would be safe and would build a new life, but what kind of life would it be? Could her mother and the rest find happiness in this strange land? Her heart suddenly felt sad as she looked at the lodges that dotted the west bank of the river. Across the river were the lodges of the Arapaho. Both villages stretched as far as Bonhist could see. She knew that just past their camps would be the white men with their fort, which they called Cantonment.

The village was not typical. They could see little activity, and the stench in the air made them turn away. Bonhist saw some children playing in the river. She smiled, wondering if they were happy.

As the travelers reached the village, Bonhist searched for her mother's face and the rest. They were in shock; the People had turned their pots upside down, showing they were without food. Men and women lay sick outside their lodges. Bonhist could not see a horse or a dog.

"I thought you said that they gave you food and medicine," Star said to Big Dog.

"They do; however, we are many of us. Not enough is all they can say. Animals to hunt are everywhere; yet, without horses and weapons, we have little success."

"Why don't you move your village? It stinks," Red Leaf said.

"We have had much trouble in this land. Only seven seasons ago, the buffalo were many; now they are hard to find. White raiders from Kansas have robbed us of our horse herds, and when the pony soldiers refused to get them back, we had war. We were punished, and more of our horses were killed. Now we have no buffalo robes to trade with the white man. They have stopped bringing their whiskey, guns, and ammunition. The Arapaho and Cheyenne now eat corn and beef. We do not have the energy or desire to move our camp."

"Mother," said Bonhist, "we will erect our lodge on the far end away from the other lodges and the fort."

By mid-afternoon, two new lodges appeared along the west bank. Star, Bonhist, and Carmen helped set up the third lodge for Whirlwind and Roaring Waters. Red Leaf, Soft Winds, and Charging Bull had their lodge close to Bonhist, Star, and Carmen.

"You are now with your own people," said Bonhist to Whirlwind. "They will need your experience and leadership."

"We would have never made it without your vision and strength. You have strong medicine," Whirlwind replied.

Bonhist turned to Soft Winds, who stood beside her brother and Roaring Waters. Bonhist opened her arms to the girl, and Soft Winds ran into her arms. Charging Bull and Roaring Waters joined them, and the four held each other with tears rolling down their cheeks.

The Cheyenne held council the following evening. Chiefs, sub-chiefs, medicine men, and prominent warriors were present. Big Dog Fletcher, Willie Fletcher, and Whitebird Fletcher took their places. They brought Whirlwind and Star as their guests. Star, as a proven warrior of the Lakota Sioux, was allowed to attend. As usual, they debated the usual discussion about their situation. This was the darkest hour that any Southern Cheyenne could remember. They suffered from disease and hunger. They were poor with few horses. Hunting was not good, and their days were long and empty. They were losing their pride and self-worth.

Chief Spotted Horse was encouraging his followers to join him in a different area with canyons, hills, and a good water supply. Chief Heap of Birds spoke against such a division of the tribe. Two medicine men had a vision; still, there was no solution. Finally, Big Dog rose and introduced the old, blind Whirlwind and Star. Spotted Horse smiled and asked Whirlwind to speak. Whirlwind stood before the council, leaning on his heavy walking stick. He turned, showing his sightless face. Many around the council had known Whirlwind when he was a young and fierce warrior. He had always been reckless and daring. For a moment, they felt the old pride they once knew. This sightless man, who had walked from Colorado leading the small traveling party of mainly women, stood before them. They shouted his name, and in his honor, yelled the Cheyenne war cry. Finally, Whirlwind began to speak. "My heart is warm and happy tonight. I believed that I would die alone in a land where my people were hated. It is not easy to live in darkness, never seeing the light of day or the stars at night. When a person is blind, they learn to listen, touch, smell, and hear. Gradually, you adjust to a new life without sight. Tonight, I listened to your counsel and realized that the Cheyenne are now blind as I am. You must adjust to this white man's world so the young can live. I have a message from the blind world for you. The Cheyenne has among us one who possesses great medicine and power. She is only a child of fifteen winters; yet, without her, we would never have made it to your camp. She has great and true visions. She has vanished into the air. She walked into the Comancheros' camp and walked out with their prisoner. She once made a canyon appear before us when we were almost dead from lack of water and food. The canyon was full of clear running water, and berries grew in great abundance. I was not the leader; she was my eyes and helped me every step. Angry white men threatened us for killing one of their steers; it was she who went to their chief and held council. He gave us two more steers and the pretty red pony. She has summoned the Trickster to fight the Comancheros. Yesterday, she summoned the spirit of the ancient ones, those medicine men who used to wear robes and walk among the buffalo to guide them to the hunters. With their spirit, she wore an antelope hide and walked among the herd, guiding them toward our arrows; we killed six.

As she was my eyes, she is now the eyes of the Cheyenne. Listen to her well, my brothers. Her name is Bonhist. She is the daughter of Star and Crow. Many of you remember Crow. He once spoke of his daughter in council and how she would help us learn to live with the white man. From this day forward, we will call Bonhist, Medicine

Woman." The council was very quiet as old Whirlwind turned to find Star and sit beside her. Timber Bear stood and looked around the council. He was a young medicine man with strong medicine and a growing reputation. "A medicine man is not just announced. It takes years of work and training. You must first be chosen as an apprentice. Has Bonhist ever gone through any training? You know that usually a medicine man passes his skills and medicine down to his son. Was Bonhist's father a medicine man? I hope none of you are taking this old blind man seriously."

Suddenly, Gray Owl, an ancient medicine man, stood. He had not spoken in council for three seasons. His teeth hurt, and he was not usually in a good spirit. Everyone straightened their backs and paid attention, for his counsel was great.

"Many seasons back, I had a vision about a golden snake. It was a great puzzle to me. We were at war with the white man, and no one knew what to do. The great Chiefs, Black Kettle and White Antelope, were both present at this council. It amazed me to see a warrior wearing a golden snake around his upper arm. It was Crow, the father of Bonhist. No one wanted to listen to Crow since he had never proven himself. Still, my vision demanded his voice be heard. He got up that night and told of his vision. He was not certain what the golden snake meant, but his wife, Star, had understood the medicine of the white man's gold and had shaped it with her own hands. He said that he would one day carry a warning to the People and that he would have a daughter that we would call Medicine Woman. You all remember Sand Creek. Crow brought a warning. He said the golden snake was the pony soldiers, and the People were like field mice. Had we listened to Crow, the golden snake would have found an empty camp the following morning. He fought bravely and courageously that day, leading many of us to safety, and he died. Now, his daughter comes to us. Will we ignore her as we did her father? I can only speak for myself, but I feel my spirit calling her Medicine Woman."

The leaders of the Cheyenne stood and, with arms raised high, declared that, from this day forward, Bonhist would be known as Medicine Woman.

"Where is this child? I would like to see this girl who has such powers," Chief Spotted Horse said. Everyone turned to Star and said, "Where is Medicine Woman? We would like to see her."

Star did not respond until they were all quiet. She then said, "My daughter was playing along the river with her red horse at sunset. I will see if I can find her."

Bonhist was sitting in her mother's lodge talking with Carmen. Carmen was beginning to speak some Cheyenne while Bonhist was learning Spanish. "Bonhist, they want you at the council. They are calling you Medicine Woman. Come!" Star said.

Bonhist could not believe her mother and hesitated to respond. "Did you hear me? They wait for you."

"Mother, you know I am not a medicine woman. I am the Sage Woman—Bonhist."

"Your father once had a vision that you would one day be called Medicine Woman. That day is here. Come with me."

"Mother, I have no powers. I only play games. I do not want to go before the council. Tell them they are mistaken."

"Old Whirlwind has told them of your games. He has declared your name to be Medicine Woman. If you do not honor his vision, he will be hurt. What will you do?"

Bonhist jumped up in anger and said, "They want to see the Medicine Woman. I will come." She threw the antelope hide over her shoulders and went outside. Walking to the red pony, she mounted and rode to the council.

Chapter 23

Halfway to the council, Bonhist stopped the red pony and returned to her lodge. She had forgotten something. Digging into her pack, she moved aside the bag of gold dust, and her magnificent treasure lay before her—the eagle feather. It was a special gift from her grandfather, Chief Sitting Bull. She fastened it to her hair with a red strip of cloth. Smiling, she now felt ready to show her medicine.

Approaching the circle of seated men, she tossed the antelope hide over her body as she had done before and galloped her pony into the arena. Stopping suddenly, she slid from the back of the pony as lightly as a cat jumping from a stool. She lifted the antelope hide, showing herself. Star addressed the council, "This is my daughter, Bonhist."

Chief Spotted Horse rose and walked to Bonhist. "So, this is Bonhist," he said. Spotted Horse looked closely at their new medicine woman and said to the council, "The Cheyenne are still the beautiful people. Look at this young maiden; a more beautiful one cannot be found." He turned quickly to Bonhist and asked, "Tell us of your medicine. We have heard many strong words. If you are to be our eyes, tell us what we must do."

Bonhist smiled at these commands. The leaders of the Southern Cheyenne instantly took a liking to her, and they were not concerned with the talk of Timber Bear. It was a delight to see one such as Bonhist standing among them. Everyone grew quiet, anticipating her words, while some wondered whether she would be too nervous even to utter a sound. Bonhist removed the twin medicine bags from her neck and held them high. "This is my father's medicine. His name was Crow. Some of you may still remember him. He gave me his medicine just before his death. My mother tells me that he died bravely at Sand Creek. They tell me that he had a vision during his youth, many seasons ago, even before he met my mother. He told of a time when the People would have to adjust to the white man's world. We are now living in that time. He said that his vision showed he would have a daughter who would be called Medicine Woman. I am his only child."

Bonhist reached up and lifted the feather. "This feather is a gift to me from my grandfather, Chief Sitting Bull." This statement caused a hum throughout the council. It surprised them to hear that the spirit of Bonhist and her mother were so closely linked to the great war chief of the Sioux. "He gave this feather to me and said that it had been his medicine since his youth and had made him strong. My mother and I were at his side during the Battle of the Little Bighorn. We witnessed the mighty victory of the Sioux and Cheyenne over Yellow Hair." This statement stirred excitement among the council, and the Cheyenne war cry lasted for a couple of minutes. Bonhist did not speak again until silence fell across the council.

"I cannot tell you what to do. My visions and the spirits move me, not my head. You see before you a young, inexperienced girl. I have visited your camp and am aware of the problems. The sick get weaker each day. Joy and happiness have escaped you, and you cannot read their trail. Your village gives off an unpleasant odor. Move the village up the river past the Arapaho. Medicinal plants are growing everywhere. Eat the plants and roots as our people have always done. With your permission, I will go on my vision quest. Then, I will know what path I must take."

Chief Spotted Horse smiled and nodded his approval of Bonhist's words. "I now give you the name of Medicine Woman. You are no longer a child. You are now a woman. Go on your quest and follow the vision revealed to you by the spirits. We will move the village, eat the medicinal plants, and take some of our people to set up another camp. We will go east to a place I know."

The following morning, Bonhist prepared for her vision quest. She planned to be gone for three or more days and sat thinking about her supplies. Star placed her arms around her daughter and hugged her. "Where will you travel, Medicine Woman?" Star smiled at the sound of Bonhist's new name.

"I will go up the river for perhaps a sleep or two."

"You will need food. After your vision, you will be hungry. I went four days without food on my quest," Star said.

"Tell me of your vision quest. Were you scared?"

"I was a warrior and not allowed to be frightened." Star hesitated with a smile then admitted, "Yes, I was afraid. Still, the most fear I ever had was the first time Crow took me climbing."

Medicine Woman smiled. "I remember the story. I, too, am a little scared; yet, I can hardly wait. I hope my vision will help the People."

"Will you take the red pony?"

"No, Mother, you will keep the red pony. The pony would be only another distraction." Medicine Woman threw her pack over her shoulder, hugged her mother, and was gone.

Staying in sight of the river, she walked in a northwesterly direction. The terrain was flat with occasional hills cropping up before her. Cottonwoods, cedars, willows, sweet grass, sacred sage, and occasional dogwood trees lined the North Canadian River. Deer were in great numbers, and once Medicine Woman saw a large flock of turkeys. Coveys of bob white quail ran everywhere. She watched a small column of pony soldiers ride along the river. They did not notice her as she knelt beside a yucca plant. As she watched them ride on, she cut a piece of yucca to wash her hair and body. Gathering the sacred sage, she placed it in her sleeping robe and her fire; after all, she was the sage woman. She smiled, thinking of her new name—it was a joke. "Do they really believe that I have powers?" That made her laugh. Medicine Woman was still on her first day, and already she felt a hunger pain. She drank from her water skin and walked on. That evening, she found a well-hidden place to camp. It pleased her to know that she had left no trail. Feeling tired and hungry, she settled into her robe and fell asleep.

Day two began early. She sat for a moment to watch the river, as always. Thinking of the Great Spirit for life and the beauty of nature. Smiling, she watched a raccoon run out on a log over the river. Deer appeared, and ducks were gliding into the water from the sky. "This territory has its own beauty," thought Medicine Woman. Gathering her robe and pack, she continued her quest. No longer feeling hungry, she saw before her a small hill overlooking the river valley. Suddenly, she knew this hill would be the site of her vision.

The hill offered a high elevation above the river. She believed that very few people would go to the trouble of climbing to the very top. The top was flat, and Medicine Woman made a small fire and offered a piece of dried meat to the spirits. She spread her robe and sat in meditation. Looking as far as her eyes could see, there was no sign of another human. She felt alone with nature and the spirits of this new land as sleep came, then day three began. Her hunger had left, and she felt strong and alive. She thought of the time when they had run out of food and water on their journey from Colorado. Everyone believed they would die; yet, something led them into the canyon country. Medicine Woman thought of David and Crow Wings. They are happy. She could feel it. Pretty Dove and White Dove were also happy on Milburn's ranch. She had not had her vision, perhaps tonight.

The vision came during the third night. When the Medicine Woman awoke, she sat up with wide eyes. Now she knew what a real vision was. A true vision was different from others she had experienced. When she had told the others of visions, it was only her way of manipulating. Sure, she had a keen, intuitive mind and premonitions, but a true vision was much stronger. The Medicine Woman had always been brilliant, yet totally unaware of her keen mind. She sat, starry-eyed, feeling a sense of guilt about how she had misused the word vision. Her vision was clear and frightening. Vividly colored pictures came to her as she slept—they were real. She would marry a white man. It was so frightening, something she had not even dreamed of or thought about. She almost hated the whites as much as her mother and would surely never speak of this part of her vision again. He was a cowboy, and they would own a large ranch. Still, she could not see his face. A stream ran down the middle of their ranch, and on either side were the lodges of the Cheyenne stretching for miles. Fields of corn and other crops were on the ranch, and horses were in great numbers. The People were happy. The Medicine Woman could see a school for the Indian children. They were learning to speak the white man's tongue and to make paper talk.

Gone were the times when a Cheyenne would be honored for counting a coup, taking a scalp, or stealing horses or women. No longer would hunts make a man valuable to his family. Now, making a good horse trade, taking a job, or learning a trade such as blacksmithing, cowboying, or even farming would bring more honor. Gold was the same as paper money, and both were the same as power. Her spirit animal was the big-horned owl. The owl would guide her. She would use the gold in her medicine bags for her people, and she would do business with the white man. She would learn to speak the white tongue.

CHAPTER 24

The vision was not what Medicine Woman was expecting, and she did not like it. *It is a vision from the Trickster*, she thought. *I will tell no one of these things, and perhaps they will go away.*

Gathering her pack and robe, she began the journey home. Medicine Woman lowered her head and thought about her vision. "How can the Cheyenne ever live in the white world? It will take several generations to change their complete value system. Perhaps it will never happen. How can anyone expect a complete change of behavior? The whites will kill us all. Still, the Cheyenne cling to the white fort like a baby to its mother."

Walking along the river, Medicine Woman came upon several persimmon trees. They were full of fruit. She ate one, and its taste surprised her. It was good. She ate and picked a good supply of the juicy fruits. Continuing, she saw a deer that would be an easy kill. Knowing that she was still a long distance from the Cheyenne camp, she did not try fresh meat. She walked on, taking her time and observing the river. At dusk, she walked away from the river and made camp. She ate some of her dried meat and slept.

The following morning, after her usual routine of talking to the Great Spirit, all the wandering creatures, the trees, the rocks, and

Father Sky, she went to the river to wash. She had hardly cleared the area when she saw a lone rider. It was a white man, a cowboy. He rode down the river at full speed, mounted on a beautiful steel gray stallion that almost appeared blue in the early morning sun. Medicine Woman hid quickly and looked to see who was chasing him. He surprised her since no pursuers followed. He was giving his horse exercise and enjoying the early morning. Medicine Woman watched with interest, noting that he was totally unaware of her. She smiled to herself and thought, *I am invisible; he cannot see me.*

The rider rose high in the stirrups as the gray stallion came to an abrupt halt. Dismounting, he led the horse to the river. Medicine Woman thought, *He loves his horse.* The cowboy talked and fed the horse from his hand. He dropped the reins, allowing the horse to drink, and walked along the river chomping the sweet prairie grass. Medicine Woman was shocked to see the man remove his boots and clothes and walk into the river. "He looks very funny—white men are so white—and he still wears his black hat." He turned, removed his hat, and sailed it back to the bank. Reaching down to his left hip, he removed a dirty bandage. The hip had an ugly wound as if something had fallen on him. It was infected, and he touched it very tenderly. "He needs wild yarrow to heal his hip. I must remember to gather some for the People." She again appraised the cowboy. "He has the shoulders and arms of a strong warrior and is a handsome one with his golden hair," she observed with a smile.

Diving in the river, he swam for a few minutes, then returned to the bank. Walking on the bank, he ran his hand through his wet hair and put on his hat. Medicine Woman almost laughed aloud. He looked around, then slipped on his blue trousers. Sitting on a stone, he yanked on his worn brown boots. The cowboy wore a light blue shirt and a dark blue bandanna around his neck. Turning, he stepped toward the horse. Medicine Woman could hear the squashing sound from his wetness, and this time she laughed aloud. He quickly turned facing north, but did not see her. After several minutes, he turned again to his horse and whistled. The horse responded and galloped toward him. He reached into the saddlebag and fed the horse again from his hand. Removing a silver object from his bag, he stuck it to his mouth. A joyful tune from the cowboy made Medicine Woman smile widely. It was great medicine, and she felt a touch of disappointment when he rode away. The rider rode toward her village. He would no doubt ride past the Cheyenne and Arapaho camps to the fort. As he rode around the bend, a big horned owl flew from a tree and glided between the Medicine Woman and the cowboy. Her spirit guide had given her a sign.

It was just past midday when Medicine Woman reached the Cheyenne village. Her mother was gone, so she entered the lodge and laid down her belongings. She was not there for more than a minute when she heard her name scream out. "Bonhist! Where are you?" It was Roaring Waters.

"I am here! What is wrong?" Medicine Woman asked as she stepped from her lodge.

"I am sorry, I meant Medicine Woman—your mother is in trouble! The pony soldiers have taken her to the fort."

"What has she done? Why have they taken her?"

"They claimed that she stole the red pony from a white man. I am afraid that they will put a rope around her neck and hang her. We must hurry! Bring your little fire stick; we will kill them all!" Roaring Waters swore.

"Where is Carmen?" demanded Medicine Woman as she stepped from her lodge.

"They have taken her along with your mother. Red Leaf, Soft Winds, Charging Bull, and Whirlwind are also arguing with the whites. Many are gathering. Big Dog Fletcher and his brothers are about to start a big fight."

"We must hurry, Roaring Waters, before the white men make a terrible mistake."

Fort Cantonment was not really a fort. It was a post built to counter Indian trouble. It was midway between Fort Reno and Camp Supply on the North Canadian River. A few years earlier, Darlington had moved the Cheyenne and Arapaho agency to a place near Fort Reno. Fort Cantonment, however, had an Indian agency that supplied the Indians.

Colonel Richard I. Dodge had established the fort, and he did not want trouble. Now he was faced with an incident that could spark another Indian uprising like the one they had only three years ago. Old Gus Miller had brought in a string of horses from Texas. When Star rode in on the red horse, Gus went crazy. "That is my damn horse. Them thieving redskins robbed me right under my own eyes!"

Colonel Dodge had Star taken into custody, and with Raven, one of his scouts acting as an interpreter, they were trying to get to the truth. "She said that she traded for the horse in Texas from a white man," Raven said.

"That's a damned lie! Have you ever heard of an Indian buying a horse? Anyone can see that this horse has been grain-fed and has shoes. It wears my brand, the flying 'M.' I have raised this horse from a colt, and I want him back!" Gus screamed.

"Settle down, Gus. I will get to the bottom of this without your help," the Colonel said.

Colonel Dodge looked at Star. She was pretty and maybe the wife of a chief. He had to be careful before this whole thing got out of hand. "Ask her what she traded for the horse."

Raven turned to Star and asked her in the Cheyenne tongue what she had traded for the red pony. Star knew that her daughter had talked to Milburn about the horse and the three steers. However, she feared that the pony soldiers would kill the horse's owner, so she admitted to owning the horse to protect Medicine Woman. "I traded a buffalo hide," she answered.

Raven turned and gave her answer to the Colonel. Gus busted out laughing, "That is another damn lie. Anyone can see that this woman is lying; that hoss is worth fifty buffalo hides. I want my hoss, and this woman arrested and punished," Gus said.

"Not so fast, Gus. We will have a trial, and a lawyer will represent this woman. You will have your chance in court to prove the horse is yours," Colonel Dodge answered.

"This is an Indian. You know she stole my hoss. Forget the trial, I will just take my hoss and be gone. You and I have done some business. You got a fair deal on them ten hosses, now fair is fair. Give me that hoss!"

Many Indians were present, including Timber Bear, who was enjoying the situation. "Now the People will see how strong the new Medicine Woman is with the white man," he thought with a grim smile.

At this precise moment, Medicine Woman entered the stockade with Roaring Waters. As Roaring Waters started to notch an arrow, Medicine Woman held his arm. "No, Roaring Waters, we will talk."

<h1 style="text-align:center">CHAPTER 25</h1>

Austin H. Todd, at twenty-four, was boyishly handsome. Toddy, as his friends often called him, was of Irish descent and stood over six feet in height. He grew up on an Indiana farm, raised by Christian parents. His father was not only a farmer but also a stone mason. Austin worked with his father during the winter months, building stone fireplaces. Their farm, near a large limestone quarry, offered many business opportunities. Austin and his father once worked with a brilliant stone mason from Italy who built the community church. By the time Austin was fifteen years old, he was an accomplished stone mason, and growing crops was second nature to him. The hard work had developed his muscles and body with extraordinary strength.

Austin's mother, Mary Elizabeth, played the piano, and she expected Austin, along with his brothers Thomas, Jacob, and Adam, and his sisters Maggie and Ida, to all sing in the church choir. Austin's love of music gave him great pleasure as he was always humming, whistling, or singing a tune. He grew up playing the guitar and the harmonica.

Joining the army as a teenager, Austin requested a position in the cavalry because he loved horses. Instead, they assigned him to construction in charge of stone masonry. Oklahoma Indian Territory was his first assignment. There he served at Camp Supply, Fort Reno, and finally Fort Cantonment. He constructed the stone building of the Cantonment Fort and completed his duty as a lieutenant. Austin was happy to be out of the army and to begin a new career as a businessman. He had saved enough money to buy a partnership in the general store at Cantonment. A Cheyenne/Arapaho agency run by Agent Miles operated out of Cantonment, and a heavy concentration of Indians camped near. Once a month, the government issued each family a ration of food, a meager amount of money, and blankets. The Indians would take their money to the general store where they would buy tobacco, salt, sugar, coffee, calico cloth, and other goods that were new to them.

For the first time, Austin Todd was making good money; however, his ambitions did not end there. He also owned a freight line. His business consisted of two wagons. He had strong connections with the military, and with his good name, the government awarded him a contract to transport building materials. His freight line required him to travel throughout the western part of the territory.

His grandest dream was to one day have the money to buy a horse ranch. Taking a wife and raising a family were important parts of that dream. He had not married because of the army, but now he had more time to think about this aspect of his dream.

He was the most sought-after bachelor in the territory. One could watch him at work and see his light blond hair flopping above dark brown eyebrows. He would look up with piercing, deep blue eyes and a quick, friendly smile, capturing the hearts of young women. Still, the territory was not overflowing with pretty young Irish women. His prospects were few. Nellie Young, the daughter of a high-ranking officer at Ft Reno, was high on his list.

Austin liked the father, and Nellie was better than average in looks. Nonetheless, Nellie was headstrong and used to having things her way. Though she was eager enough, Austin feared that she would be hard to live with.

Helen, the daughter of Harold Woods, was another candidate. Her dad had a government contract to raise cattle. They lived on an isolated ranch above Camp Supply, close to the Cimarron River. Helen was a pleasant black-haired young woman, yet a little too wide through the hips to please Austin.

Finally, Sybil White was young, strong, and loving. She truly cared for Austin. She would laugh at his witty Irish ways and delight over his guitar and harmonica playing. Sybil was the daughter of the blacksmith, Joe White, at Cantonment, and could put up vegetables or work in the field like a man. She was almost pretty except for her flat chest. Yet, Austin preferred her to the other two.

Something in Austin's heart would not allow him to discourage any of these young women; nevertheless, he secretly believed that, when the time was right, he would return to Indiana to find a wife.

Austin and his partner, Boonie Thompson, lived in the rear of the general store. Like the other buildings Austin had constructed, this one was made of the calumet stone. It was warm in winter and cool in the summer months.

The Indians liked Austin Todd. He showed an interest in them and was generous with his supplies—especially tobacco. They constantly hung around his store, and the ones who spoke English kept him informed about the Indians.

This day had started much like any other. He had saddled up his prized Blue Boy. The steel-gray stallion carried him up the North Canadian for several miles. Austin loved the early morning time when he could think and ride. He had taken his normal dip in the river and returned to the store. Rubbing a horse salve to his sore, infected hip, Austin applied a fresh bandage. He was concerned about the injury since it was not healing.

Boonie had opened the store, and the regular customers were hanging around. Then, just past midday, all hell broke loose with old Gus Miller. Screaming and shouting, he got everyone's attention, including Colonel Dodge. According to Gus, an Indian had stolen one of his horses. Now, excitement mounted as the colonel tried to get the facts. Austin could see a mature Indian woman holding the horse. She was pretty yet ready to fight. The horse had all the markings of being raised by a white man. Of that, there was no doubt. It was a beautiful sorrel, red and shiny with an intelligent expression in its eyes. It was a horse that anyone would be proud to own, with the brand "M" on the left rump for all to see. Gus Miller was in an ugly mood and was making a good case for himself. As the rage went on, Austin spied Big Wolf leaning against the stockade fence and waved him over. Big Wolf was a leader among the Cheyenne and could speak a little English. He was friendly and was one of Austin's best customers.

"What's happening?" Austin asked.

"The white man is trying to steal the horse. This will cause trouble," Big Wolf responded.

"Are you so sure that they did not steal the horse from Gus?" Austin asked.

"This woman is a Lakota warrior. She was married to a Southern Cheyenne who died at Sand Creek. She and a small group from Colorado walked in last week. They had the horse then."

"What is this woman's name?" Austin asked.

"We call her Star. They once called her Elk Cow. Her daughter has great powers and is named Medicine Woman. She is a beautiful one who was once called Bonhist—the Sage Woman. The horse belongs to those two."

"Where is her daughter?"

"Here she comes now," said Big Wolf as he lifted a finger toward a young woman who had just entered the stockade.

Austin Todd stood frozen in his tracks. She was the most beautiful woman he had ever seen. The sight of the Medicine Woman walking toward the fight stirred an emotion in Austin that he had never felt before. It was love at first sight. Without thinking, he walked toward Colonel Dodge and, before Bonhist could speak, said, "That brand is strange, Colonel."

Colonel Dodge looked at Austin Todd with amusement. "Do you have some facts that will help?" he asked.

"Well, I am not sure, sir. But that brand has a bar below the "M". The Miller brand has a bar at the top. Miller's brand is the flying M," said Austin as he pointed toward the brand.

"Well, I'll be damned," shouted Gus. "Who in the hell asked you. You're a damned storekeeper. What the hell do you know about brands? I reckon you don't know a damn thing about horses. We have several branding irons on my spread. That their brand was my first. I later got the idea of The Flying M. One of my new hands used the earlier brand. It's still mine, and that's my hoss!"

Medicine Woman walked up and hugged her mother. "Do not worry, mother. Everything will be all right." She turned and faced the Colonel, saying in the Cheyenne tongue, "This horse belongs to me and my mother. Why are you trying to take it?"

Raven smiled and turned to the Colonel and said, "This is Medicine Woman. She is the daughter of Star—the one who holds the red pony. She claims the pony is hers and her mother's."

The Colonel looked at Bonhist. She was no more than a child. While Gus Miller was shouting and spitting tobacco, this young woman looked him straight in the eye with a pleasant smile. He turned to Raven and said, "Ask her where she got the horse."

Raven interpreted, and Medicine Woman replied, "I bought the horse from Milburn. He owns a ranch on the Canadian River in the canyon country."

Colonel nodded and asked, "How did you pay for the horse?" As Raven started to ask the question, Gus shouted out, "Are we going to listen to more damn lies? Hell, give me my hoss. I will never come back here again!"

The Colonel could see more Indians gathering. Many were carrying weapons and looked ready to use them. "Gus! I am conducting this investigation—not you! Give this young woman a chance."

"Are you saying that an Indian's word is as good as mine?" Gus shouted.

The Colonel turned to two of his men and gave an order. "Restrict this man. I do not want him talking until I ask him." The two soldiers responded and stood next to Gus, who was now quiet but spitting his tobacco toward the Indians.

"Ask her how she paid for the horse?" the Colonel repeated, sighing and looking a little tired over this whole affair.

Medicine Woman turned from Raven and, with a big smile, looked into the Colonel's eyes and said in English, "With gold."

CHAPTER 26

"More damned lies," Gus shouted. "Them Indians have no morals. If she ever had any gold, she cut some white man's throat for it."

Colonel Dodge turned to the two troopers and gave another order. "If he opens his mouth again, hit him over the head and incarcerate his carcass."

"Yes, sir," responded one trooper with enthusiasm.

Gus Miller sulked, yet he shut up. His face was as dark as a thunderhead, and his eyes were as lightning as he darted glances toward Medicine Woman.

Colonel Dodge turned toward Medicine Woman. "Where did you get your gold, and do you still have any?" Raven translated, and Medicine Woman reached into her sash and removed a single nugget. "I still have this golden stone. It was the last gift my father gave me before he died at Sand Creek."

Gus was about to explode, but he said nothing. The Colonel looked at the stone for a moment, then said, "Do you mind if we examine it?"

Raven translated, and Medicine Woman smiled and gladly offered the stone. "Mr. Todd, since you are a storekeeper, perhaps you would be kind enough to validate this nugget."

Austin walked slowly toward this rare beauty. *This is the cowboy,* Bonhist thought. She smiled at Austin and handed him the nugget. Austin looked it over; he bit down on it and examined it more closely. "This is as good as any I have ever seen. It's worth a couple of good horses," he said, handing the stone back to Medicine Woman.

"Still, that does not prove that she bought the horse. I'm afraid that I'll need some facts before I can allow that horse off the compound."

Medicine Woman then faced the Colonel and said in perfect English, "My name is Bonhist; you look at paper, please."

Everyone was shocked to hear these words come from the mouth of the Medicine Woman. The Colonel hesitated for a moment, then said, "If you have a paper, I will be happy to look it over."

"Thank you, please," Medicine Woman said. "They call it a bill of sale." Bonhist again reached into her sash, brought out a folded piece of paper, and handed it to the Colonel.

Colonel Dodge slowly unwrapped the paper and read it. It was a legal bill of sale that described the horse and the transaction that occurred with Bonhist. They dated and signed it, James Milburn. "This bill of sale is legal, and it gives an identifying mark on the horse. According to this paper, the horse has a nick cut in the shape of a 'V' from its left ear. Check the horse. Look at its left ear," Colonel Dodge commanded.

"Sir, the left ear has a nick in it."

"This horse belongs to—Raven, what did you say her name is?" the Colonel asked.

"She is Medicine Woman and has strong medicine."

"Yes, the horse belongs to Medicine Woman. Gus, I want to see you in my office. I think you are the one who doesn't know horses."

Austin Todd looked around the stockade. The Indians were in awe of Medicine Woman and of the great powers she had shown over the whites. Austin smiled to himself. "I do not know if she really has powers, but none is more beautiful or smarter," he thought. "Big Wolf," he said. "I will give you a plug of 'bacca if you will introduce me to Medicine Woman."

Big Wolf smiled and held out his hand. Austin slapped it with the tobacco as promised, and Big Wolf led him to Bonhist. Bonhist saw them coming and suddenly felt nervous. It was the handsome cowboy. He had tried to help her and her mother, and for this she was grateful. Big Wolf smiled and spoke in Cheyenne. "Medicine Woman, this is Austin Todd. He is a friend and would like to know you and your mother." He then spoke in English. "Austin Todd, this is Medicine Woman. Austin Todd, this is Star." Star did not even acknowledge the introduction, but her daughter—Medicine Woman—did.

"I am Bonhist. I am pleased to meet you, Cowboy," said Medicine Woman in the white man's tongue. Her sparkling black eyes and smile captivated Toddy. He could not believe it, but even his knees were getting weak. He was trying to think of a way to keep this young maiden around on a regular basis.

"My name is Austin, but you can call me Toddy. Would you like to work in my store? I will pay you a lot of paper money." Austin could see that the Medicine Woman did not understand, so he called over Big Wolf. "Big Wolf, will you translate for me and Medicine Woman?"

Big Wolf smiled and answered, "Another plug of 'bacca, you please."

After Austin agreed, Big Wolf explained to Medicine Woman what the white man had said.

Medicine Woman looked at Austin without speaking. Finally, she said, "Cowboy, how much paper money?"

"Big Wolf, tell her that my name is Toddy or Austin, and I will pay her three dollars a month." Big Wolf turned and translated.

"Cowboy, one steer in Texas is worth ten dollars. Am I not worth as much as a steer?" Big Wolf howled with laughter as he translated.

Austin took a step backwards; this he had not expected. After a slight pause, he nodded and said, "Yes, you are worth many steers. I will pay you ten dollars a month, but my name is Toddy."

Big Wolf translated, and Bonhist quickly spoke up, "Cowboy, you will also teach me the tongue of the white man?"

After the translation, Austin agreed and said, "Yes, I will teach you the white man's tongue—my name is Toddy."

Now, Medicine Woman smiled with joy and said, "Cowboy, I have a gift for you." Big Wolf again translated. Austin was now puzzled since he could not imagine what the young woman meant. She handed him a small rawhide bag. "Cowboy, inside is the medicine plant. We call it wild yarrow. You will put it on your sore hip." As Big Wolf translated, Medicine Woman pointed to his left hip.

"I'll be damned," Austin said. "She does have great powers."

Boonie Thompson was less than pleased with Austin. "You mean you hired an Indian to work in our store without consulting me? Did I hear you say we are going to pay her ten dollars a month? Have you lost your senses?"

"Take her wages out of my half of the profits; however, she will be worth twice that amount," claimed Toddy.

"That may be; still, I do not want her around the money. Find something for her to do besides handling any money."

"Don't worry, Boon, plenty can be done around here besides counting your money. I will train her and teach her English."

"Good God, she can't even speak English; she must be something special."

"Yeah, she is. Now come on out and meet her." Boonie got up from his books and followed Austin. Austin made the introduction, and Boonie bowed to Medicine Woman as if she were the queen. Looking at Austin with a side glance, Boonie nodded his approval and said, "If she could cook, we would pay her twenty dollars a month."

Boonie was not the only one upset with Austin. Sybil White looked like she had just eaten a sour lemon, and Star gave her daughter and Austin a cutting glance that would match any Sioux warrior who had ridden against Custer. Still, the following morning, Medicine Woman rode the red pony to the general store to begin her first day.

CHAPTER 27

The hot, windy days of summer forced everyone to the river and into cool attire. Star and Medicine Woman continued to dress in their traditional buckskins, spending hours making sure the beadwork and colors were just right. They noted, however, that many Cheyenne women were wearing calico dresses. Medicine Woman decided that they, too, would soon buy the cooler material for thin dresses.

Slipping into a sleeveless Buckskin skin dress, Medicine Woman enjoyed her new summer outfit. She had dyed the upper part of the dress yellow—beadwork of white and blue formed rectangles across her shoulders. The skirt was short, and the helm was dyed a burnt orange with matching beads. Rawhide fringes hung from the armholes and the middle part of the skirt, which was a natural tan. Her moccasins matched her skirt, all sewn with a threadlike sinew. The white man's thread would have done the job more quickly and easily, but they preferred the old way.

Dressed in this manner, she would turn any man's head and be the envy of any woman. Medicine Woman was tall and slender and well-shaped. Her black shiny hair bounced as she rode her red pony toward Fort Cantonment. As always, she wore a bright, joyful smile, and her eyes sparkled with anticipation of seeing her cowboy. As she reached the juncture in the river where Cantonment Creek joined the stream, she saw him.

He was riding his horse along the sandy bank.

Smiling as she watched, Medicine Woman thought that his hip was still bothering him. An impulse to follow stirred her emotions so that she playfully spurred her mount.

With his steel gray stallion maintaining a leisurely pace, Bonhist could see that her red pony would have to work to keep up. After several minutes, the cowboy spurred his mount to full speed, and Medicine Woman began to fall back. Suddenly, dust shot up as the horse came to a stop. Austin Todd dismounted, fed a handful of grain to the gray, and turned him loose to graze. He lowered his pants and removed the bandage, looking at his sore hip. The medicine plant was working. He finished undressing and, wearing only his black hat, walked out into the river. Watching, Medicine Woman laughed to see that he was still standing knee-deep in the water, wearing his hat.

A sound from Medicine Woman's horse cut through the air, sending Austin into alarm. He was unarmed and, worst of all, his horse had wandered. Memories of the battles with the Cheyenne Dog Soldiers were still fresh in his mind. He sighed with relief when, looking, he saw the prettiest sight imaginable—Bonhist. As she rode in smiling, Austin Todd knew then that there could be no other woman for him. This was who he wanted. He then realized that he was standing naked before her and jumped back into deeper water in panic. Bonhist laughed since all that was visible was a black hat and two blue eyes peering out. *The cowboy wants to play*, she thought.

It was as if two cultures directly opposed to each other were moving at full speed toward a collision. The Indians had taught their children to swim at an early age. They loved the water, and many were excellent swimmers. They swam in the nude and thought nothing of it. Austin Todd, on the other hand, was relatively modest. He was not a strong swimmer, and he had never swam with women. The only exception was back in Indiana when his sister and cousin joined him and his brother at the old swimming hole. Even then, the girls were covered from the ankles to the neck in what they called a swimming suit. It was all very proper, and of course, the girls behaved as if no boys were around. Now, he was buck naked, and the woman he loved was standing on the bank laughing. From Austin Todd's point of view, this situation could not have been worse. But as he had that thought, it did get worse. She slipped off her dress, and with a kick, her moccasins flew into the air. Laughing, she dived into the river and swam like an otter. She had been wearing nothing under her dress. Austin could feel his excitement rising.

Medicine Woman thought this was a fun game, splashing water on the black hat. As the cowboy rushed from the water, hiding himself with his black hat, she wondered if other white men took such brief baths. She swam back to the bank, slipped into her dress, and put on her moccasins. Flipping back her wet black hair, she gathered two big handfuls of yarrow and returned to the cowboy who was jerking on his boots. "Good morning, cowboy, these medicine plants are for your hip." She said the "good morning, cowboy" in English. The rest was in Cheyenne. His red face showed his embarrassment, while she acted as if nothing had happened.

As they rode back, Austin took out his harmonica and began playing a lively tune. Occasionally, he would stop and sing a verse of "O' Suzanna." Medicine Woman loved the melody and tried to hum along. Austin offered her the harmonica, suggesting she try it. She flatly refused, since among the Cheyenne women were not allowed to touch musical instruments. It was bad medicine. Hunching his shoulders, he acted as if he did not understand and continued playing. That morning was one of the most exciting moments either of them could remember. Back at Cantonment, Medicine Woman was delighted to see how it pleased Cowboy to show her his trading store. Austin soon discovered that he and Bonhist had different systems of counting. He began trying to explain. "One, two, three," he said as he counted apples from a barrel. Medicine Woman picked up an apple and said, "One." Picking up another, she said, "Two." On the third, she took a bite. "Good," she said in English.

Austin smiled as she finished off the apple. Bonhist looked like a wolf watching a fat rabbit as she glanced at numbers one and two. *I'll try a new approach*, he thought. "Look," he said. "These are cards. Watch—ace of spades is one; two of spades is two; three of spades is three. Do you understand?"

The cards fascinated Bonhist. She immediately picked them up and spread them on the counter. Laughing with delight, she said, "Paper talk, yes?"

Watching, Boonie shook his head with a smile and walked to the back room for another spool of calico cloth. Austin picked up a sheet of paper and wrote, "You are the most beautiful woman of all." Pointing to his scribbling, he said, "This is paper talk."

"This," waving to the playing cards, "is a game of chance–like a horse race." That comparison was to be complicated for Bonhist to follow in English, and Austin could see a confused expression. As he was trying to explain in sign language, Star and Carmen came into the store.

Turning to them with a smile, she motioned them closer, "See what I have learned. Paper talk," she said, pointing to the note Austin had scribbled. Then, with a wave of her hand over the playing cards, "Game of chance. What does game of chance mean?"

"We need to talk," Star said. "Come with me."

Medicine Woman stepped outside with her mother and said, "You do not like me here with these white men, and you are going to ask me to come back to the Cheyenne camp."

"Yes," Star admitted.

"Mother, I am now a woman and must follow my own heart. Do you understand that my heart and my vision lead me here?"

Star looked hard at her daughter. She saw herself. Those were almost the exact words that she had once used with her own mother about Crow. She nodded her head and said, "Yes, you are a woman now, and you need to follow your own heart. But remember who it was that murdered your father and his parents. We will talk more tonight." Star turned and walked toward the village.

"Mother," Bonhist called. "Take the red pony. We will talk tonight."

Carmen approached Bonhist. "Can I cook your dinner or do anything else for you?"

Bonhist spoke to Austin, trying her best English, "Cowboy, this is Carmen. She cooks. Can she cook a meal for us?"

Boonie was delighted with this new prospect. "Yes," he said. "Let me show her our kitchen."

As Boonie was showing Carmen the kitchen, Sybil White stormed into the store. There, before her, was the man she loved, making eyes and flirting with this Indian. "What are you doing? Do you actually prefer this Indian to me? I want her out now! You do not fool me, Austin Todd! I know you're smart enough to know that these Indians are not like us. Have you already forgotten how they fight? She will stick a knife in your heart and laugh." Sybil then noticed Austin's note on the counter.

CHAPTER 28

Sybil read the note before Austin could even move. Wadding it into a ball, she threw it at him. Giving Bonhist one last look, she burst into tears and ran out the door. Bonhist immediately turned to Austin and said, "Cowboy's wife?"

"My name is Austin, and she is not my wife. Sybil is only a friend. Why she is so mad, I don't know."

"Sybil loves you. She is white like you and will give you many fine sons." Bonhist then turned and walked from the general store. Her words were mainly in Cheyenne; however, enough English was spoken that Austin got the idea.

"Big Wolf! Raven! Where are you?" Austin shouted. "I need a translator." No one answered, so Austin followed and tried to make Medicine Woman understand.

"This is my business. I wanted you to work here because you can help the Indians. You want to learn the white tongue. I can teach you. Sybil had no right to interfere. She is jealous since you are so beautiful. I do not have a wife, and if I had one, it would not be Sybil." Austin desperately talked to Medicine Woman as she silently and swiftly walked back toward the Cheyenne camp. Still, he was getting nowhere, and he had no idea how much Medicine Woman understood. Finally, he pulled out the deck of cards and said, "We will have a game of chance. It is like a horse race. We will draw for high card. If I win, you will come back now. If you win, I will pay you ten dollars for your trouble, and you will not have to work a day for me. Do you understand?" Bonhist could not resist the offer to play Cowboy's game. She turned to him and, using sign language, indicated that she wanted to play.

Austin was now encouraged and walked over to a wooden barrel. He spread the cards face down on the barrel. "Now, pick a card." Bonhist smiled and turned over the three of hearts. "Remember," Austin said, "this is three-like the apple." He then looked at the cards and said, "Now I will choose one. This is a game of chance, and maybe you win, or maybe you lose." Austin had the cards carefully marked. He used these marked cards only with Boonie to settle arguments. Now he looked over the cards and reached out and turned over the ace of spades. "Oh, this is my lucky day. This is the highest card in the deck. I win."

"No, cowboy," Bonhist replied. "I win. This is a one, my card is a three. My card is higher. You will pay ten dollars." Suddenly, it dawned on Austin that she was repeating exactly what he had told her. He could think of no way to explain how number one was higher than three. She had beaten him at his own game, and he would probably lose her as well.

"Yes, you have won. Come with me, and I will give you ten dollars. Remember, Carmen is cooking our lunch. We will eat, and I will teach you more about the game of chance and the white man's tongue."

Bonhist nodded in agreement, and with great relief, Austin led Medicine Woman back to the store. Once there, Austin pulled his guitar from behind the counter and began strumming a tune, his favorite religious song, "Rock of Ages." It brought an instant smile to Medicine Woman's face. As Austin was singing and strumming his guitar, Raven walked in, looked around, and, when the music stopped, asked, "Do you need an interpreter?"

"No, not now," Austin answered.

"Yes," Bonhist said. "I need an interpreter. Cowboy, do you have cigars?"

"Yes, but is something bothering you? What do you need?" Austin asked.

"Give me cigar."

Austin reached under the counter and removed a cigar from a box. He handed it to Medicine Woman with a puzzled expression. She gave the cigar to Raven and said, "You will be my interpreter?"

Raven nodded his head and smiled as he lit the cigar. "Come, we will go talk with white girl."

Sybil White lived with her mother and father. Her father, Joe White, was a government blacksmith and was quartered by the military. Their home was a stone structure built by Austin Todd. Not large but powerfully built, it offered good protection from Oklahoma's weather. Sybil was nineteen, not much older than Bonhist, but she felt like an old maid. All the other young women her age were already married. She believed that her best and perhaps only chance was Austin Todd. Now he would probably never speak to her again. She lay on her bed sobbing when a sharp rap on the door caught her attention.

"My father is not here. You will find him at the blacksmith shop," Sybil shouted from her bedroom.

"You are the one we wish to speak to," said Raven from the front step. Sybil quickly checked her hair and wiped away her tears. As she stepped from her bedroom, they surprised her waiting at her front steps.

"Why do you want to talk? I have nothing to say to either of you," Sybil said.

"This is Medicine Woman. She would speak with you," Raven said.

"What does she want? She has no business talking with me."

Bonhist did not wait for a translation but said, "I worry that your feelings were hurt. I have come to see if there is anything I can do to make you feel better. I will do nothing to interfere with your plans with Cowboy."

Raven translated as best he could and waited for an answer. "Tell Medicine woman that it was not her fault. Losing my temper was dumb, but I do not have any plans with Austin Todd. She can have him."

Raven took a couple of puffs from his cigar, smiled, and made the translation.

"Tell Sybil that I only agreed to help in the trade store since I thought it would help my people. The cowboy has not asked me to be his wife; he has only asked me to work at his trading post. He has agreed to teach me the white man's tongue."

Sybil smiled at Bonhist and said, "Tell her that I am sorry

for my anger. I had no right to get mad at Medicine Woman or Austin. He is free to do whatever pleases him."

The translation was quickly spoken, and Bonhist smiled at Sybil and said, "Can we be friends?"

The yes that followed needed no translation. Sybil and Bonhist hugged each other. "It is my custom when I make a new friend to give a gift. I would like you to have my new moccasins," said Bonhist. She removed her moccasins and asked Sybil to sit. She slipped them on Sybil's feet, and both smiled since they were a good fit.

"And I have a gift for you," said Sybil. She smiled, took the golden chain from her neck, and snapped it around Bonhist's. Both young women were very pleased with their gifts and their new friendship. They hugged again, and Bonhist asked, "Will you come with me back to see Cowboy? He waits to hear my answer. I will work for him if it does not make you sad."

"Yes, I will come with you. I owe him an apology anyway," Sybil said with a smile.

Austin was very relieved to see both young women enter his store smiling. "Cowboy, I will work for you. Sybil and I are now sisters. See my necklace; is it not pretty?" said Bonhist with sparkling eyes and a slight smile.

"You are very lucky to have Medicine Woman working for you. I am sorry for my temper. I was wrong, and you were right."

"What was I right about?" Austin asked .

"Your note! She is the most beautiful of all. Nevertheless, it was I who was wrong. I should never have gotten mad and thought you wanted Medicine Woman for your wife. Why, it would be a miracle if you could get such a smart woman."

Carmen had prepared a delightful lunch from the poorly stocked kitchen. The meal impressed Boonie greatly. Bonhist insisted that Sybil stay. They ate, laughed, and enjoyed the meal.

"I did not know the Cheyenne could cook like this," said Boonie as he was taking second helpings.

"I am not Cheyenne," said Carmen. "I am Mexican, and cooking has always been my job."

"What in the world are you doing in the Cheyenne village?" Boonie asked.

"I follow Bonhist wherever she goes."

"Who is Bonhist?"

"Bonhist is Medicine Woman."

"Medicine Woman owns you, I suppose," Boonie said.

Carmen hesitated for a moment, then answered, "Yes, she owns my heart."

"Since Medicine Woman is now working in our store, would you be our cook? I will pay you two dollars a month," Boonie said.

"That is much money; however, the decision is Bonhist's. I will do whatever she says."

Everyone looked toward Medicine Woman, who was listening. No one knew how much she understood. Since she sat in silence, they assumed that she understood little of the conversation. Austin looked over at Carmen and asked, "You could help me teach Medicine Woman English, and could you explain to her that my name is Austin?"

"Austin is a senseless word to Bonhist. It means nothing! She has given you a name with meaning—it is a great honor. Beware of Medicine Woman. She has great powers and knows more than you would believe."

"Yes, but I am a storekeeper—not a cowboy. I have never been a cowboy; I do not even like cows," stated Austin.

This statement brought a response from Bonhist. "Cowboy will own a big ranch—many horses. Cowboys love horses. Carmen will cook five dollars a month."

This statement overwhelmed Austin and Boonie also. Austin had never revealed his dream, not even to his parents. Now, Medicine Woman exposed his deepest desire with no more concern than if she had been swatting a fly. She truly had some powerful intuition that was almost frightening.

Boonie shook his head with a sigh. *Five dollars a month! So far, Medicine Woman has done nothing but cost money*, he thought.

Sybil changed the subject, saying, "We women will clean up."

"No," said Bonhist. "Game of chance; cut cards. If I win—men clean; if Cowboy wins—women clean."

Austin flipped his blond hair back with a grin. His handsome face studied Bonhist for a moment. "Okay, we will have a game of chance. Sometimes you win, and sometimes you lose."

Austin spread the cards across the table face down and said, "Pick one."

"No," Bonhist replied. "You pick."

With a broad smile, Austin turned over the king of diamonds. "Very high card," he said.

Bonhist studied the cards carefully, then flipped over the ace of spades. "Oh, this is my lucky day, the highest card in the deck," she said with a twinkle in her eye.

CHAPTER 29

"We have a break in the weather, and it is not yet the moon of falling leaves. This cooler weather will encourage our hunters," Star said to Medicine Woman.

"Mother, good hunting can be found up and down the river. However, except for the few arrowheads that we pick up from the ground, our arrows have no sting. I have an idea," Medicine Woman responded.

Medicine Woman walked over to the lodge of Whirlwind and Roaring Waters. "Have you seen Charging Bull?"

Whirlwind was beating a ceremonial drum, and its rhythm echoed throughout the camp. Soft Winds sat beside Roaring Waters, sewing beads on a pair of moccasins. "Yes," Roaring Waters responded. "He is down in that ash grove trying to find limbs that are suitable for arrow shafts."

"I have had a vision. It is about you, Charging Bull, Whirlwind, and Soft Winds. Can we talk?" Bonhist asked.

"Yes, I will go get Charging Bull," Roaring Waters said.

As he left Soft Winds turned to Bonhist and asked, "How do you like working for the white man?"

"It is good. They trade paper money for my work. I am also learning to speak the white tongue."

"Roaring Waters and I will soon marry and have our own lodge. I see you looking at the white man; will you marry him?"

"Neither has he asked me to marry him, nor have we walked along the river and talked from the heart. Perhaps one day we will marry," answered Medicine Woman.

"Do you remember David? Are these two alike?" Soft Winds asked.

"Cowboy is like David in some ways. They are both strong warriors and handsome, but Cowboy is different. Something inside drives him; he is determined to have much gold. I believe he dreams of a horse ranch. David's path was chosen for him by his father. He will inherit Milburn's ranch and sit under the veranda watching his children play. Cowboy is more exciting since he is uncertain of his path."

"When will you tell Cowboy his path?" Soft Winds said with a smile.

Medicine Woman laughed and answered, "We women must be careful in the way we lead our men."

"I see Star in the evenings walking along the river, talking with Big Dog Fletcher. They laugh and act as if they are the only ones on the river. Could it be that you, I, and your mother will have a Cheyenne wedding by winter?"

"Soft Winds, you and my mother could marry soon, but Cowboy is not ready to marry an Indian. Many of his white brothers warn him against such folly."

"He would never find anyone prettier or nicer than you," Soft Winds said.

"You forget, Soft Winds. White men are led by the sight of gold, not the sight of women. Cowboy fights against his heart. His desire for gold and to have a horse ranch are first in his mind."

"He could have both—you and gold," said Soft Winds.

"Yes, maybe you are right," answered Medicine Woman.

Just then, Charging Bull walked into camp, dropped an armload of limbs, and looked at Bonhist with a smile. "What do you want, Medicine Woman?" he asked.

"The People need arrowheads. You and Roaring Waters can work in the blacksmith building and make metal ones. Whirlwind and Soft Winds can sharpen them and trade them for paper money. We will go talk with Sybil's father."

Everyone was excited about this idea. Even Whirlwind stopped thumping his drum and smiled.

The small congregation of Cheyenne, led by the Medicine Woman, entered the blacksmith shop that very afternoon. Joe, the blacksmith, looked up from his work. He had horses to shoe and a wagon wheel to repair. He liked Medicine Woman, yet he was short on time, and talking was not something he could afford. "'You want to see Sybil. She is working in the field. Good to see you, Medicine Woman," he said as his eyes returned to his work.

"Mr. Joe, you please talk with Medicine Woman," Bonhist said as her dark eyes met his.

Medicine Woman surprised Joe. She had come around often to spend time with his daughter, and now it occurred to him that a business deal was in the making. He laid his hammer down and turned to the young Cheyenne maiden. "Can I do something for you?" he asked.

"Yes, Mr. Joe, these are my friends. We have come to talk business. Do you have time or should we return later?"

"Right now is as good as any for talking. What's on your mind, lass?"

"My people need arrowheads for the fall hunt. They have trained Roaring Waters and Charging Bull to make them with metal. They need both metal and a blacksmith shop. They could trade the arrowheads for paper money and pay you for the metal and the use of your shop," said Medicine Woman as she waved toward the two young warriors.

"There was a time when the Indians were rich with furs. Now that the buffalo are mainly gone, not even the whiskey traders or the horse raiders from Kansas come around. I understand that the Indians need arrowheads, but there's not enough money in it for me. It would be a waste, I suspect."

"Mr. Joe, with your training, these two could help you like I help Cowboy in his store. You would get more work done and have more gold," Bonhist pointed out with a smile.

"What can this blind one do, or this young woman?"

"They could sharpen the arrowheads and trade them to the People for paper money," answered Medicine Woman.

"I have an idea, come let me show you." Joe walked to an old barrel and tilted it over. "This here is scrap, not much good for anything.

If these two would spend two days a week working for me shoeing horses, hell, they could make all the arrowheads they wanted."

Bonhist smiled and nodded her agreement. She turned and spoke in Cheyenne, explaining to the rest. Turning, she said to Joe White, "Now we make paper talk—you call contract. I will have Cowboy read it to me, and we will all sign; this is good, you agree?"

Joe White raised his head and, leaning back, laughed. "Medicine Woman, you should be one of them damned lawyers," he said. And so it was that the Indian branch of the blacksmith shop got started.

That evening, after the signing of the contract, Austin Todd said to Bonhist, "Medicine Woman, the paper money that your blacksmith shop will make from the arrowheads will cost my store. Now, many of your people will spend their money on arrowheads rather than the supplies in my store. You are going to make me a poor man."

"Do not worry, Cowboy," Bonhist answered with a smile. "You will still get your horse ranch. All the money will come to you in time, like the water from Cantonment Creek always moves toward the river."

Austin thought for a minute and smiled. "Let's play a game of chance," he said. Spreading out the cards, he added, "If I win, we will walk along the river and talk of the future. If you win, I will owe you another paper dollar." The turn of the cards amazed Austin since he won. So with his guitar slung over his shoulder, he walked hand in hand with Medicine Woman to the river.

Austin had never been so happy. If this moment in time could freeze, he would be content. He had never seen such an outstanding woman as Bonhist. She was everything he had ever dreamed of and more. He knew he loved her, but was it really right? What would his parents think, and what would the white people in the territory think? Would it ruin his businesses? And what would his children look like? They would be breeds... half Cheyenne. Is this what he really wanted? He looked deeply into Bonhist's dark eyes. They sparkled as she smiled at him. *Yes*, he said to himself. *Nothing else matters. I do not even care about the horse ranch... only Bonhist.*

"Austin Todd! What in the hell are you doing with that... that redskin!" Nellie Young screamed. Looking up, Austin was shocked to see her and the Colonel riding up on horses on route to Fort Cantonment from Fort Reno. He had not expected visitors, and now he sheepishly sat quietly beside Bonhist as Nellie and her father passed on toward the fort.

CHAPTER 30

"Toddy, I don't want to pry, but you have always seemed like a son to me. You could be one of the most prosperous and influential men in the territory. With hard work, you have the drive to get to the top. The problem, Austin, is marrying the wrong woman; it could pull you down. You'd be wise to marry a woman of class, someone who would promote your career… a good Christian white woman. You don't have to settle for a Cheyenne. Good Lord!"

"Colonel Young, the woman you're referring to is a leader among her people, very powerful. They call her Medicine Woman. She works at my store and has helped me with the Indians while I am teaching her English. You and Nellie rode up on one of our lessons."

"Toddy, it looked like more was going on, but if you say that's all there is to it, I'll take your word for it."

"Colonel, I don't want to leave you with the wrong impression. I am fond of Medicine Woman; however, we are not courting. I think her mother would shoot me with an arrow if we were," said Austin with a laugh.

"Well, son, I've come to offer you a big freight job. You will make a handsome profit, too. I want you to go by the Okarche rock quarry and pick up a load of stone, enough for a fireplace. If you'll bring your hammers and cut the stone, I'll double the price. Then go by Fort Reno to the sawmill and take a load of lumber to Camp Supply. You'll clear a hundred and twenty dollars."

"That sounds like a good deal; still, I'll need to hire a man or two. It'll take me away from my store for about three weeks I suspect. Make it hundred fifty, and I'll personally shape each stone that goes into that fireplace."

Colonel Young laughed and agreed. Early next morning, Austin hitched the horses to the wagons and pulled them to the front of the store. He had already talked with Boonie and made arrangements to hire Steve Adkins to drive one wagon. Wanting to explain his freight contract to Medicine Woman, he waited until she arrived. He was shocked when she appeared dressed in the white calico that Marie had made back on Milburn's ranch. Her hair shone, and she wore a necklace and bracelets made of red and black corn. Beautiful! Austin's eyes showed his pleasure. Realizing this, a big smile spread across Bonhist's face as she greeted him. "Good morning, Cowboy. Whose wagons are these?" she asked.

"My wagons. I'll be gone several days. I'm carrying building supplies from Fort Reno to Camp Supply. It's good business. You can help Boonie with the store while I'm gone."

Nodding her understanding, Bonhist looked up to see Colonel Young and Nellie come around the corner of the store. Nellie immediately saw in Bonhist's face her affection for Austin. She walked straight to Austin, threw her arms around him, and with a kiss said, "Toddy darling, I'll see you at Fort Reno."

Turning, she gave Bonhist a frown. Then, lifting her chin, she walked away.

"I can see," Medicine Woman said, "that you have made good business." Abruptly, Bonhist walked back to her village.

Climbing on the wagon and heading east toward the rock quarry was hard for Austin. The image of Bonhist's face and the hurt look in her eyes haunted him. He wanted to follow after her, hold her in his arms, and tell her of his love. Yet he kept riding, thinking of nothing more than his beautiful Cheyenne maiden. Remembering back, he recalled how Bonhist had given him the yarrow that had quickly healed his infected hip. Her smiling face was etched in his brain. With every mile, he felt more miserable! "What am I doing?" he thought as he pulled the wagon off the dirt road and walked back to the rear where Blue Boy was tied. "Steve, I've got urgent business back in Cantonment. I'll hire another man to help you and pay you another ten dollars. Go on to the rock quarry and load the stone, and I'll meet you in Fort Reno to work on the fireplace. Will you take lumber from the sawmill to Camp Supply?"

Steve smiled, thinking of the extra ten dollars, spat a stream of tobacco onto the ground, and nodded. Austin threw a saddle to the back of Blue Boy, and in minutes, was heading back to the Cheyenne village. Riding on past the fort and up the river, he reached the lodge of Star and Bonhist, dismounted, and walked to the entrance flap. When he called for Medicine Woman and rapped on the flap, there was no response. The lodge was empty. No one was in the immediate vicinity. Pain shot through his stomach. How could I be such a fool?" Then a woman stepped from a nearby lodge. Red Leaf could see that he wanted something, yet she knew none of the white tongue. After a few minutes of his best sign language, Austin could see that any form of communication was impossible. He mounted Blue Boy and rode in a gallop back to the fort to find Big Wolf. "You'll come with me to translate." It was a command, not a question.

"Two plugs 'bacca," Big Wolf answered, smiling.

"Okay, you'll get your tobacco." Austin gave Big Wolf a hand, swinging the Cheyenne up to the back of Blue Boy to ride double back to the lodge of Bonhist.

"Red Leaf says Medicine Woman went with hunting party," Big Wolf said.

"Which direction, when?" Austin asked.

Big Wolf smiled while talking with Red Leaf. She moved her hands up and down, then finally pointed up the river. Before Big Wolf could translate, Austin was already in the saddle, riding at full speed.

Two days later, Austin realized that his efforts to find Medicine Woman were useless. Not a trace of the hunting party could be found. Returning to Cantonment, he spoke to Carmen who was staying in a small shed until she heard something from Bonhist. She knew nothing of the hunting party. Finally, Austin walked on over to the blacksmith shop looking for Roaring Waters and Charging Bull.

"They took off this morning," Joe said.

"Going with a hunting party, I suspect. Took five of your horses. Medicine Woman said she'd pay you later."

"Did you talk to Medicine Woman?" Austin asked.

"Yep, but she didn't speak her mind. Just took five of your horses and left. You want to report it to Colonel Dodge? He'd send a detail after them."

"No, I don't care about horses. She'll bring them back. Thanks, Joe."

Saddling up his last horse, a black mare, Austin rode Blue Boy back to the store, leading the mare. "Carmen, when Medicine Woman gets back, tell her that I have something very important to discuss with her. I have a job in Fort Reno, but I'll be back in a few days." To Big Wolf, he said, "Get on that black mare. I have a big job for you. You can make big money... lots of bacca."

CHAPTER 31

The fireplace took more time than Austin had anticipated. He spent two full weeks at Fort Reno. Nellie had invited him over for supper on his first day.

"I've made an important decision," Austin announced. "Pass the biscuits, please."

"You look so serious, darling. What in the world could be so important?" Nellie asked.

"I have decided to marry Medicine Woman if she will have me."

Nellie choked on her food, coughing. Excusing herself, she ran from the room.

"My God, man! Do you know what you're saying?" Colonel Young responded in a heated voice.

"You may not understand my thinking, but I know that I deeply love Medicine Woman and could not be happy without her. I only pray that she feels the same."

"Toddy, I hope I'm wrong, but you're in for a hard life if you marry that Indian. I have dealt with the Plains Indians for many years; they're different from us. Things that you hold important mean nothing to them, and things that they hold dear are not significant to us. I hope you realize that in taking an Indian for your wife, you will break my daughter's heart and will have a rival in me."

"Sir, I have always respected you for your fairness and leadership. Nellie and I have been good friends, and the last thing I want is to hurt anyone. I've thought hard about this resolution. It is the most difficult decision I have ever made. Still, my heart would break if I were untrue to myself. I'm sorry, sir." Austin then excused himself and returned to his quarters. When the job was finished, Colonel Young aloofly paid Austin the agreed settlement. Austin loaded the wagons with lumber, and he, Steve, and Big Wolf set out on their journey back to Camp Supply. When the wagons were on the road and under control, Austin rode ahead with his heart set on seeing Bonhist. It had been two weeks, and he could hardly wait. Riding up to the general store, he heard his heart pounding and his stomach felt sick. He whispered a little prayer.

"She's not here. We haven't seen her; I understand that she, her mother, and a small band haven't returned since you left for Fort Reno. No one seems to know their whereabouts," Boonie said calmly.

Bonhist looked around the camp. The others were happy over the twenty wild horses that they had captured, yet her heart was heavy. Perhaps her intuition had been wrong after all. She had not actually seen the face of the cowboy in her vision. Her spirit animal had given her a sign—was the big-horned owl also wrong? Medicine Woman had tried her best to win Cowboy's heart; nevertheless, he seemed to want another woman. She had liked his boyish, handsome face and his warrior-like body, but more than anything else, she had come to love his gentleness. Medicine Woman was used to a stern, hard style that she often saw in men. Cowboy was the most gentle man she had ever known, and he had captured her sad heart. She thought back on that last morning. How foolish she felt in her new white dress! She had hoped that Cowboy would notice, but he only had eyes for the white woman.

The hunting party consisted of Medicine Woman, Star, Soft Winds, Charging Bull, Roaring Waters, Big Dog Fletcher, and his two cousins, Flyingman and Bear Track. They had left the territory and returned to the canyon country. Capturing the horses had not been too hard. They now corralled them in a box canyon where plenty of grass and water were available. The scheme was simple. Big Dog, Flying Man, and Bear Track were to stay and work the horses; the rest rode to Milburn's ranch. They hoped to drive a small herd of cattle and horses to the Cheyenne camp. They had already felt the cold sting of the fall weather, so they knew they must work fast. Bonhist wanted to return quickly for another reason; her heart ached for Cowboy. She swore to herself that when she saw him again, she would open her heart and hope for the best. A full moon had passed since they left Fort Cantonment, and it would be another moon before they would return.

"Bonhist, where is your mind? What are you thinking?" Star asked.

"My mind is clear and here. What do you want, Mother?"

"If that is so, why are you burning that rabbit? It is black on one side and raw on the other. You have been acting very strangely. Would you like to talk?"

"Oh, the rabbit! Well, never mind, it is the way Big Dog likes it," answered Medicine Woman with a sheepish grin.

"Big Dog and I have decided to get married if he does not die first from eating your cooking. Are you worried about seeing David again?"

"No, Mother, David is married to my sister Crow Wings. They are happy; I only want to conclude our business and return to Cantonment."

"Why is this so? The People will be happy over the cattle and horses, but you seem heavy-hearted like a mother dog that has lost her litter. Are you not excited for the return to Milburn's ranch?"

"Yes, Mother. It will make me very happy to see them all, but my heart drags the ground because I am in love and the one I love is back in Cantonment."

"Who could that be? I have not noticed you walking along the river with a man, nor have I heard the flute of a suitor."

"Mother, you might as well know. I love Cowboy, and my heart is heavy," said Bonhist as she dropped the rabbit in the fire and rolled over on her robe.

"Bonhist! Your words hurt my ears. Your father would be deeply hurt to think his daughter would marry a white. White people are not like us. They would destroy the moon for a handful of gold nuggets. You are the Medicine Woman, a leader among the Cheyenne. You would betray your own for the love of a white dog? Tell me this is not so," Star pleaded.

"Mother, I must tell you of my vision even though I swore that I would tell no one. I saw Cowboy in my vision. We will one day marry and build a horse ranch. I saw the lodges of the People living on this ranch and working with the horses. The real owl, the one with the big horns, who is my spirit guide, gave me a sign when I first saw Cowboy. Mother, if I do not follow my vision, how can I help the People?" At this, Bonhist broke into sobs, hugging her mother.

"Oh my poor daughter, your path is a bitter, hard one like your father's. May the Great Spirit guide you and watch over you."

"Mother, it is a trick on me sent by the trickster. Cowboy does not love me the way I love him, but he is the only man I have ever known who does not think I am good to look upon. What must I do to win his heart?"

Star hugged her daughter and said, "Worry not, my daughter, for your vision will have its way."

The following morning, the small band that Star led rode to the ranch. By late evening, they arrived to the great excitement of everyone. Star laughed to see that Pretty Dove, Crow Wings, and White Dove were all with children. That evening, they dined in the big house with Marie's kitchen turning out the food laced with jalapeños. Finally, Milburn asked about their plan in the territory. Medicine Woman surprised him by answering in the white man's tongue. "The People are not happy. Giving up our ways is hard, and we have very little food. The Cheyenne once had large herds of ponies, but now almost everyone has to walk to the white man's fort for supplies."

"Have you found a husband?" David asked.

"No," Bonhist answered with a straight face.

"Don't go back," Milburn said. "Stay here. We have plenty for all."

"We cannot do that. We must hurry back before winter. Our plan is to bring back wild horses and steers for the People."

"Will you get in trouble for leaving the reservation?"

"Yes, we take a great chance. They will probably take away our horses and punish us."

"I'll help you," Milburn said. "I'll write you a bill of sale. My ranch hands are just looking for something to do. They'll round up some of those wild steers and some horses to drive into the Oklahoma badlands. You'll receive them in the territory with no one the wiser." Milburn smiled as everyone looked relieved.

"Tomorrow morning, you and I will practice with the pistols," David said to Bonhist. "I want to see what you've learned. Do you still have ammunition?"

"My last box has only a few bullets. I once shot a rabbit. My aim is not good, but I can draw and shoot fast," Bonhist answered with a smile.

The following morning, David discovered that Bonhist could handle her Colt at an excellent pace. She had quick hands and a good eye, but had a hard time keeping the gun level. "Try this," David said. He picked a target—an empty Prince Albert can. With quick hands, David drew and shot twice. The sound rolled down the Canadian

River as if it were one shot. The can was ripped with two holes through its middle.

Bonhist looked at David with great admiration. You have great medicine, David, with the little fire sticks. How do you shoot so accurately and so quickly?"

"You need to practice being accurate. I have brought you three more boxes of shells. When you practice, do not worry about speed. Just keep the pistol level and squeeze off your shots. Now you try."

Bonhist smiled at David. "Why do you teach me, David? I would never shoot another person, and I prefer the bow for hunting."

"Would you shoot a man to save your mother?"

"Yes," Medicine Woman answered as she drew almost as quickly as David, while clearly missing the can.

"Just remember, level and squeeze," David repeated.

CHAPTER 32

Two weeks later, a small herd of forty steers and fifty horses crossed into Indian Territory. Milburn's ranch hands had done their job. The cowboys rode along for a short distance with the Cheyenne as the latter got the feel of handling the livestock. As soon as everything was under control, they turned with a wave. Bonhist held the bill of sale and a note from Milburn stating that the transaction was legal and had occurred in Indian Territory. She tucked the papers away in her sash.

The cattle and horses would be of great help to the Cheyenne camp. The Arapaho, who had always been growers called Earth People, had stored away corn, dried squash, and dried pumpkin for the winter. From Austin, they had learned to grow a new plant—potatoes. But the Cheyenne, who had always been hunters following the buffalo, found life much more wearisome in the white man's world.

Medicine Woman had been away from Cantonment for two moons, and her heart yearned to see Cowboy. She was determined to ride immediately to the general store and run into his arms. She had taken five of his horses and planned to return ten. They divided the rest of the horses and would trade them to the People for paper money or other valuables. The few horses would be greatly prized and increase the spirit of the People.

Following the Canadian River for four suns, they turned the herd northeasterly toward the North Canadian and the Cheyenne Camp. Moving through a dry land where the air was chilly and the wind had a bite, they soon faced the cold season, but the cattle would restore the People's health and spirit. Upon reaching the North Canadian, they followed the river downstream in a southeast direction until their village was in sight. It was evening, and Medicine Woman could hardly contain her excitement. The Cheyenne walked out to them with enthusiasm and smiles, thanking her strong medicine since she had devised the entire escapade in an hour. Spurred on by her anger with the white woman, she had wasted no time. Now her heart was happy for their success, as shown in the Cheyenne's smiling faces.

Nevertheless, the excitement she felt at the prospect of seeing Cowboy again overshadowed her happiness. Tired and hungry with the red pony tied outside her lodge, she decided to wait until morning before riding into Cantonment. It was too cold to swim in the river, so with water from her skins, she would wash her hair and body and wear her nicest dress. With a frayed stick, she would clean her teeth and chew some sweet plants. She wanted to be pretty and desirable.

Roaring Waters and Charging Bull strung up Austin's five horses and five more of equal value as Medicine Woman had directed early the following morning. With a smile, Bonhist rode the red pony to Cantonment, leading the ten horses. Riding past the general store onto the blacksmith shop, she felt a surge of excitement as she saw Blue Boy. He was in Cowboy's corral along with the black mare.

Opening the gate, Bonhist turned the ten ponies loose in the corral. Suddenly, it occurred to her that Cowboy had not ridden Blue Boy. He was not wet from a morning ride, nor was an imprint from a saddle to be seen. Since Cowboy always rode early, a chill of panic shot through her body. Turning quickly, she jumped to the back of her pony and rode to the store.

"Medicine Woman, where have you been? Toddy has looked everywhere for you. He has been crazy with worry; we had decided that you had gone back north. Seeing you again is wonderful," Boonie said excitedly.

Carmen rushed through the curtains from the storage room, screaming, "Señorita Bonhist! It is you." She instantly burst into tears and ran, hugging her.

With her first opportunity, Bonhist turned to Boonie and asked, "Where is Cowboy?" Carmen sobbed louder, her chest heaving up and down. "Is something wrong?" Bonhist asked, looking straight at Boonie.

"No, lass, nothing is wrong. Toddy has gone to Indiana. He will return in the early spring."

"Why did Cowboy go to Indiana?" Bonhist asked.

"That is where his folks live, and he has returned to find a wife."

Tears immediately sprang from her dark eyes and ran down her face. "Cowboy's horse, Blue Boy, is in the corral. Did Cowboy ride another horse?"

"No, lass, Toddy rode on the train. The one your people call the iron horse. It's all right," Boonie said. "You both can work here, and in just a few months, Toddy will return."

Joe White had walked over from the blacksmith shop. "What are all those horses doing in Austin's corral?"

"I brought back his horses," Bonhist said.

"Medicine Woman, you took five horses, but I counted ten horses in the corral. Did you make a mistake?"

"No, Mr. Joe, the extra five are payment for using Cowboy's horses," Bonhist answered as she wiped tears from her face.

"I'm not taking care of all them horses. One or two aren't bad, but twelve that's different," Joe said.

"I will take care of the horses for Cowboy," said Bonhist. Joe White nodded and turned toward the blacksmith shop. He hesitated, then asked, "Will Roaring Waters and Charging Bull be back to work soon?"

"Yes, Mr. Joe, they have been with our fall hunting party. They will come back to your shop."

Joe nodded his approval and said, "'They will make good blacksmiths one day."

He had no more than left when the sergeant from the fort and two troopers entered. "We have orders to escort Medicine Woman to Colonel Dodge's headquarters," the sergeant said.

"Is she under arrest?" Boonie asked.

"No, sir, they need her to answer questions, that's all," the sergeant answered.

When Medicine Woman entered Colonel Dodge's office, she noticed the Indian agent, a short, slender man named William Green, assigned by Darlington to help the Indians at Fort Cantonment. Star and the rest of her party were also present. Pony soldiers standing at attention around the room lent a gloomy feeling to the group. Colonel Dodge, with a forced smile, spoke to Bonhist through his interpreter, Raven. "Welcome, Medicine Woman. You are in no trouble; this is not a court. We just need an explanation of why you left the reservation and came into possession of all those steers and horses. It is against the law for any Indian to leave the territory or conduct business other than here on the lands that Congress has given you."

Raven translated, followed by William Green, who rose and spoke with a stern voice. "I want charges brought against this woman. I know she is the leader and instigator of this whole affair. A good source informed me that laws were broken. We will not tolerate this." Suddenly, the mood changed from gloomy to ugly.

CHAPTER 33

The repetitious clanking sound of the train's wheels echoed in Austin's ears. The occasional lonely whistle crying out brought back the painful memory of Medicine Woman. Even the two quarts of whiskey bought back in Kansas City and St. Louis couldn't drown the memories of her smiling face.

Austin hadn't shaved for three days. The long trip without proper food, along with the loss of Medicine Woman, added to a growing emptiness as if his life had no further meaning. He aimlessly strummed his guitar and sang as the train clicked along the tracks. An old man sitting beside him tapped his foot to the music. Other passengers gathered closer, entertained by his drunken mood and the singing.

Austin began another song with a strum of the strings.

"He said you better come and work for me. I have some land to drain. I'll give you fifty cents a day. Your washing board and all, and you will be a different man when you leave Arkansas. Well, I worked six months for the son-of-a-gun. Jess Herring was his name. He was six feet tall in his stocking feet. As tall as any crane. His hair hung down in pig tails; he had a long, lantern jaw. He was a photograph of all the gents of the state of Arkansas. He fed me on corn dodger, as hard as any rock. Till my teeth begin to loosen, my jaws begin to lock. I got so thin on sassafras tea, I could hide behind a straw. Indeed, I was a different man when I left Arkansas. I got aboard the evening train half dead and half alive. I bought a quart of whiskey, my misery to thaw. I got as drunk as two boiled owls when I left Arkansas."

As he sang the catchy tune, two elderly ladies gave him a sharp look, then turned away smiling. He was too good-looking and too good-natured to irritate them. Even the straight-laced preacher sitting three rows away tapped his foot and smiled.

Finally, Austin laid down the guitar and leaned back, closing his eyes. Then the old man spoke up. "Where you from, son?"

"Indian Territory—Fort Cantonment, ever hear of it?"

The old man laughed and said, "Thought you were from Arkansas. You must be in love. Your woman get killed by them Indians?"

"No, she is an Indian. She left me to go back north, probably to Montana. If I thought I could find her, I'd follow her all the way to Canada."

The two elderly women turned and looked at Austin again, this time frowning. The preacher also gave Austin a disgusted snarl and turned his head.

"The territory is mighty wild country, I hear," the old man stated. "You're carrying a firearm. Seen many gun fights?"

"Gunfighters are around, I guess—mainly up in Kansas or down in Texas. Ever hear of Wyatt Earp?"

"Nope, can't say I have. But how about you? You're a crack shot?"

"Myself, I couldn't hit the side of a barn with a handgun. I prefer a rifle; even then, I'm not the best shot around. I'm just a storekeeper."

"I'd never guess it. You have the look of a fighter. Out there in that Indian country, you have to stand up and fight, don't you?"

"I'm a stone mason and own a freight line. That's all the fighting I need," Austin said with a sigh. Closing his eyes, he hoped the old man would shut up so he could sleep. Yet the old man seemed to want to talk despite Austin's short replies.

"What brings a young man up here to this cold country? A businessman like you has a nice warm place back there in Oklahoma."

"Where I come from, a man who asks as many questions as you would get shot the first day. My parents own a farm in Lawrence County, Indiana. I'm going to see them and my brothers and sisters. If things work out, I may even bring a new wife back to the territory."

"You don't say. You got one all picked out?"

Austin looked at the old man for a long minute, then answered, "No, sir, but she'll be white and Christian—one that'll advance my career." That answer brought a cheer from Austin's listeners, and then, as Austin closed his eyes, the old man shut up.

The next morning, as the train pulled into Bedford, Indiana, Austin grabbed his bag and got off. He felt like a team of horses had run over his back. In no shape to face his mother, he checked into the downtown hotel, fell asleep, and didn't wake until evening. Across the street, he paid a man fifty cents for a hot bath and a shave. Suddenly weak from hunger, he walked back to the hotel to eat the specialty of the house—steak, potatoes, and milk gravy. Returning to his room, he slept soundly again until early morning. As he washed his face, Austin looked in the mirror and combed his sandy blond hair straight back. He let it fall forward, flopping almost to his eyebrows. He shook his head at his image and swore he'd never drink whiskey again. His black broadcloth suit was wrinkled in spite of his best efforts to press it with his hands. After dressing, he added his old black hat and walked to the stables, hiring a team of horses and a wagon. When he arrived at the old farm by noon, he was finally home.

"Austin Hubbard Todd!" Mary Elizabeth exclaimed.

Austin picked his mother off the ground with a hug as she started to cry. Smiling, his father emerged from the barn still carrying his hammer. The farm looked the same as Austin remembered. By evening, his brothers and sisters were all present. Thomas, Jacob, and Adam had questions about the Indian Territory and whether the land was fertile for farming. His sisters, Maggie and Ida, laughed and teased Austin, wanting him to meet one of their new friends from church.

That evening, while Austin's mother played the piano, his father sang, and the entire family joined in. Tears ran down Mary Elizabeth's face since she had never believed her whole family would be together again.

The family, never happier, was all intently interested in Austin's adventures in Oklahoma. He told them the story of Medicine Woman and his decision to find another from Lawrence County to take back to the territory as his wife.

Then on Sunday morning, as they attended church services, Austin met Deanie. He liked her appearance, although at first he thought she had brown hair and eyes. Then he realized her hair took on a red tint in the sun. She was almost as tall as Medicine Woman, but did not have the same grace and beauty. Still, Deanie would do. She had something special that Austin liked, though. It was in her eyes, and she was pretty. A plucky girl, she came from strong stock. In time, he could learn to love her, yes, Deanie would do. He should not hesitate to ask her to marry him. She'd be his wife.

Chapter 34

"Don't repeat that, Raven. Stirring up trouble is not what this meeting is about. Agent Green, your job is to help the Indians; policing them is not your responsibility," Colonel Dodge reminded.

"That may be so, Colonel, but Indians need to know that they are under white man's law. This reservation is their land, where they can move around freely as long as they don't leave. We provide them with what they need: food, blankets, and medicine. I believe the law should be enforced. For them to leave is completely wrong. What were they doing? Stealing? Killing? Who knows?" Agent Green challenged.

"I have noted your objections. Now, please sit down."

"Okay, but I want to say one last thing. These Indians need to be taught the white man's ways. We need missionaries and schools so they can learn to speak English, dress like whites, and, for God's sake, be taught to farm."

Colonel Dodge nodded toward William Green, then turned to Raven. "Ask Medicine Woman to explain the hunting party and where the cattle and horses came from." Raven turned toward the party of Indians and translated. Medicine Woman stood and faced

Colonel Dodge. She smiled and, to everyone's surprise, answered in English.

"Cheyenne people always hunt before the cold season. We need food and horses."

"Medicine Woman, how do you explain the cattle and horses?" asked the Colonel directly to Medicine Woman.

"We bought them from Milburn."

"Is Milburn the same man you bought the red pony from?"

"Yes."

"Do you have a bill of sale for the cattle and horses?"

"Yes."

"May I see it?"

Reaching into her sash, Bonhist produced the papers that Milburn had given her and handed them to the Colonel. He read the bill of sale and explanation carefully, then handed the papers back to her with a smile. "Well, again, you have produced proof that clearly shows you've done nothing wrong. Is there anything you would like to say?"

"Yes, we Indians already have our own religion, our own school, and our own language. When you ask us to learn white ways, it is like asking the birds to swim in the river or the fish to fly. I do not understand Agent Green when he said that this is our land—is this so?"

"Yes, the U. S. government has generously assigned these lands to the Cheyenne and Arapaho. You are free to move about on the reservation, but you must never leave."

"Then why are the pony soldiers here?" asked Medicine Woman.

"This fort and the pony soldiers are here for your protection. When white hunters come onto your land to hunt or to build a ranch, it is our duty to run them off. We also keep them from stealing your horses or attacking you. We are here to help the Cheyenne and Arapaho."

"Can a Cheyenne like me and my mother build our own ranch?"

"No, the reservation is for everyone. No one group can own a ranch."

"A white man has his own ranch on our land. He lives near Camp Supply," Medicine Woman said.

"Yes, but he has a government contract to raise cattle for the Indians. He is like Austin Todd or the soldiers; he is here to help the Indians. Do you understand?" Colonel Dodge asked.

"Yes, and now I can agree with the words of Agent Green. The Cheyenne can be more like whites. I have two ideas that will help us be like you."

Medicine Woman's statement brought a broad smile to William Green's face. Colonel Dodge also smiled cautiously. "We are here to serve. How can we help?" said Colonel Dodge.

"First, when the white rancher, the one you call Harold Woods, drives his cattle to this fort, you pay him twenty dollars a steer. Is this right?"

"Yes, we pay a premium price, the same as if he'd driven them on up to Dodge City."

"You then give these cattle to the Cheyenne and Arapaho?"

"Yes, the whole purpose of his government contract is to help produce food for the Indians."

"Good, you will now pay our hunting party a premium price for our cattle. Then you will give the cattle back to us, since your purpose is to help the Indians."

Agent Green's smiling face turned to stone. "That's bull, another Indian trick. They can't blackmail us into giving them top dollar for those steers and then give them right back—that's a bunch of bull!"

Colonel Dodge suddenly laughed and said, "Whatever Austin Todd is paying you at his general store, I'll double it if you'll come and work for me. I'd never thought of that. I'll give you credit for that one. Okay, how many steers you got?"

"We have forty steers."

"All right, I'll give you six hundred dollars for the lot and give them to the agency to be delivered right back to you," he said, smiling.

"You will give us eight hundred dollars for the steers. The steers and the money will be delivered to the agency to be allotted among the People."

"If I ever go into business, I want you to be my partner," Colonel Dodge said with a smile.

"You're not going to listen to that, are you?" William Green spoke up.

"Yes, sir, I am. You'll see to it that every penny is accounted for, or I'll put an end to your career," the colonel swore. "You said you had two ideas; what was the other?"

"You said the pony soldiers are here for our protection. They keep the white hunters off our land and from building their own ranches. Is this true?" Medicine Woman asked.

"Yes, that is the truth of it. What can we do? Have you seen any signs of white people moving in on Indian lands?"

"Yes, and I know we can depend on the pony soldiers to help us," Bonhist said.

As Colonel Dodge looked at this beautiful, smiling Cheyenne maiden, he thought back to a time when white raiders from Kansas stole an entire herd of Indian ponies almost in sight of the fort. The Indians had demanded that the military find the thieves and return the horses. When this did not happen, the Indians went on an uprising. Battles and outbreaks of violence swept across Indian lands, and many of the Cheyenne left the reservation for Texas, where they joined the Comanches. It was a fight to get things under control again. The colonel had gone through those hard times, and he did not ever want to chance provoking the Indians again.

"We are greatly concerned since many herds of cattle cross our lands every year, going to Dodge City. If the cowboys choose to cross our land in the future, they will pay one paper dollar for each steer. We expect the pony soldier, who is here for our protection, to collect the money and transfer it to our agency. Our wolves will watch and bring word of these intruders."

Colonel Dodge's face now turned to stone, along with Agent Green. He sat for a long time before he answered. "Texas herds have been crossing to Kansas for years. They do not cause trouble. Those cattle are shipped by rail to the east. That's not the same as someone wanting to move in and homestead."

"You have promised that this is our land and we can freely move as long as we stay on the reservation. The pony soldiers are only here to help. If the cowboys from Texas want to go around our land, that is their choice, but they will not cross without paying."

"How about Milburn? He's one of those Texas cowboys. Are you going to ask him to pay?"

"He has already paid. We traded him safe passage across our land for the horses and cattle. When the Cheyenne makes a promise, we keep it."

"Damn! All right, we will help collect a fee for crossing Indian land. Now, are you satisfied?"

"Yes," Bonhist smiled. "You and Agent Green must be happy to see how you have showed the Cheyenne to be more like the white man."

CHAPTER 35

Austin Todd's plans to return to Indian Territory with a wife had not come to fruition as he had hoped. The weather had been so cold that traveling conditions were near impossible. Still, he had managed to spend time with Deanie, and he found himself liking her. She was smart, perhaps a little smarter than Austin himself. However, each time he started to talk with her about the future, something constantly interfered. So, today, when an exciting new opportunity presented itself, Austin felt he had to take advantage of it. Deanie was coming home with his family after church. She and his sister Ida were friends. They had planned for Deanie to spend a couple of days on the Todd farm.

Lunch was pleasant enough; however, Austin was very taken aback when Deanie offered to do the dishes with Austin's help. Stacks of dirty dishes and metal pots waited. The family thought it quite funny, and chuckles could be heard throughout the house.

Austin found himself talking of Oklahoma and the west. His dream of one day owning a horse ranch and having a wife and kids was discussed as he scrubbed the pots. Wiping his hands on a towel, he rolled it to form a loop and flipped it over Deanie's head. As he pulled her closer, she looked up into his eyes and said, "Good roping, cowboy."

The face of Medicine Woman instantly came to mind. "Why did she have to say cowboy?" he thought. He tried hard not to let his mind wander, spoiling his opportunity. Pulling her even closer, he reached over, closed his eyes, and kissed her. During the kiss, all he could think of was the smiling face of Bonhist.

Deanie smiled, saying, "I've always loved you, Austin."

"I love you too, Deanie, and want you to be my wife. We can get married and, as soon as we can travel, go back to my store in Oklahoma. Two years from now, we'll have our own horse ranch."

Deanie exclaimed, "Yes, I'll marry you! You don't know how long I've waited to hear those words. We'll be so happy."

Austin held Deanie tight in his arms and tried to remove Medicine Woman from his thoughts. As they kissed again, Deanie said, "Let's tell our folks now. I want everyone to know that I'm going to be Mrs. Austin Todd. Austin, you have made me so happy."

That evening, as the fireplace roared with a hot blaze, Elizabeth played the piano while everyone sang 'Sweet Betsy From Pike.' Austin looked around the room at his family. They were happy for him; this was going to work.

"Austin," Deanie whispered, "I love you, but there's one thing you need to know before we make our wedding plans."

Austin turned to Deanie. She was very beautiful and everything that he should have in a wife. "What is bothering you?"

"Austin, I hope this won't annoy you or alter our plans. I love you so much, but I could never go to the Indian Territory, not even for a visit. I have heard about what happens to young women in the West. They look old before their time if they survive at all. The Indians are so brutal; you could never trust them. There is a farm for sale near my parents' home; we could live there. I cannot live on a horse ranch. I'm afraid of horses, darling. You were born to be a farmer, and this country is settled and civilized. We could have such a wonderful life here in Indiana."

Winter was passing at a snail's pace for Bonhist. Her mother, Star, had married Big Dog Fletcher. The one-time Lakota warrior now carried a white man's name—Elk Cow or Star Fletcher. The thought of it made Bonhist laugh; yet, her mother was smiling for the first time in years. Soft Winds and Roaring Waters were also married and had their own lodge. Even Carmen was in love with the older Boonie, and lately Charging Bull and Sybil had been seen talking along the river. Everyone was happy except Medicine Woman. The man she loved, Cowboy, was gone. He would soon return with his new wife during the moon when the buds turn green.

Bonhist had made friends with the big Chief of the fort, Colonel Dodge. He seemed to respect her and often asked questions about the People. After her mother married Big Dog, Bonhist moved into the rock house with Carmen; nevertheless, a day did not pass without Star and Bonhist seeing each other. Whirlwind took care of Austin's horses as well as Bonhist's red pony and, of course, Medicine Woman kept him well supplied with cigars. Good things were happening; yet, Bonhist's heart was heavy, dragging the ground.

The snows came and left and came again. Winters in Oklahoma were not nearly as harsh as in the northern states. Many days were pleasant, and with the new metal arrowheads, hunters were up and down the river. With their extra money from the cattle, some of the warriors had bought horses. Bonhist practiced with her Colt until her bullets were gone. She purchased more from Boonie and one morning shot a large buck. "Keep the pistol level and squeeze," she told herself with a smile.

One evening, as she sat with her mother making a beaded robe and moccasins for Big Dog, there came a rap on the lodge flap. Thinking it was Red Leaf or Soft Winds, Star called out in Cheyenne for the visitor to enter. To their surprise, the mighty Chief Stone Calf and Chief Bear Robe entered with a handsome young warrior, Running Buffalo. "We would speak with Star Fletcher," the stoic Chief Stone Calf said.

"I will leave," Medicine Woman said, thinking that these great chiefs wanted a private session with her mother.

"No, our visit concerns you," said Chief Stone Calf. "Star, we have come to talk with you about Medicine Woman and Running Buffalo. We speak for Running Buffalo, as he is an orphan with neither a father nor an uncle to speak on his behalf. It is time for Medicine Woman to take her place of leadership among the People. We want her to marry Running Buffalo. He is fierce among the People and will one day be a chief. Running Buffalo has expressed his love for Medicine Woman and wants her to share his lodge. They would raise many strong warriors. Running Buffalo is not rich, but he will give you five fine ponies for your loss."

Star looked up into the face of the young warrior. Tall, handsome, and bearing a slight resemblance to her late husband, Crow, Star liked him immediately. "To own five horses in these days is unusual. Where did you find these horses?" asked Star.

"I found the horses up the river. They were running wild, and I was able to capture them," he answered.

Medicine Woman was in shock. She could not believe her mother was so calm. She did not want to marry anyone, and this young man, she did not even know. Marrying a total stranger was out of the question—that was sure. Bonhist noticed that he wore a Colt revolver and carried it in a fancy holster with a Mexican design. "Where did you get your fire stick?" Bonhist asked.

For the first time, Running Buffalo smiled. Bonhist had to admit to herself that he was handsome, but what kind of a man was he? "I traded with a white man from Robert Bent's ranch," he said.

"What did you trade for such a fine fire stick?"

"My fastest pony," he said in answer to the question.

Stone Calf cut in, "Will you accept these five fine ponies for your daughter?"

Bonhist looked sharply at her mother. Star smiled at the young warrior and said, "It would please me greatly to see my daughter marry such a fine warrior. Still, I know my daughter. She will not marry anyone she does not love. My daughter, Medicine Woman, follows her visions. They are very strong and true. I cannot speak for her heart. You will have to ask her yourself."

Chief Stone Calf turned to Bonhist, saying, "It would be good for the People if you consented to this marriage. Running Buffalo is young and strong; he is a leader. The two of you will provide strong guidance to our brothers and sisters as we learn to live on this reservation. What is your answer?"

Chapter 36

Bonhist looked at the stoic faces around her, seeing the earnest expression on Running Buffalo's face and feeling the chiefs' tension. Her mother waited with the rest for her answer.

"Your visit pleases and honors me and this lodge. I am excited about your offer. Any young maiden among the Cheyenne would be fortunate to be the wife of Running Buffalo. You wait for my answer—my answer is yes. But we must get to know each other. Have we walked along the river and talked with our hearts? Have we ridden our ponies, hunted, or worked together? Until I know who this one is who would be my husband, we will not share a blanket or marry. I will soon be sixteen winters. When I reach my seventeenth, if our hearts are as one, we will then marry."

For the first time, the men smiled, and Running Buffalo quickly agreed to the arrangement. As the men turned to leave, Bonhist grabbed Running Buffalo's hand, saying, "Come, we will walk by the river while the weather is good."

"Medicine Woman, I have seen you ride the red pony and work in the white man's store." Looking for something to say as he walked along beside Bonhist, Running Buffalo declared, "My heart is full of love for you."

"I admire your fire stick. The holster is very pretty. Where did you get such a weapon?" she responded.

"A white man whom I met only two days ago traded a fine pinto pony and this little fire stick for my fast black stallion. I made a good trade, don't you agree?"

"Yes, but have you fired your pistol?"

"No, I will try it when I go hunting. Medicine Woman, is that a pistol you carry under your robe?"

"Yes, this is a Colt revolver, much like your fire stick given to me by a friend."

"Do you know how to load the bullets?" Running Buffalo asked very sheepishly.

Bonhist laughed and looked into Running Buffalo's eyes. He laughed with her, but she could see that he was embarrassed. "Let me show you how to load your fire stick."

"I am sorry I do not have bullets."

Again, Bonhist laughed, this time to herself. She could see that Running Buffalo could not take much more teasing so she said, "Give me your pistol. I have bullets and will show you how to load them."

Running Buffalo removed his fire stick from its holster, looking at the ivory handle grip and rubbing his hand down its barrel. Bonhist could see how he admired it. She removed six bullets from her holster and loaded the revolver. It was a short Colt .45, and she noticed that someone had notched its handle. She then removed several more bullets from her belt and placed them in Running Buffalo's gun belt.

"The white man calls this a Colt .45, the same as mine," said Bonhist as she handed the loaded revolver back to him.

"Do you just pull this trigger?"

In an instant, the firearm discharged with a loud explosion, recoiling so hard in Running Buffalo's hand that he dropped it.

"Aiee, be careful! You will shoot your foot off! This Colt is strong medicine. First, you must cock the fire stick, then aim and shoot. It is best to keep the fire stick level, then squeeze the trigger," Bonhist said as she picked up the Colt and handed it back to Running Buffalo. "Watch." Bonhist then drew her own Colt and shot twice at a knot hole in a cottonwood tree. Her target was about thirty feet away, and she placed both bullets within an inch of the knot.

"Aiee, you are good. Are you good at everything, Medicine Woman?"

"It took many days of practice to shoot that well."

Running Buffalo then drew an arrow from his quiver and with his bow shot it precisely to the middle of the knot. "I think I will hunt with my bow."

"Yes, that was a great shot, now try it with your fire stick."

Running Buffalo drew his fire stick, cocked it, and shot. The bullet whistled through the branches at the top of the tree, and a few leaves floated to the ground. Bonhist laughed, and this time Running Buffalo laughed as well.

"Come, I will now show you how to clean your Colt."

Jimmy Bennet was a professional gambler who had drifted down into Oklahoma Territory from Kansas. Like many gamblers, he had learned it was not healthy to stay in one place very long.

Bennet, with his brown derby cocked to one side, had a look about him of being a sucker or an easy mark. But under that cover, he was like a fox in a hen house. His favorite game was dealing Monte. He appeared a little clumsy with the cards and would carelessly allow someone to 'catch port' or see their next card. He would then turn up the deck, and, to the amazement of his opponent, the card would be gone! He could jump cuts without being caught or deal a layout and make you win or lose as he wished. At the Sac and Fox Agency, he got away with $800 and left them puzzled and mad. Two nights later, he made his first big hit, cleaning out the officers at Fort Reno for twenty-five hundred dollars. There, the United States Marshal, Billy Lee, who worked out of Fort Reno, was on to Bennet, so he quickly moved on. Several ranches with government contracts to raise cattle for the forts and Indian Agencies had men working for them who were little more than outlaws and cattle rustlers. They would steal Indian ponies or hijack easy targets. Taking advantage of this, Bennet was in and out of the camps, always leaving with four or five hundred dollars or more.

One evening, he drifted onto Robert Bent's ranch, told them his name was Jim, and that he was passing through. He watered his horse and offered to pay for a meal. He showed a wad of money and, of course, was invited to stay for dinner. Later that night the subject of cards came up, and ole Jim was invited to play. The game was played on one of the beds in a dugout where the ranch hands slept. Billy

Horton sat in the middle of the bed with his back to the wall. Henry Overby sat on the edge of the bed with Andy Puckett to his left and Bennet to the right. As the game progressed, Bennet saw at once that Billy and Henry, secretly cousins, were teaming up and would no doubt split their winnings later. Andy was a greenhorn with no idea what was going on. Bennet dealt Puckett a couple of winning hands early. He then sat back and watched Billy and Henry cheat. They were average players, but in a couple of hours had taken Andy for four hundred dollars and Bennet for two hundred, which he had thrown in to add heat to the fire. At that point, Andy got up and announced that he was beaten fair and square and was going to leave while he still had a horse and saddle. Bennet pulled out a couple of hundred dollars, threw it on the bed, and asked if anyone cared for a game of Monte. The two tinhorn gamblers quickly agreed. Within the hour, Bennet raked in a thousand dollars. This development caught the cousins by surprise when Bennet announced, shoving the derby back, that, "Nothin' like this has ever happened to me before; chucks hadn't even planned on playing." Before the cousins could regain their wits, Bennet had pocketed the money and was gone.

Early next morning, Henry saddled his pinto and rode out looking for Bennet. By midmorning, he found the gambler riding along the river toward Texas. Henry pulled a gun on him, pure and simple—hijacking. Henry wanted all that money, and he had no intention of splitting it with Billy. He would knock this dummy in the head and bury his body with no one the wiser. As Bennet got off his horse with his hands in the air, Henry, his face covered with a bandanna, ordered him to drop his revolver slowly. Unknown to

Henry, Bennet had four other concealed weapons, three pistols, and his pride—a tinker's knife from back in Tennessee made for fighting and as sharp as a razor. As Henry reached into Bennet's jacket for his wallet, the gambler, with the same hand speed he had used the night before to jump cut, slipped the dagger from behind his neck and lunged it into Henry's heart. The victim never knew what had happened. He wanted to pull the trigger, but somehow his body would not respond, and in the next second, he was dead.

Chapter 37

Bennet quickly appraised the situation. He had just killed a man, but so what—the hijacker had it coming. He was not concerned about life, merely the consequences. Surely, the man had friends, a partner, relatives who would avenge his death. But worst, if it got out that he had killed this man, it could tarnish his image at the gambling tables. Bennet was as much a con man as a gambler, and a reputation for killing would ruin his game. No one must ever know about this.

Bennet evaluated Henry's valuables: his pinto horse was of high quality, and his Mexican-designed revolver and holster would bring some money. He rolled them up and put them in his saddlebags. He looked again at the dead body, and in an instant, scalped the man and cut off an ear. Smiling, he realized that when the body was found, it would appear to be the work of an Indian. He then rolled the body down into a gully. Riding away in a gallop, he smiled as he led the pinto. Bennet had gone no more than five miles when his horse pulled up lame with a split hoof. Bennet thought hard before throwing his saddle on the back of the pinto, but there was no other choice. As he swung his leg over the pinto and into the saddle, he looked up and noticed an Indian watching. He was only a short distance away and appeared to be a young Cheyenne warrior. He held a string of average-looking horses, but sat on a fine-looking black stallion. Bennet alertly waved the young man over. "Do you speak veheo, the white man's language?"

The Indian held up his hand, indicating peace as he rode closer and said, "Little talk."

"I have heap mu kite (money) for the black horse."

The Cheyenne quickly shook his head, "No."

"My name is Jim. What's yours?" Bennet asked as he tried to use hand signals to talk.

"My name is Running Buffalo. Do you have pone bread or black coffee?"

"No, I have not eaten for two days. Would you trade your black pony for this pretty paint?"

Running Buffalo jumped from his black pony and looked over the pinto carefully before saying no.

Bennet smiled at the Cheyenne. He wished he had time to teach him cards; he would be good. "Are you a hetaneka eskone (boy) and the black pony belongs to your father?"

"No, I am a warrior; the black is mine."

Bennet then reached into his saddlebags and brought out the pistol. The inlaid silver on the holster shone as it hit the sun. Bennet presented the pistol to Running Buffalo. "Would you trade your black for this beautiful pistol and the pinto?" It took only a heartbeat for Running Buffalo to agree to the trade. Minutes later, Bennet was riding the black stallion toward Texas while Running Buffalo was riding the pinto and wearing his new holster and pistol as he moved toward the Cheyenne village at Fort Cantonment.

Three days later, the body of Henry was discovered. His friends swore over his grave to find the killer. Three weeks later, the hands from Bent's ranch drove fifty horses to Fort Cantonment to be sold to the cavalry. There was not much going on at the Fort, not even a saloon, so the ranch hands planned to get back on. They would make one stop to the general store. Coffee, sugar, and tobacco were in short supply so that they would stock up. Henry's pinto was in plain sight, tied outside the store. The pony carried an Indian saddle and markings. Inside, they found Running Buffalo talking to Bonhist. He was wearing Henry's pistol! Billy Horton and Andy Puckett had planned to ask about the horse, but seeing the holster and pistol left no doubt in their minds. "You! I'm talking to you—horse thief and killer! Draw!"

Running Buffalo turned from Bonhist. He looked at the two men in amazement. Why were they attacking him? One of them was going for his weapon. Instantly, Running Buffalo drew, but not his Colt. Instead, he pulled his hunting knife and threw it from his hip in a backhand motion. The knife caught Andy Puckett in his right shoulder before he could clear leather with his pistol. Horton's shot immediately followed, and in the next second, Running Buffalo clutched his chest, falling to the floor. Bonhist had never witnessed a gunfight before. It was the most brutal act she had ever seen. Running Buffalo had no chance at all. Bonhist, in a cry, ran to Running Buffalo. Turning him over, she could see an expression of dismay in his eyes as he looked into her face. In the next second, his eyes went blank. He was dead. The last thing he saw was the face of Bonhist.

Carmen was screaming, Boonie had already run for help, and in minutes, Horton was arrested. The next day, the Cheyenne built a burial platform for Running Buffalo. The pinto lay dead below him, and the Colt pistol and holster hung from a supporting post. His bow and quiver were lying across his chest. He was a warrior who had crossed over into the spirit world, maybe to Spirit Mountain with Crow. Bonhist looked up at the western sky, tears running down her face. As she watched the beautiful designs of orange and purple, she wondered how much more grief the People would endure.

The next day, a council was held at Fort Cantonment. Billy Horton and witnesses explained that a white man had been killed on their ranch. Witnesses told of the pinto and holster, which clearly showed that the killer was Running Buffalo. He had drawn a knife on them, and they were only defending themselves. Charges were dismissed, but Horton was ordered to leave the territory. The Indians were in an uproar when they heard of the verdict. They did not understand the white man's justice for they had clearly told the officials that Running Buffalo had killed no one and had traded for both the pinto and the holster.

The following day, Bonhist, Chief Stone Calf, Bear Robe, and Spotted Horse met with Colonel Dodge. It was not a pleasant meeting, and Bonhist did most of the talking.

"You have said that this is our land; we are not allowed to leave it, and your pony soldiers are here to protect us. But you have allowed these cowboys to kill one of our people right here in Cantonment, and you have freed him?"

"Now, Medicine Woman, you must understand. This terrible incident was out of our control. A white man was killed on Bent's ranch, and these men believe that it was Running Buffalo. When he threw his knife, these men had the right to defend themselves. I know that some of them may be nothing more than outlaws, but that is our law. This man, Horton, has been ordered out of Indian Territory."

"I will not rest until the great white chief in Washington has ordered all these cattle people off Indian lands."

"Medicine Woman, that would be impractical. We hold one thousand steers here every winter to feed the post personnel and the Indians. We need cattle."

"Perhaps, but we do not need these ranches. We can buy cattle from Texas cattlemen."

"Yes, but remember—you want us to charge those Texas cattlemen one dollar a steer to cross your land to Kansas. Do you think they will do business with the Indians?"

"We have come to ask three things of you."

"Medicine Woman, I will do whatever is in my power to help. What do you want?"

Bonhist took a pack of cards from her sash and put the ace of spades on Colonel Dodge's desk, saying, "One, we want a new agent. We liked and trusted Agent Dyer; bring him back."

She then laid down the two of spades. "Two, we want all cattle ranchers off Indian lands." The three of spades next hit Colonel Dodges' desk as she said, "And three, the ranchers will pay the Cheyenne and Arapaho grass money."

"What the hell is grass money?"

"The thousand steers that you hold eat Indian grass. These cattlemen who hold government contracts use Indian grass. You will all pay one dollar paper money for each steer and horse."

Two years after that meeting, Agent Dyer reported that the Cheyenne/Arapaho had $250,000 in their budget. In 1885, President Grover Cleveland issued a proclamation ordering all cattlemen out of Oklahoma. The government soldiers carried out those orders.

Ho-e-ma-ha, the Winter Man, had again played his flute and brought ice and snow to the Indian lands. However, little by little, Grandfather Sun was winning the battle and slowly driving Winter Man back to his home in the north. Finally, the day came when Boonie announced that he had received a telegram from Austin. "Toddy will be home soon. He is now in Kansas City. When he gets here, Carmen and I will marry and go on a long honeymoon."

This news brought a thrill of excitement to the heart of Bonhist. She turned with a smile, asking, "Did the paper talk say anything about Cowboy's wife?"

"No, I guess we'll all meet her when they get here."

CHAPTER 38

Bonhist could not forget the gunfight. Waking during the night, she would be in a sweat, fighting her robe, having another bad dream. If only she had been wearing her Colt, she could have saved Running Buffalo. Unarmed, she could not stop the men from Bent's ranch. Never again would she be without her pistol, nor would she be totally relaxed. This she promised herself.

Cowboy should come in from Indiana any day with his new wife. Bonhist had decided that she would no longer work at the general store. She feared that her presence would be a problem. Feeling a deep sadness sweeping over her, she walked to the river to be by herself. She had hardly found a place to sit when her mother walked up and joined her. "Medicine Woman, your heart is heavy and drags the ground. Would you like to talk?"

"Mother, I am very sad. I never had a chance to know Running Buffalo. I feel alone and mad at myself because I could not even help during the fight. To make things worse, soon, Cowboy will return with his wife."

Star hugged her daughter without saying a word. After several minutes, Star spoke, "Your vision quest will come true. During my sleep last night, Crow spoke. He said that Running Buffalo is free and happy and joins the others on Spirit Mountain. He thinks that I should listen to you—it is the way. Keep strong and believe in yourself."

"Mother, you give me courage to face tomorrow, but I feel that you have something else to tell me. What is it?"

"I hope you will be happy with me when I tell you that I am with child."

"Aiee, Mother, I hope the baby will be a little girl! I would like a sister. Will you name your child Fletcher?"

"Perhaps I will also name you Fletcher," Star answered with a laugh.

The following week, Austin came home. He was tired and unshaven as he walked into the store and dropped his bags to the floor. "Toddy, where is your wife?" asked Boonie.

"Couldn't find one that's suited to this country. I suspect it'll be a while before I try that again. What are all those horses doing in the corral with Blue Boy?"

"Medicine Woman brought them back from their hunting party. She said it was payment for the use of your horses."

"Medicine Woman! Is she here? Where is she now?"

"She quit us only three days ago. Said she had other things on her mind. She's out at the Cheyenne village."

"When did she come back? I can't believe it. I've got to find her right now."

"She'll be glad to see you, too, but I'd shave and bathe if I were you."

Within the hour, Austin had shaved, washed up, put on some sweet-smelling rose water, combed his hair back, and was on his way to see Bonhist. With a heart full of joy, he couldn't believe his good luck. Some of the Indians waved, happy to see him. Reaching the lodge of Star and Big Dog, he dismounted and rapped on the lodge flap. It was late evening, and the western sky was streaked with colors of orange and shades of dark gray and purple. *Oklahoma has beautiful sunsets*, Austin thought as he waited. A little surprised as Big Dog stepped from the lodge, Austin announced, "I have come to see Medicine Woman."

Big Dog nodded his understanding and pointed up the river. "Away, she hunts. Her lodge over there, but she hunts."

Austin's eyes looked past the lodge Big Dog had pointed out and followed the river's path. It was lined with trees of all sorts, mainly cottonwoods, willows, and cedar. Finding Medicine Woman would not be easy along the river, which ran northwesterly. He turned to Big Dog, saying, "You lead me to Medicine Woman. One plug 'bacca."

At this point, Star stepped from the lodge. Austin was very surprised to see a rare smile on her face. Returning the smile, he could see where Medicine Woman got her uncommonly good looks. She spoke in Cheyenne, and Big Dog interpreted. "My wife has said that we will both take you to our daughter. She has missed you."

Bonhist had hobbled the red pony in a meadow of yellow and brown grass, then walked to a spot along the river among the cottonwood trees. She leaned back against a tree and watched the North Canadian River. The spirits of the river were peaceful. Seeing the signs, she knew the deer were plentiful. And she would be able to take one back to camp. Bonhist wanted the deer as much for its hide as for the meat. However, she did not want to disturb the spirits, so she promised not to hunt in this area again until another moon had passed. She would make herself invisible to the deer and wait. Looking up the stream, she saw five coming to water. They were too far for a shot, so she just watched. Lately, she had been practicing with her Colt and now decided to use it in her hunt. Her mind drifted back, thinking of Cowboy. Eager to see him again, even if he were married, she would try to be a friend to his new wife. Suddenly, she heard movement. Turning her head, she saw the white tails of four deer.

Instantly, her target flashed before her, a large buck with three does. With the natural quickness and keen eye that is born to only a rare few, she drew her revolver and fired two shots. The third doe fell with both bullets striking through the shoulder of its left front leg, then ripping into its heart.

Bonhist lifted her hands to the sky and repeated the hunter's prayer. It pleased her to see that the doe was young, and its skin could be tanned into a beautiful white dress. It was also fat and would provide many good steaks. She removed her hunting knife and cut the deer's throat, allowing it to bleed freely. Next, she carefully dressed out the deer, leaving its guts for the coyote. Steam rolled from the hot cavity, and the blood was hot. She would have to fetch her pony and build a travois. It was almost dark, so she had to hurry. As she rose from her kill, she heard noise. In a flash, almost quicker than the eye could see, her Colt appeared in her hand. It was her mother, Big Dog—and Cowboy! Just as quickly as she drew the pistol, she returned it to its holster. A wide grin spread across her face, then she remembered two things. Cowboy had a wife, and she was standing before him, dirty and with blood from her elbows to her hands.

"Bonhist," called Star. "The one you call Cowboy has come to see you."

Bonhist had been waiting for months to see his face again. She had missed him terribly, and now all she could do was stand there with her knees shaking. Finally, she said, "Where's your wife, Cowboy?"

Austin slid from Blue Boy and walked to Bonhist without a word. He stopped in front of her and lifted her from the ground with a hug. Tears began to run down her face, but she protested, "Cowboy, I have blood all over me, and I smell like a deer."

With this, Austin leaned down and kissed her. She had never been kissed like this before. She hugged him back, returning the kiss. Finally, Austin said, "I didn't marry; there was no one in Indiana to compare to you. I only went because I believed you'd gone back north, and I'd never see you again. I have missed you!"

Noticing her mother and Big Dog, Bonhist turned and said, "I need the red pony. Help me, Cowboy, I need two poles for a travois."

Austin smiled at Bonhist. Reaching down, he lifted the deer over his shoulders, and with a turn, walked to Blue Boy. With ease, he placed the doe in front of his saddle. "No, you don't need any poles. Blue Boy can carry your little doe back to the tepee. Why didn't you shoot the buck?"

"Because this doe will make a beautiful white wedding dress."

Austin froze; his heart sank. *Could it be that Medicine Woman had been promised to another man?* he thought. With slight hesitation in his voice, he asked, "Who will you marry?"

"You," she said as she leaped to the back of her red pony.

CHAPTER 39

A year had passed since Bonhist had escaped from the pony soldier near the corn field where the Squirrel had been shot. Lieutenant Henry Bartholomew Fry had not forgotten that beautiful Cheyenne girl whose smiling face and long legs haunted him. She had slipped through his fingers that night on the Arkansas River when his men told him that an Indian had struck him with a club in the darkness. He had never believed that lie, suspecting that it was one of his own men who had done it.

The girl and her party had traveled on to their people in Oklahoma, and Fry insisted on following. Unexpectedly, a turn of events due to several complaints from his men on the post relieved him of his duties at Bent's Fort. Shortly afterwards, he resigned his commission.

Lieutenant Fry had not returned to his father's home in the east since his trouble with the law had never been resolved. Instead, his father had wired him money—enough for a ranch, but in place of making a wise investment, he squandered the money.

Drifting into Kansas from Colorado, he looked for opportunities to turn a quick profit, but nothing he tried worked. At last, he, under the cover of a black hood and darkness, found an opportunity to prey upon easy marks among travelers. He had also once robbed a stage line and its passengers. With each success, he grew bolder quickly, changing from a black flannel shirt and hood into his military uniform to pass himself off as an officer.

He would gamble and live the good life until his resources ran low, then he would strike again. He was chased out of Medicine Lodge, Kansas, for killing a man in a gun fight, even though witnesses claimed it was fair. Being fast with his hands, Henry continued killing another man in Wichita. Soon, he had built a reputation.

One night in Dodge City, he was sitting in a poker game and having uncommonly good luck. He had won over five hundred dollars, and only two men remained in the game. One looking like a professional gambler was dressed in a black cloth suit, and another, seemingly simple-minded sucker, was named Jim. When Henry won two more big hands, the professional gambler pulled stakes and left the table. "What's your name?" Henry asked the other one.

"Jim," he answered.

"You have a last name?"

"They call me Bennet."

"Well, Bennet, would you like to play Monte for some real money?"

Bennet threw four hundred dollars on the table, answering, "I'll play till that's gone."

A grin spread across Fry's face. "Go ahead and deal," he said.

It took less than an hour for Bennet to clean out Fry's entire bankroll. "Twelve hundred dollars—you're cheating!" the lieutenant shouted as he jerked his chair back and reached for his gun. Before he could pull the Colt from its holster, though, Bennet had deftly slipped a Derringer from his coat sleeve and leveled it. Fry froze as he stared into the eyes of Bennet.

"You made a mistake about cheating," Bennet said. "A strange thing about cards; sometimes they fall in your favor—sometimes they don't. I won fair. Don't make me pull this trigger." Bennet carefully raked in his winnings, tilted his brown Derby hat to the back of his head, and backed out of the saloon.

"Who is he?" Fry asked, facing the other gamblers.

The one in the black cloth suit spoke up, saying, "He's a damn good card cheat."

"He will soon be a dead card cheat," Fry answered.

The next morning, he inquired about Bennet everywhere in Dodge. No one had seen him. Finally, he talked to the blacksmith. "I'm looking for a scrawny man in a brown derby hat. You see him?"

"Yep."

"Where can I find him?"

"Don't know. He saddled up late last night and left town."

"You know which direction?"

"Nope, but it was mighty cold last night. I don't think even a drinking man would go north into that wind. He's drifting down into Oklahoma."

"What kind of horse was he riding?"

"Brown Bay. Nothing fancy."

Henry Fry had wanted to try the territory anyway. There was a pretty little Cheyenne there, and now he had another reason to go into Indian country. He promised himself that he would follow

Bennet to hell if it came to that. Knowing Bennet had at least sixteen hundred dollars, Henry would hijack him and take the money back.

He planned to forge a legal document that appeared to be a warrant for Bennet's arrest. He planned to get Bennet in chains. Then rob and kill him. Who would ever know or care? The beauty of his plan was to get the military to do the dangerous work. He still remembered Benanet's quick hands when Benanet pointed the derringer at him.

Henry polished his brass, cleaned his uniform, and, with his official papers, rode east. He had no idea why he was riding east except that the likelihood of meeting someone who had seen Bennet seemed better.

He soon rode into Fort Dodge. They had heard of Bennet, but no one had seen him. After eating a good meal, he rode on, taking a southeastern route. Three days later, Henry rode up to Medicine Lodge, one of the towns where he had shot a man. Since this was a good town to stay clear of, he rode on.

As the late evening approached, he was feeling cold and a little hungry. At a ranch just ahead, he asked for a place to hold up for the night and something to eat. "Mind if I water my horse and eat? I'm Lieutenant Smith, U.S. Army, on the trail of a wanted man."

"You're welcome, Lieutenant. One of my hands will take care of your hoss. Come on in, name's Harvey," spoke an elderly, white-haired man.

Henry was glad to accept a big helping of fried bacon, sourdough biscuits, and milk gravy. "Who ya chasing?" asked Harvey.

"A scrawny little devil in a brown derby hat; calls himself Bennet."

"Well, I'll be damned! He was here two nights ago and wanted to pay for his lodging with a big roll of money. We suckered him into a card game. Damn, if that little weasel didn't take us for four hundred dollars. I thought about killing him, but let him go on his way—to the territory."

"You're lucky you didn't try anything. He doesn't look it, but he's a dangerous man. Left a trail of dead men all the way from here to Colorado—he's a card cheat!"

The next morning after a hearty breakfast, Henry crossed into the territory. The trail to Bennet was getting hotter. If circumstances were right, he'd shoot Bennet on sight—if not, the army could take him. By late evening, he rode into the Kaw Indian Agency near Newkirk. No one having the description of Bennet had been seen. While Henry stayed the night, they fed him and cared for his horse. Continuing south the next day, he reached the Pawnee Agency, but Bennet had not been seen. But two days later, when he arrived at the Fox and Sac Agency, Bennet had been there. He had taken them for eight hundred dollars. One of the troopers reported that Bennet was headed for Fort Reno.

Lieutenant Carl Riley wired ahead and confirmed their suspicion. Bennet had just left after winning $2,500 from the officers. He was following the North Canadian River into Cheyenne/Arapaho country. The next morning, Henry watched Gus Miller collect his money for a string of horses, planning to head west toward Fort Reno and then back to Texas.

Henry asked if he could ride along since they were both going in the same direction. Gus agreed and, by late afternoon, he was lying in a shallow grave with a bullet through his back. His money was tucked neatly in Henry Fry's pocket.

<h1 style="text-align:center">CHAPTER 40</h1>

Bonhist knew that she deeply loved Cowboy. Now, for the first time, she realized that he felt the same about her. Sensing this, she was glad to see that even though she was Cheyenne with skin darker than his, he found her good to look upon. She felt light as a feather, and her smile told the world of her happiness.

With the news that Bonhist and Austin were to be married, Boonie and Carmen decided to change their plans. They had wanted to go on a trip. Boonie had worked the store during the winter while Austin was in Indiana. Now it was his turn to take time off. Boonie also knew that Carmen wanted to attend Bonhist's wedding. Austin and Bonhist might be forced to postpone their wedding until they have more time.

"No," said Bonhist. "Cowboy and I will not marry until I have completed my wedding dress. It will take two moons. We will need this time to make plans. Carmen, you and Boonie should go ahead with your wedding. When you return from your trip, then Cowboy and I will marry."

"Sí, Medicine Woman, but you do not have to wait. Boonie and I can marry next year."

"No, you should go ahead. Cowboy and I will marry on the moon when the buds turn green. Now, how can I help with your wedding?"

"My wedding, my happiness, and my life are possible only because of your courage. You have given me life, and that is enough."

The next week, Carmen and Boonie were married and left for San Francisco. Bonhist and Austin worked at the store and hired Soft Winds to help. The three spent the day laughing as they worked. "Carmen is not here. Can you cook?" Austin asked.

"Cowboy, you are going to marry a woman, and you do not even know if she can cook? We will cut cards, you, me, and Soft Winds. High card cooks; low card cleans up kitchen; and middle card does nothing."

Austin turned to Soft Winds with a sly grin and asked, "Soft Winds, can you cook?"

"Yes, she can cook as all Cheyenne women can, but are you afraid of the game of chance?"

"Darling, you play with me like a cat with a mouse. But I'll get the cards."

This brought a laugh from both Bonhist and Soft Winds. Austin spread the cards on the counter. "You choose first, Cowboy." Austin drew the nine of clubs and slowly turned it over. "You draw your card now," Bonhist said to Soft Winds. Soft Winds picked out the five of hearts.

"Now it's your turn," Austin said with a big grin. Bonhist smiled as she ran her slender fingers over the cards. She stopped at one for a moment, then moved on to the next. Turning it over with a laugh, she looked up with her black, sparkling eyes.

"The eight of diamonds! I'm the middle one; now I can sit back and watch to see how my future husband cooks."

"You've cheated—somehow," said Austin jokingly. Bonhist laughed so hard that tears came to her eyes.

"Cowboy, do not you remember—I am Medicine Woman, not darling. But since I love to hear you sing, I will make a trade. I will cook while you play and sing 'Around Mountain.'"

"You mean, 'She'll Be Coming Around the Mountain.'"

"Yes, that one. Is it a trade?"

"Yes, darling, that's a good trade."

"My name is Medicine Woman, not darling." This response brought a big grin to Austin's face.

"If you can call me Cowboy, I can call you darling."

Bonhist responded to Austin's words by running into his arms. She then pushed him away and handed him his guitar.

The business was going well as the Indians always spent their small allotments on tobacco, coffee, sugar, and salt. The extra horses that Medicine Woman brought back from their hunting trip to Texas were sold at a low price to young Cheyenne warriors. "Darling, we have saved money, but are still a long way from having enough for a horse ranch. I'm afraid that we'll have to stay in this store much longer than I thought."

"No, Cowboy, I have a plan. We will get the horse ranch after we marry."

"Darling, you don't understand. In the white world, it takes money—not a plan or a vision."

"I will show you, Cowboy, how we will get our horse ranch with my plan from my vision." Austin looked at Bonhist's beautiful, sincere face and shook his head, but said nothing more.

The wedding dress was coming along nicely. Tanning the doeskin was hard work, but, at last, it was soft and white. The sight of it made Star smile. "It will be the most beautiful of all wedding dresses. It is soft with a pleasant odor and as white as snow."

"Mother, will you help me with the beadwork?"

"Of course, my daughter."

"I want blue beads for the Great Spirit of the sky, brown beads for the Great Spirit under the earth, and red beads because I think they're pretty."

"Yes, and we will cut the metal from the Prince Albert cans and roll them around the fringes so you will jingle as you walk."

"Aiee, Mother, that is good. You are very smart."

"I wish that your father had lived to see this day."

"Mother, don't you know he is here. He is always with us, and sometimes I talk with him." Star reached over and hugged Bonhist without a word, a tear forming in her eye.

The following evening, the Cheyenne called a council. The chiefs were concerned about overcrowding and living conditions right next to the Arapaho. The sun had set, and a large yellow moon rose in the eastern sky. Leaders sat around a large campfire, wrapped in their robes, as each gave his ideas on what must be done. Finally, Chief Stone Calf looked at Bonhist as she sat between her mother and old Whirlwind. "We have not heard from Medicine Woman. Do you have any words for this council?"

Before she could respond, Timber Bear let out a loud grunt and stood immediately. "You would call for the counsel of this white girl that hides in the body of a Cheyenne before me! It is said that she has great powers, yet I see nothing but another white person."

Everyone looked toward the angry medicine man. He had never agreed with her title since she had never been an apprentice or earned the name of medicine woman. He was obviously jealous of Bonhist and in a rage. Chief Stone Calf then nodded toward Timber Bear and said, "Speak, Timber Bear."

"I have little to say about the overcrowded conditions. Some of us could move to Fort Reno. Darlington has an agency there, and it is on this same river. But I have much to say about this one." He turned and pointed straight toward Bonhist. "You honor her by calling her Medicine Woman. You ask for her counsel before mine. Now I will tell you what she has done for us." With incredible showmanship and arrogance, he walked to the center of the council next to the fire. From under his robe, he took six lances and stuck each one with a loud thud into the ground in a line. He then went back to his position in the circle and lifted a rawhide bag. Walking to the first lance, he placed the skull of a rabbit on the top of the shaft. "This rabbit skull reminds us that Running Buffalo died in Medicine Woman's arms. If she has powers, why didn't she save him? On the second lance, he placed the skull of a bobcat. "This skull reminds us that she cooks and works for the whites." The third lance struck the raccoon's skull. "This skull reminds us that she talks the white language." On the fourth lance, he placed the coyote's skull. "This skull reminds us that she wears the white man's little fire stick on her hip and uses it rather than a Cheyenne bow." On top of the fifth lance, he placed the skull of a deer. "We are reminded by this skull that she is a friend with the big white chief and counsels with him about the People." And finally, on the sixth lance, he placed the skull of a buffalo. "This last skull reminds us that she will soon marry a white man and bear his children!" Timber Bear looked down the row of lances with satisfaction. Each skull from the rabbit to the buffalo grew progressively larger than the one before. With a grave smile, he looked around the council and sat down. The council members turned at once, looking toward Bonhist as Chief Stone Calf spoke, "Medicine Woman, do you have words for us?"

Bonhist rose from her buffalo robe, covered by the antelope skin that she wore as a poncho. With the head skin hanging from her long, flowing black hair like a hood, she looked at the row of lances. Everyone sat waiting for her rebuttal. How would she answer? They knew that she had done many good things: her hunting trip to Texas, the fees for cattle crossing Indian land, charging grass money, promising to rid the Cheyenne/Arapaho lands of cattle ranchers, and helping learn to live in this white world. The chiefs, medicine men, and high-ranking warriors who formed the council settled into their robes, waiting with great interest.

"During the third night of my quest, I saw a vision that was so horrible and strong that I have only talked about it with my mother. I wanted to forget it and never think of it again. Surely the Trickster himself must have been responsible for what I saw. Agreeing to marry Running Buffalo was what my heart wanted, not my vision. The spirits clearly showed another way that would bring a solution to the crowded conditions we now face. Running Buffalo had to go away so my vision could come true." Bonhist then moved her antelope robe, and with hands so quick that few even saw, she drew her Colt and shot the rabbit's head from the first lance. The skull burst into a hundred fragments and was gone. She then twirled the gun on her finger and replaced it in its holster in a flash. The men jumped in their robes from the shock of the sound. Looking around, they settled with not even a smile.

Bonhist then looked at the bobcat skull and said, "Yes, I cook and work in the white man's kitchen and store. It is a good lesson for our children if they want to survive." She then drew in a flash and shot the skull from the second lance as she had done the first. Timber Bear started to interrupt, but the chiefs gave him a quick hand signal to sit and remain quiet. Bonhist glanced at the third lance. "I am proud to speak the white tongue. It gives me the power to talk for the People." Again, almost faster than the eye, she drew, shot, and returned the pistol to its holster. "The white man's little fire stick has six teeth. The Cheyenne bow has but one; you have to reach for the quiver for another tooth." With this remark, she whirled and shot the coyote skull from the fourth lance. "The white chief that you accuse me of being an ally with can be either an enemy or a friend who helps us. I will use him to help the People. The fifth shot rang out, and the deer skull disappeared. "You all know Cowboy. He is the key to the solution for our crowded conditions. I love this man and will be his wife as I follow my vision." Bonhist then shot the buffalo skull between the eyes. It split right down the middle and fell to the ground in pieces. Medicine Woman turned with a whirl, covered her head with the antelope hide, and walked to her robe. She wrapped her buffalo robe around her body, and with her mother and Whirlwind, left the council without another word.

<h1 style="text-align:center">CHAPTER 41</h1>

Timber Bear was now the joke of the Cheyenne village. Since he had been opposed to naming Bonhist as Medicine Woman from the start, he had spent many hours preparing the skulls, believing they would have strong medicine. Now the People dared to question him and laugh as he walked by. To escape this ridicule, he decided to move downriver to the Darlington Agency near Fort Reno. They would all be sorry when they needed his medicine and counsel, he told his wife. And so Timber Bear moved.

It would be several weeks before Boonie and Carmen would return for the wedding. Plans for the ceremony were slowly progressing.

"Medicine Woman, your wedding dress is beautiful, and it's not even half finished," said Red Leaf. "Will you also wear the eagle feather that Chief Sitting Bull gave you?"

"That eagle feather and my father's medicine bags will be the most important parts of my wedding attire."

"Will you have a white man's wedding or a Cheyenne ceremony?"

"Both," answered Bonhist as she continued the careful process of beading the trim on her dress.

The following morning began much as any other, with Bonhist and Austin taking an early-morning ride. The weather was chilly, with a strong southwest wind. Blue Boy and the red pony, that Bonhist was now calling 'Shorty' because the gelding was shorter than the steel-gray stallion, grazed as Austin and Bonhist sat together on the banks of the river.

"How does the wedding dress look? Is it ready?"

"Cowboy, I did not have time for the wedding dress last night. It is coming along so slowly that perhaps we won't be able to get married until the next cold season."

"That dress better get done! I'm not waiting. When Boonie and Carmen get back, we're getting married. I don't care what you wear!"

Bonhist's head fell back as she laughed. "You are fun, Cowboy. I was only kidding; the dress looks good and will be ready."

As Austin and Bonhist rode to the store and dismounted, they were being watched by a pair of officers eating breakfast across the street. "Who's that girl?"

"You mean the pretty Indian?"

"Yes."

"They call her Medicine Woman, but you can forget about her. That's Austin Todd she's riding with. He's a former lieutenant and will marry her this spring."

"What is her real name? I recognize her from Colorado."

"Well, sir, I can't say that I know her real name, but I can find out if it's important."

"This is my lucky day. I believe she's wanted for thievery and the death of a rancher. Don't let this out, as someone might warn her. She's slipped through my fingers once, but it'll not happen again."

"Lieutenant Smith, are you sure? Dodge runs this post, and he puts stock in that girl. He wouldn't believe it."

"Yes, but as you have already told me, Dodge is in Texas and can't be reached. This is even more important than Bennet. I need to know her real name. Can you handle that?"

By midmorning, Henry Fry had the information that he required and had forged a warrant for the arrest of Bonhist, known as Sage Woman. He walked from his temporary quarters that Lieutenant Hamilton had assigned, past the blacksmith shop, to the headquarters of Fort Cantonment.

"I knew this warrant was somewhere in my papers. As you can see, it's legal. Send a couple of troopers to the store and arrest her."

"Sir, I think it will work better if we send for her. We can then apprehend her in this office. Austin Todd will cause trouble if we try to capture her in his store."

"Well, I'll let you handle that. One more thing, I'll need two troopers to help me until we reach Dodge City. I can get assistance once I'm in Dodge."

"You might need more than two troopers. Medicine Woman is powerful. Still, the law has to be enforced."

Lieutenant Hamilton made the mistake of sending three troopers to summon the Medicine Woman, which alarmed Austin.

"What do you want?" he asked them.

"Medicine Woman is ordered to report to Colonel Dodge's office."

"Colonel Dodge is in Texas."

"Yes, but Lieutenant Hamilton is in charge in the colonel's absence."

"What business does Hamilton have with my future wife?"

"We were not told."

"Go back and tell Lieutenant Hamilton that my future wife is not subject to being ordered around at his command. If he wants to speak to her, he can come over here."

"But sir, we have orders to bring her to his office."

"Do you have a warrant for Medicine Woman's arrest? If not, carry my word back to the lieutenant."

"We will be back." The troopers turned and left the store without another word. They had hardly gone when Charging Bull slipped in the back door.

In Cheyenne, he reported excitedly, "I have seen him! The crazy pony soldier who chased us from Colorado. He has seen you, Medicine Woman, and still wants you as his woman. Do not worry, we will fight for you." Immediately, Bonhist reached under the counter for her pistol. She quickly buckled on her belt and threw her antelope hide over her head, wearing it as a poncho.

"What's going on? What did Charging Bull say?" Austin asked.

"Cowboy, there is an evil man here. He is a lieutenant from Bent's Fort who chased us from Colorado to get me as his woman."

"He's not taking you anywhere. Calm down, he has no authority here."

"They are coming back," Charging Bull said, pointing out a window.

"Charging Bull, go get my mother." As Charging Bull left in a run, Austin turned to Bonhist.

"What did you say?"

"Cowboy, I told Charging Bull to go get my mother. They are coming after me."

"You stay right here. I'll handle this. Don't come out." Austin then strapped on his handgun and stepped out onto the porch. The same three troopers approached.

"Austin Todd, we are sorry to inform you that we have a warrant for the arrest of Bonhist, the one known as Medicine Woman."

"What are the charges?"

"Stealing and killing a rancher in Colorado."

"That's a lie."

"Get her a good lawyer and let the courts decide that."

"She's not going anywhere. If they want to try her on those false charges, they can come here to Fort Cantonment. She's not leaving."

"Sir, you have no choice. This is a legal warrant, and it is our duty to take her." Austin drew his revolver and shot twice at the men's feet.

"You men have known me a long time. You know I mean business! Now get! If you want Medicine Woman, you'll have to walk over my dead body." The troopers turned and started back in a rush, meeting Hamilton and the lieutenant from Colorado.

"Sir, we're not fighting Todd!"

Lieutenant Hamilton turned to Henry Fry and said, "It would be better if we waited until Colonel Dodge returned. He can handle Austin."

"That may be your way, but it's not the law. I have a warrant, and I'm taking that girl back to Colorado for trial, even if I have to walk over her lover. Give me the warrant."

Henry Fry held the warrant for Austin to see while reaching down to release the hammer guard on his Colt revolver. Walking toward the general store where Austin stood in the doorway, he shouted, "This is a warrant for the arrest of Medicine Woman. I am taking her now. Do not force me to use my weapon!"

Austin stepped from the porch and faced Henry Fry. "Don't take another step! You will not arrest or take my future wife anywhere. She is not going with you. If there are charges against Medicine Woman, the lawyers will make arrangements for a trial here."

Henry stopped and placed the warrant in his pocket. He then flexed his hand, lowering it to his weapon. "Okay, if that's the way it is, you make your move."

Chapter 42

A scene all too common in the early west was playing out in the street in front of Todd's store. Two men stood facing each other. Each had a pistol strapped to his waist. Only one would survive, or perhaps neither. Henry Fry had been in this situation before; he was quick and sure of himself. This tall man he faced was obviously not a gunfighter. He noted the position of Todd's gun. It hung too low on his hip and was not even tied down. It was clear he was acting out of emotion rather than reason. He would be easy to defeat and, since he was resisting arrest, totally in the wrong.

To taunt Todd, he called out, "Why would a store clerk like you die for a redskin? She's not worth it; probably sleeps with half the bucks on this reservation. She'll cut your throat one day just for your horse."

Smiling at the reaction he saw in the greenhorn's face, Henry thought to himself, *He's too angry and out of control to find his pistol.*

Suddenly, Bonhist appeared on the porch and stepped to Austin's side. She positioned herself four feet behind him and eight feet to his right. Soft Winds moved with Bonhist and stood at her side. Roaring Waters joined them, standing next to his wife.

Henry again cried out to Austin, hoping to force the issue, "Well, Mr. Loudmouth, either go for your gun or get out of my way. I'll probably bed the bitch myself before we get back to Colorado." On hearing those words, Austin lost all restraint as he went for his gun. With too much wasted motion, his right hand fumbled clumsily. As he managed to draw and fire, his first shot kicked up sand in front of him; a second whistled well above Henry Fry's head.

Henry's draw was fluid, clearing leather as swiftly as ever. As his finger closed on the trigger, two shots rang out in rapid succession, blending with his so that the three sounded as one. His bullet flew harmlessly through the air. Checking his gun, he knew something was wrong! His hand moved to his chest and felt the wetness of blood. He was shot! Looking at Austin in astonishment for one brief moment, he doubled up and fell to the red dirt of the Indian Territory—dead. Henry had been hit twice, once through the third brass button on his coat and second an inch to its side—both penetrating his lungs and heart.

Remarkably the two shots were indistinguishable to the onlookers. Bonhist had fired them from under her poncho and returned the Colt to its holster with only Soft Winds and Roaring Waters aware of her action. They now stepped in front of her to hide the smoke left by her Colt. The witnesses blinked, trying to figure out what had happened. Suddenly, as if on cue, Star and Charging Bull rode up on their ponies, followed by twenty-five Cheyenne warriors led by Chief Stone Calf.

"Lieutenant Todd! You've just killed an officer of the U.S. Army who was trying to perform his duty," Lieutenant Hamilton snapped. "You're under arrest."

Austin froze in shock, unable to comprehend the situation. He stood there with his gun smoking. "Give me that weapon, Austin. It will go better for you if you surrender peacefully." Austin handed over his gun, shaking his head, not believing what had just taken place.

"Why are you arresting Cowboy? According to your law, he has a right to defend himself. When Running Buffalo was shot, Colonel Dodge said that a man has this right. That man's gun is out of his holster and in his hand. Cowboy had to defend himself." With these words, she turned toward Soft Winds and Roaring Waters, her look saying they should keep quiet.

"That is so, but Austin Todd just killed an officer who was carrying out his duty. You are both under arrest." Lieutenant Hamilton then realized that many angry Cheyennes had him surrounded. He looked at Austin, "Don't make this incident worse."

At those words, Austin regained his wits and turned to Bonhist, "Medicine Woman, tell your people to back away. Everything will be okay."

The Cheyenne warriors needed only a hand signal from Bonhist to retreat and allow Lieutenant Hamilton to take both Austin and their Medicine Woman into custody.

The week that followed was especially stressful for Austin. People from across the territory rode over to get a look at the gunfighter. Business at the general store tripled, and a journalist from Wichita traveled down to take a picture of Todd and write the story. *The military personnel at the post were also acting strangely,* Todd thought. They had known him as a gentle man, a peaceful person who built and grew. He had been a storekeeper; now they looked at him with fear in their eyes—he was a celebrity—a warrior. The army confiscated his weapons and horses and kept him well-guarded while he operated his store. People were also interested in Bonhist. They wanted a look at the woman that Austin would kill for. After all, she was the cause of the gunfight. Bonhist, they discovered, was exceptional, and all the men could see that she was worthy of his protection.

Hamilton sent a dispatch via telegraph to Bent's Fort for information regarding Lt. Smith's identity. A week passed, and there was still no response. Near the end of the week, Bonhist and Austin were relieved when Colonel Dodge returned to the post. After questioning both Austin and Bonhist, he found a lawyer to represent them. They were held under house arrest during the day so they could operate the general store. To the amazement of everyone, when the reply came from Bent's Fort, it revealed Lieutenant Smith to be an imposter. A report followed stating that Smith was actually Henry Fry, who had resigned his commission over a year ago. His family was notified, and the case was closed with Austin and Bonhist cleared of all charges.

A month later, Boonie and Carmen had returned from their trip. "I hear you're a dangerous man," said Boonie. "Where's your pistol? Strap it on, I want to see a real hero."

"Sorry, partner, I buried it a month ago. Never want to have another gun in my hand."

"You buried a perfectly good fifteen-dollar Colt? Why? They all say that you're as fast as anyone in the territory. I didn't know you were that good."

"Boonie, I don't want to talk about it! I can't explain what happened any more than the men standing around watching. Except for a miracle, I'd be dead right now."

As the chickadee finally burst into its song, "Summer is near," and the buds turned green, the wedding of Bonhist and Austin was set for the following Sunday. The army chaplain, Roy Harding, agreed to perform the ceremony in the store with all the post personnel present. Everyone wanted to see the gunfighter—Austin Todd—marry the Cheyenne girl. The Cheyenne ceremony was a puzzle to Austin. He didn't know what to expect. "Darling, what is a Cheyenne wedding like? Will I have to do anything unusual?"

"Yes, Cowboy. First, you must bring my mother and Big Dog many horses. This arrangement can only be made by your father, an uncle, or even a good friend. You cannot speak for yourself."

"But why are the horses necessary?"

"To make up for their loss. You are taking me from their lodge. This is a tradition among my people. Second, my mother has made you a Cheyenne buckskin shirt trimmed with beads. You can wear this during our wedding."

"I have a donkey; will that be good enough?"

"Cowboy! I will bite your ear off if you think I am only worth one donkey." With this, Austin laughed and hugged her.

"Who will I get to speak for me? I have no family here."

"Get one of the translators. They like you and would speak to my mother and Big Dog."

"I'll ask Big Wolf. He'll do anything for 'bacca."

"Yes, Big Wolf would gladly speak for you."

So Big Wolf and Austin Todd rode to Big Dog Fletcher's lodge. The Indians knew in advance why Austin had come to their lodge, yet they played their parts well. Austin kicked his foot nervously into the ground as Big Wolf spoke in Cheyenne to the parents of Bonhist.

"They say they are honored that you have come to their lodge. What is your offer for their daughter?"

"Tell them that they can have all my horses except Blue Boy. That's seven good horses."

Big Wolf turned with a twinkle in his eye and spoke in Cheyenne to Big Dog and Star. "He can do much better. I will tell him no. Do you agree?"

Big Dog nodded his agreement, and Big Wolf turned back to Austin, saying, "I am sorry, my friend, but this gift is not acceptable for one as outstanding as Medicine Woman."

"Okay, I have a new Winchester; I'll throw that in with ten plugs of 'bacca."

Again, Big Wolf turned to Big Dog and Star and spoke in their tongue. "He holds out still. I will tell him no."

"I am sorry, Austin, but Medicine Woman is worth even more."

Austin looked to the sky and kicked his foot again. This time, he said, "I will include Blue Boy."

Big Dog smiled even before Big Wolf made the offer. "He has given you the thing he loves most; this is good. The 'bacca will be mine."

"Your gift has been accepted. You are a strong warrior and a lucky man."

When the day finally arrived, Bonhist was striking in her wedding dress. The eagle feather from Chief Sitting Bull hung from her black, silky hair, and the twin medicine bags from her father proudly adorned her slender neck. The white man's ceremony took place first, followed by food, music, and Austin playing the guitar and singing. By late evening, the wedding party moved upriver to the Cheyenne village. Austin led Blue Boy and his seven mares to the lodge of Big Dog Fletcher and Star. He handed over the horses to Star. "Brought this one as a colt from Kentucky," he reflected as he turned and gave Big Dog a new Winchester rifle and a box of shells. Star accepted the horses and nodded her approval.

"Your horse will receive good care," said Star as Big Dog held up the new rifle with a smile. The traditional Cheyenne ceremony was performed, and they agreed to share their lodge. The blinded Whirlwind, acting as a priest, performed the short wedding. Star, as a Sioux, added a touch common among the Lakota but not generally part of a Cheyenne wedding. She laid her mink robe over Bonhist and Austin. This was the same robe that Chief Thin Face had presented to her and Crow as a wedding present many years ago. It was still in good shape and shone richly in the evening sun.

Austin and Bonhist stepped inside their specially built wedding lodge with the entire village whooping and hollering the Cheyenne war cry. It had been built from more than thirty cow hides. Only certain women among the Cheyenne knew how to bead and paint the tepee. One of the hardest workers was Red Leaf; it made her heart full to do this small thing for the daughter of Crow.

As the crowd began to move back down the river, Bonhist and Austin sat quietly for a while listening to the sounds. It was hard to believe they were finally together, safe and happy.

CHAPTER 43

One month after the wedding, Bonhist and Austin entered Colonel Dodge's office. The colonel met the two with a big grin. "Well, you look happy enough. How can I help you?"

"Sir, my wife insists on meeting with you. She has something on her mind, and we might as well hear her out."

"Sit down. Let's talk. How are things with the Indians?"

"The Cheyenne are concerned about such a large number of people camping so close together. We do not like living across the river from the Arapaho, and sickness will not leave our village."

"Medicine Woman, I am also concerned over the health problems of the Indians. Can you offer any solutions?"

"Yes, I would like to start an Indian settlement horse ranch. Many Cheyenne could live on this ranch and work with us. If we could get a government contract, we could raise good horses for you and the other forts. This would spread the Indians over a larger area while they learned a new trade." Austin looked at her in surprise as silence fell on the room following her proposal. Finally, a big grin spread across Colonel Dodge's face.

"I like it. I want you and Austin to scout the Cheyenne/Arapaho territory. Report to me when you find the land you'll need, and we'll draw up a contract."

The word of an Indian settlement ranch spread rapidly among the Cheyenne. Each wanted to help by finding the exact location that would be perfect. Austin and Bonhist rode here and there on several excursions, examining different sites, only to reject them for one reason or another. Finally, Charging Bull came forward with a suggestion. Austin, Bonhist, Charging Bull, Roaring Waters, and Big Dog Fletcher rode out to the area proposed by Charging Bull. Indeed, it was a nice location for a ranch, and while Austin was very excited, Bonhist stood in amazement. This was the very spot where she had experienced her vision. They rode their horses upon the high hill where she had made her camp many moons earlier. As they looked over the land from this high vantage point, Austin turned to see if she approved. "Well, Darling, I like it. What do you think?"

"The spirits are trying to tell me something. Let's sleep here tonight and talk about this location tomorrow."

"You Indians are just plum spooky. What's wrong with this? We have everything we need."

"Cowboy, you are a white man. It is hard for white people to understand spiritual things. Have patience, for the right location will soon be revealed."

During the night, Bonhist saw her spirit animal, the great horned owl. Led by the owl, with remarkably clear vision, she saw the site of their ranch. "Cowboy, during the night, I had a vision. I now know the location of your horse ranch."

Riding east, Bonhist led the party away from the North Canadian River. Everyone looked at each other and shrugged their shoulders. Where was Medicine Woman leading them? Austin, riding beside her, said, "It's hard to find good water like the North Canadian in these parts. Why are we heading away from it?"

"We are going where the spirits lead."

Nothing else was said. That evening they camped, and Big Dog reminded Bonhist that their water supply was low. "Do not worry, my father. We will soon have water."

The next morning, Bonhist continued leading the group east by south into the rising Oklahoma sun. By noon, they rode upon a small settlement called Okeene, where they watered their horses, and Austin bought some coffee for the party. "How much farther will the spirits lead us?" he asked.

"Cowboy, you will soon see your ranch."

After lunch, they continued east for two and a half miles when Bonhist abruptly lifted her hand. "Here, where these two creeks join, we will build the headquarters of the Todd Indian Settlement Ranch." The creeks were called Big Springs and Little Springs. As they rode up on the creeks, Charging Bull pointed to a spring of fresh water gushing upward about the size of a man's arm, cold and sweet. The clear water flowed abundantly and was the best that they had seen in the territory. They explored the area, riding down the creek all the way to the Cimarron River. The creeks were lined with trees, and the soil was rich. When night fell, they returned to the main spring, filled their water containers, and camped for the night. Everyone was excited, talking about their discovery.

Two days later, a detail from Fort Cantonment approved the site, and Austin signed the government contract. He was now the owner of a horse ranch and the founder of the first Indian Settlement in Oklahoma. Bonhist approved the Cheyenne families who volunteered for work on the ranch, including all the Fletcher, Flyingman, and Beartrack families. Charging Bull, Roaring Waters, Soft Winds, Red Leaf, and, of course, Star, all moved their lodges to the ranch. When assembled, the group accounted for almost one-third of the Cheyenne village.

The contract provided pay for the Indians to fence the ranch with red cedar posts from Roman Nose Canyon. The government allowed a strip of land one mile wide, or one-half mile on either side of Big Spring Creek, all the way to the Cimarron River, for the ranch. Altogether, it covered twenty-six sections.

After completing the fence, Austin approached Bonhist. "Now, it's time to bring in the horses. It will take all the money I have to afford a few of good quality. It will be necessary to live in your lodge a while longer. I will dig us a dugout where we can eat and sleep on stormy nights. Then, when we can afford it, I will begin to build the ranch house and barns."

"My husband, have I ever shown you my gold? My father, Crow, once filled these twin medicine bags with gold nuggets from Spirit Mountain, where I was born. I also have this small bag of gold dust from my brother, David. Take your wagons, buy the supplies you need, and get the horses as well."

Within a year, Austin had built a large ranch house. It included a massive fireplace and kitchen, bedrooms, a dining room, and a large screened back porch. Within the first year, two barns, a blacksmith shop, a stockade with holding corrals, a windmill, a corn grinder, and a spring house over the creek were added. Cheyenne tepees lined Big Springs Creek all the way to the Cimmaron. The families worked to provide for their needs. Vegetables of all kinds were grown, cattle roamed the area, and small game was available around the river. The Todd Ranch became known for its beautiful horses, and the venture prospered.

"Medicine Woman, your father once said that you would show the Cheyenne how to survive in the white world. Look at what you've done," Star said, pointing. She sat with Bonhist on the back porch as they looked as far as the eye could see on the lodges of the Cheyenne. Happy children were running and playing along the creek while smoke drifted upward from the cooking pots.

"Yes, mother, it is good to see the large horse herds and hear dogs barking again in the Cheyenne camps. The women and children once again have smiles. Cowboy also happy with the gold he makes from the ranch. It is good."

Epilogue

It was summertime and warm in Oklahoma, the year was 1898. The Austin Todd family was eating breakfast prepared by Bonhist and her mother, Elk-cow.

Austin could hear the wild horses the Cheyenne brought in. "Those horses will tear down that corral; I'm going to throw in some hay. Maybe that will calm them down."

In his rush, he left the door open. Austin ran an Indian Settlement Ranch, which was the first in Oklahoma. His horses were sent by train to Fort Reno. He had about twenty-two sections of land that ran all the way to the Cimarron River from the Watonga area.

Austin was tossing hay into the corral when he noticed his two-year-old child crawling into the corral. At the same time, the horses turned on the child. "Oh my God," Austin shouted.

Then, out of nowhere, was Bonhist. She used her body to shield the child while taking a death blow.

The doctor looked from his stethoscope and shook his head. Bonhist would only have a few days to live. Bonhist was bedridden and surrounded by family, who tried to make her feel comfortable.

Austin had ordered a plow from the blacksmith in Ark City, Kansas, some months ago. A few days after the Bonhist incident, the Todd family had a visitor: a Blacksmith named Mr. Nicholson. While Mr. Nicholson was waiting in his wagon to unload the plow, he watched the Indian girls slide down a mudslide and into the creek. They were all nude! One of the girls especially caught his eye! It was Mary Elizabeth Todd.

The next day, Mr. Nicholson found himself standing before the dying Bonhist, asking her permission to wed Mary. Bonhist smiled and nodded yes.

Mr. James Neuton Nicholson and Mary Elizabeth Todd are the grandparents of Jack Frazier, author of *Bonhist: Cheyenne Medicine Woman*.

L-R: Author Jack Frazier with his sister (Judy), dad, and mom (Montana, 1952)

Jack Frazier's daughter (Lynn) in Bonhist's wedding dress, passed down from Mary Elizabeth Todd

ACKNOWLEDGEMENTS

I would like to thank my parents Ray and Marie Frazier for their family knowledge and Native American heritage.

I would like to thank my son Ricky Frazier for his technical knowledge and computer skills.

I would like to thank my Great Uncle Thomas Todd for the summer he spent with my family teaching and telling many stories of his Mother Bonhist. He made me my first Indian bow!

About the Author

Jack Frazier was born in Blackwell, Oklahoma and raised in west Texas. He completed college at Pittsburg State University at Pittsburg, Kansas. He played basketball for Pittsburg State. He had a career as a guidance counselor, teacher, and basketball coach at the high school level. Jack is a registered member of the Cheyenne Arapaho Tribes of Oklahoma. His debut book was *Five Gallon Bucket*.

At 88 years old (2025), he's proof that it's never too late to publish! Jack loves basketball, but he wasn't always good at it. In fourth grade, he made his first attempt at a free throw and failed. For his birthday, he asked for a basketball. He realized he didn't have a basket when he went outside to shoot.

Out in the garage was an old rusty 5-gallon bucket—back then, they were made of metal, short and wide. Jack quickly cut out the bottom with a chisel and hammer, creating a basket, and the rest is history.

Basketball was in his bones and his dreams. He played in college at Pittsburg State University. At 5'11 3/4" tall, Jack was told he had the skills but not the height to play pro basketball. Instead, he pursued coaching and became a high school basketball coach.

In his short story, *Five Gallon Bucket*, Jack shares his experiences and thoughts on the sport, particularly from the lens of a basketball coach. His musings are endearing and Quill Hawk Publishing looks forward to giving basketball lovers a glimpse into this retired coach's story of how the five gallon bucket gave him purpose.

Jack is retired and lives in New Mexico with his wife. They split their time between Angel Fire and Alamogordo. When he's not dreaming about basketball, you can find Jack on the golf course.